COLONIAL
CHRISTMAS BRIDES

This Large Print Book carries the
Seal of Approval of N.A.V.H.

COLONIAL CHRISTMAS BRIDES

FOUR ROMANCES GLOW FROM THE WINDOWS OF OLD WILLIAMSBURG AND JAMESTOWN

LAURALEE BLISS & IRENE B. BRAND

THORNDIKE PRESS
A part of Gale, Cengage Learning

GALE
CENGAGE Learning·

Detroit • New York • San Francisco • New Haven, Conn • Waterville, Maine • London

GALE
CENGAGE Learning

© 2007 *Jamestown's Bride Ship* by Irene B. Brand.
© 2007 *Angel of Jamestown* by Lauralee Bliss.
© 2007 *Raven's Christmas* by Irene B. Brand.
© 2007 *Broken Hearts* by Lauralee Bliss.
Scripture quotations are taken from the King James Version of the Bible.
Thorndike Press, a part of Gale, Cengage Learning.

Thorndike Press® Large Print Christian Fiction.
The text of this Large Print edition is unabridged.
Other aspects of the book may vary from the original edition.
Set in 16 pt. Plantin.
Printed on permanent paper.

LIBRARY OF CONGRESS CATALOGING-IN-PUBLICATION DATA

Bliss, Lauralee.
    Colonial Christmas brides : four romances glow from the windows of Old Williamsburg and Jamestown / by Lauralee Bliss & Irene B. Brand.
        p. cm. — (Thorndike Press large print Christian fiction)
    ISBN-13: 978-1-4104-2047-3 (alk. paper)
    ISBN-10: 1-4104-2047-7 (alk. paper)
        1. Christian life—Fiction. 2. Christmas stories. 3. Large type books. I. Brand, Irene B., 1929– II. Title.
    PS3602.L575C65 2009
    813'.6—dc22   2009026471

Published in 2009 by arrangement with Barbour Publishing, Inc.

Printed in Mexico
1 2 3 4 5 6 7 13 12 11 10 09

JAMESTOWN'S BRIDE SHIP
BY IRENE B. BRAND

In memory of Dr. Herschel Heath,
Dr. Charles Moffat, and
Dr. Elizabeth Cometti,
my history professors at Marshall
University, who made a profound
impression on my life and helped
prepare me for a writing career in
historical fiction.

CHAPTER 1

Jamestown, Virginia Colony, 1620

Susanna Carter could hardly believe that she had survived the long sea voyage to Virginia. When Captain Trent bellowed from the quarterdeck that the colony was in sight, she left her cabin and hurried on deck as fast as her weak legs would carry her. She had lost count of the days they'd been on the voyage, but it seemed a lifetime since she had left London. The days on shipboard had been frightening enough, but after the ship left the Atlantic and moved slowly up the James River, the thick forests bordering the river had reminded Susanna of huge giants ready to pounce on their victims.

The sails were furled, the progress of the *Warwick* slowed to a crawl, and waves splashed against the tree-lined riverbanks. Susanna leaned against the bulwarks and stared in dismay and disappointment. Surely this village of squalid huts couldn't be

Jamestown — England's prized possession in America! Advertisements had circulated in London for several years claiming that the New World offered opportunities for a life surpassing anything to be found at home.

As she turned her weary head and slowly surveyed the area, Susanna wondered if she had made a wise decision when she left London. Jamestown was the most woebegone place she had ever seen. She saw nothing except a fort constructed with tall, wooden posts enclosing a few houses and a church, with several homes and other buildings outside the palisade. It seemed incredible that she had endured weeks of seasickness, hunger, and every discomfort imaginable to reach the Virginia colony — a place she hadn't wanted to visit in the first place.

And regardless of her grandmother's plans, it would be a *visit,* and a short one at that. She touched the soft leather bag hanging inside her garments, which contained enough coins to pay her return fare to England. Even if Grandmother no longer wanted her, Susanna didn't doubt that her maternal uncle would be happy to give her a home.

In spite of her disappointment in Virginia,

after a rough ocean crossing, Susanna was pleased to see something besides water and trees. She welcomed a few days of respite from the rigors of sea travel.

Ada Beemer, a friend Susanna had made on the voyage, joined her. "Are you feeling any better?"

"Not much, but at least I haven't been sick at my stomach since we left the Atlantic and sailed into Chesapeake Bay."

"Have you eaten anything?"

"I tried some cold gruel this morning, but I'm not sure it's going to stay down."

"It's good you didn't eat any of the pork. In spite of the thick salt packing, it's rancid now. I can hardly force it into my mouth."

Looking to the left, Susanna saw a large group of women surging toward the bow of the ship. Women were so scarce in the colony that for the past two years, the Virginia Company in England had recruited women to travel to the New World as brides for the colonists. The *Warwick* carried fifty potential brides, and Susanna scanned their faces, which mirrored a wide range of emotions — excitement . . . fear . . . resignation . . . hope . . . determination.

Riveting her attention on Ada, one of the prospective brides, Susanna tried to judge her friend's feelings, but her face revealed nothing. "Aren't you scared? Apprehensive of what's waiting for you?"

With a brave little smile, Ada admitted, "Of course I am. But whatever's waiting for me in Virginia can't be any worse than my life would have been if I'd stayed in England. When my father gambled away his inheritance and then took his own life, our whole family could have ended up in debtors' prison. My mother's brother was kind enough to settle our debts and give us a home, but there are three children younger than I, and I wouldn't add to his burden. Coming to America seemed to be my only option."

"Well, at least you had someone who wanted you. Grandmother lost all patience with me when I refused to marry the second man she chose for me." Bitterly Susanna added, "And treating me like a criminal, she transported me to Jamestown to live with my aunt."

Ada laughed softly. "But adults always arrange marriages. Why did you expect anything else?"

"I expected to marry someone I can love. My parents were devoted to each other, and that's the kind of marriage I want."

"The kind of love you're seeking is very rare in marriages. I hope I can learn to love the man I marry, but if not, I'll try to respect him."

"Aren't you taking a terrible risk? The man who chooses you might be a terrible person."

Ada shrugged her shoulders. "That's a chance I took when I made my decision. The men were screened by representatives of the Company, even as most of us were. But some of these women are convicts, and the English authorities are shipping them to Virginia to get rid of them. The settlers are taking a risk, too."

"From what I've heard of London's poor, many people are put in jail simply because they had to steal to feed their families."

Nodding, Ada agreed. "That's true, and that's why I've been kind to those women. But I pray that everybody finds the right mate. The two chaperones who sailed with us will talk to the men before they're allowed to approach us and will refuse anyone they consider unacceptable."

"The chaperones will be returning to England, won't they?"

"Yes, they're supposed to go home," Ada said, her eyes twinkling merrily. "But with women so scarce in this colony, they might decide to stay."

Observing the stern face of the stout,

middle-aged woman who was beckoning Ada to join the other brides, Susanna doubted that she would stay behind. Which suited Susanna's purposes, for it would be impossible for her to return on the *Warwick* without another female on board. As strict as the chaperones had been with their charges, Susanna knew they would provide all the respectability she needed.

With a deep sigh, Ada said, "I'll soon learn what my future is. And I'm selfish enough to wish you *would* stay in Jamestown. I'd like to know that you're on the same side of the Atlantic I am, but I understand how you feel."

"You've been a good companion. I don't believe I would have lived through the voyage if you hadn't befriended me. I pray that God will lead you to the right husband," Susanna said.

"I believe He will. I'll try to let you know how I fare."

"Until the *Warwick* returns to England, I'll be with my aunt, Eliza Wilde, and her husband, Lester, but I don't know where they live." Gazing again at the few buildings, she added, "The settlement is small, so we shouldn't have much trouble finding each other."

Susanna returned to the tiny cabin where

she had slept, picked up a small chest, and returned to the deck. The ship's captain, an acquaintance of her family, would see that her larger trunks were delivered to the Wilde home.

The ship was gliding closer toward the bank, and even that small movement nauseated Susanna. She clutched her stomach, which was sore to the touch. Whether from lack of strength or because she'd lost her land legs after so many weeks at sea, she felt dizzy, and her stomach heaved. Determined not to lose the food she'd eaten earlier, she turned her attention to her destination.

Although this colony had been established for several years, it seemed to Susanna that there weren't enough houses for the more than one thousand inhabitants reported to be living here. But Captain Trent had told her that some settlers lived in outlying districts. Above the squeaking of the ship's timbers and the snapping of the rigging, she heard him barking orders at the sailors.

The ship listed sharply to the left when it nudged roughly into the long wharf that jutted out into the river. When it righted itself, Susanna lost her balance. She grabbed at the bulwark and didn't fall, but the nausea returned. Without time to return for the pan she had used in the cabin, she leaned over the rail and lost her breakfast into the muddy water of the river.

Hearing loud laughter, she looked up to see several men looking her way, amused at her distress. Anger overriding her embarrassment, Susanna stared at them with a haughty expression meaning, "How dare you laugh at a woman of quality," a glance her grandmother would have approved. The men looked away quickly.

She scanned the large crowd waiting on the riverbank to see how many others had witnessed her distress, but most of them were looking toward the women waiting to disembark. The ship stopped, and two sailors jumped out to tie it to palings on the wharf.

Susanna's gaze rested briefly on the compassionate gray eyes of a handsome man standing close to the ship, who must have noticed that she was ill. Thankful for his apparent sympathy, she nodded to him but turned away when Captain Trent approached.

"Miss Carter, as soon as the other women get off, I'll take you to your family. I'll send your trunks later on in the day." He carried a small chest, but he leaned over and picked up the one at her feet. "Stay close beside me," he said. "I don't want these men to think *you* are a prospective bride."

Susanna made an effort to stay beside him, but her legs seemed to have a mind of their own, defying her efforts to move forward. Determined, she forced one foot after the other until she reached the wharf, which didn't have a rail for her to hold. The water swirling beneath the narrow wooden structure brought back her dizziness. She looked toward the captain for help, but he had his hands full already. Unable to control her legs and sensing that she was falling, she uttered a weak cry.

The *Warwick* was already in sight when Joshua Deane left the forest path. He wended his way among the wattle-and-daub structures of Jamestown, dismounted, and tied his horse to the hitching post in front of the stockade. When he shipped his hogsheads of tobacco several months ago, he had stipulated that the tobacco be exchanged for household items and seeds. He hoped this ship had brought them.

A ship's arrival was always a time of rejoicing, but he was surprised at the size of the crowd, as well as the excitement. As the ship neared the shore, Joshua noted the large number of women standing near the bow.

Suddenly realizing the reason for the men's eagerness, he chuckled softly. The importation of wives was probably one of the best things the Virginia Company had done for the colonists. By experience, Joshua knew how lonely a man could get without female companionship, but he wasn't desperate enough to wed a complete stranger even if other considerations weren't involved.

Speaking to the colonists he knew, Joshua worked his way slowly toward the river. He reached the bank just as the ship nudged into the wharf. Three men beside him laughed uproariously, and he followed their pointing fingers. A woman, hardly more than a girl, leaned over the side of the ship, losing her dinner. He turned angrily on the three men who found her predicament amusing, but she didn't need his help. Imperiously, she lifted her head and stared scornfully at the men until, shamefaced, they looked away. Her eyes shifted to his, and she must have realized that he hadn't shared their amusement, for she inclined her head toward him. She looked away, but Joshua was concerned about her, for she looked as if she were going to faint.

A man approached the woman, and when Joshua saw that it was Captain Trent, he knew she was in safe hands. Eager to have a word with the captain about his shipment, Joshua worked his way toward the wharf, where several sailors held the prospective grooms at bay. They formed a path allowing the women to make their way unhindered up the bank and into the meetinghouse.

Joshua wended his way toward the captain just as the woman swooned. The captain saw her stumble, but before he could drop the chests he carried, Joshua leaped forward and caught her, swinging her upward into his arms before she fell into the shallow water.

"Thank you," the captain said. "That was quick thinking." He wagged his head sympathetically. "Poor girl! She's been sick most of the trip, but I thought she looked better today or I'd have been watching her more closely."

Joshua nodded toward the church. "Shall I take her up there with the other women?"

"No, she's not one of the brides. Her name is Susanna Carter, and she's come to visit her aunt, Eliza Wilde. Her grandmother, Lady Carter, put her in my custody to assure her safe delivery. I'm glad you caught her. I wouldn't want to get in bad with a family of quality!"

"I know where the Wildes live. I'll carry her there. It's only a short distance."

Susanna stirred in Joshua's arms and opened her eyes. Her eyes shifted from him to Captain Trent, who peered anxiously at her.

"Oh! What happened?"

"You almost fell off the wharf. Mr. Deane caught you. Are you strong enough to walk to your aunt's home? It's not far."

"I think so. I'm sorry I've been such a nuisance to you."

"After several weeks at sea, it takes awhile to learn how to walk on land again," Joshua warned. "With your permission, I'll carry you."

Susanna's eyes looked like black satin as she studied his face. Seemingly satisfied, she said, "Thank you. I am tired, and I don't believe I can walk."

Her lids slipped down over her eyes as she settled more comfortably into his arms. Joshua tightened his grip, feeling a strange sense of possession as he walked up the bank. Susanna's small, embroidered white cap had loosened, freeing her thick auburn hair to fall over her shoulders. A stiff breeze from the James twirled some of the loose tendrils around Joshua's face. He gazed at the dark lashes that swept across her delicately carved cheekbones. She was very pale, and he sensed that several weeks of seasickness had caused her smooth skin to lose color. Still, considering the sweetly curled lips set in an oval face and arching eyebrows just a shade darker than her hair, Joshua thought she was the most beautiful woman he'd ever seen.

So intent was he on his appraisal of Susanna, Joshua had forgotten the captain's presence. He looked up quickly when the captain said, "I've got two crates for you on the ship."

"I'm glad to hear that. I thought a ship was due, and I hoped it was bringing my supplies. I came on horseback today, but I'll bring a cart tomorrow to haul them to the plantation."

"That's soon enough. Your boxes are far down in the hold. It will take awhile to get everything unloaded."

Joshua had thought Susanna must be asleep for she hadn't moved, but without opening her eyes, she said, "When will you be leaving the colony, Captain?"

"A week or more. Why? You planning to go back? Your grandmother indicated that you were going to live in the colony."

She opened her eyes and gazed at the captain, and Joshua noted another facial feature — her determined chin. "That is *her* idea. Please don't leave without seeing me," she said.

The captain cast a puzzled look at Joshua, who had noticed that Susanna hadn't answered the captain's question.

Susanna lifted her upward curving eyelashes, and she managed a small smile. "Are we almost there?" she asked.

"Yes."

"Then please let me try to stand. I'd prefer that Aunt Eliza doesn't think that I'm unable to walk. She doesn't even know I'm paying her a visit, and I don't want her to think I'll be a burden to her."

Joshua looked at the captain uneasily.

"That might be best," the captain agreed. "But take it easy, Miss Carter."

Still holding her securely, Joshua set Susanna on her feet.

"Lean on Joshua until you're sure you can stand," the captain advised.

Susanna staggered slightly when her feet touched the ground, and Joshua tightened his hold. When her legs seemed to support her, she took one tentative step and then another. "I believe I'll be all right," she said, looking up at Joshua. "Thank you. I won't delay you any longer."

"We're almost to the house. I'll walk along behind you, and if you have trouble, I'll be here to help."

She accepted his help with a slight smile, and although Joshua could tell it was an effort, she walked with determination. He admired her slender body and straight back, as well as her courage. The cap fell to the ground, and her auburn hair swayed around her shoulders. He picked up the cap and handed it to her.

Although all of the Jamestown houses were similar in construction, the Wilde home was larger than most of them. Huge logs shaped the oblong structure covered with a sod roof. Walls were made of smaller branches, which were daubed with thick clay found in the river marshes. Smoke drifted upward from a stone chimney. A narrow porch ran the length of the home.

As Captain Trent stepped up to the front door, Susanna leaned against a post for support.

"I'll leave you now," Joshua said.

"Thank you again."

He walked away, but he glanced back just as Eliza Wilde opened the door. He took one more glance at Susanna before he forced himself to look away. Five years ago he had made up his mind that there was no place for a woman in his life. What was there about Susanna Carter that made him question if he had made the right decision?

CHAPTER 2

While she waited for the door to open, Susanna realized that all of her trembling wasn't caused by seasickness and fatigue. What if Aunt Eliza didn't welcome her? She was a long way from home to find out that she wasn't wanted in Jamestown either. She remembered her uncle as a large, brusque man. What if Uncle Lester didn't want an uninvited houseguest? If she wasn't physically able to go home on the *Warwick,* would she be forced to marry one of these strangers in Jamestown just to have a roof over her head?

She glanced toward Joshua Deane's straight, well-built body and his long, easy stride as he walked away. Remembering his large, gentle hands as he'd carried her, she contemplated for a moment that marriage to *him* might be all right. But was he even now hurrying away to choose one of her shipmates for his bride? Or perhaps he already had a wife.

Her musings ended when the door opened and a tall, angular woman stepped out on the porch. After five years, Susanna had almost forgotten what Eliza Wilde looked like, but happy memories with this favorite aunt revived immediately.

Eliza shifted her eyes from Susanna to Captain Trent, then back again to Susanna, recognition slowly dawning in her eyes.

"Brought you a guest," Captain Trent said.

Eliza stepped closer to Susanna, disbelief in her dark eyes. "Susanna? Is it really you?"

"Yes. I'm sorry to come without an invitation."

"Why, child, you're welcome. I've never been so happy to see anyone."

Tears filled Susanna's eyes as Eliza pulled her into a tight hug. "Come inside out of the cold. You, too, Captain, and tell me why I've been so blessed." As she closed the door behind them, Eliza asked in a startled voice, "Has Mother died? Is that why you've come to me?"

"No, she's all right . . . but she doesn't want me to stay with her anymore." Susanna managed a small, tentative smile. "We don't get along very well."

Eliza stepped back from Susanna. "And I can see why! You're too beautiful — she was afraid you'd steal some of *her* admirers! What else did you do to anger her?"

"I turned down the men she wanted me to marry."

"And I'll bet they were twice as old as you and ugly as a rhinoceros but with plenty of money."

"Yes," Susanna answered and laughed softly, recalling her two suitors and how well Aunt Eliza had described them.

"Cap," Eliza said, "excuse us for airing our family problems before you. Sit down, both of you, and I'll get you a noggin of tea. I keep water hot all the time."

"I can't stop now, Eliza. I've got unloading to do."

"Then come later on in the week for a meal."

Captain Trent took a letter from the chest he carried. "Lady Carter sent this to you."

Eliza made a face. "Full of instructions on what I'm to do with Susanna, I'll wager." She tossed the letter on a chest. "I'll read it later."

Shaking hands with Susanna, the captain said, "One of the men will fetch your trunks up later on today."

Eliza closed the door behind the captain and turned to Susanna again. "I can't believe it's really *you*. If I have my way, I'm

26

going to keep you here."

Motioning to her grandmother's letter, Susanna made a face. "I'm sure the letter will explain that's what grandmother intends, but I'm expecting this to be a short visit. If I'm feeling better, I'm returning to England when the *Warwick* sails. Uncle Felton will take me in."

"We'll talk about that later," Eliza said, and she patted a bench close to the fireplace, which Susanna sank onto wearily. "How about a cup of tea for you?"

"Tea! In Jamestown? It's a rarity in London. I've tasted it only once."

Laughing, Eliza said, "We don't have India tea either. It's sassafras tea — something we got from the Indians. It's used for medicinal purposes more than for general drinking, but when I'm tired, a hot cup of it makes me feel better."

Eliza took a pewter cup from a corner cupboard, lifted a heavy iron kettle from the crane hanging over the coals in the fireplace, and filled the cup. She handed the tea to Susanna, and she wrapped her hands around the warm cup. "Lester likes a cup of this every night for supper."

"Where is Uncle Lester?"

"In his workshop behind the house. His carpentry skills have come in handy here

27

in the New World. He makes furniture, and because very few settlers bring household items with them, he has a thriving business."

Susanna sniffed the herbal tea and took a tentative taste. It wasn't distasteful, and she sipped it slowly.

While Eliza talked about their five years in the Jamestown colony, Susanna looked around the large room. A huge fireplace dominated one wall. A musket and a harquebus hung over the mantelpiece, which had been hewn from a huge tree trunk. A powder horn hung nearby. An iron crane, projecting over the coals, held several iron pots exuding tantalizing scents. The tea settled Susanna's stomach, and the food actually smelled appetizing. A pair of boards had been nailed together to form a table that stood on a trestle in the center of the room, surrounded by several benches and stools. A bedstead, covered with colorful quilts, was built into the wall. It was a small but comfortable home, Susanna decided, but apprehensively, she looked for another bed.

Interrupting her aunt, she said, "Is this your only room?"

"Yes, except for a little storeroom where Lester can sleep. Until we make other arrangements, you can sleep in the bed with me."

"Oh, no! I'll sleep in the storeroom. I shouldn't have come!"

"Don't be concerned about it," Eliza said. "As soon as you finish your tea, you must go to bed and rest. In a day or two, you'll feel fine, and we'll find a place for you to sleep." She motioned toward a ladderlike stairway beside the front door. "The loft is a nice warm place. We can fix a bed for you up there. Want some more tea?"

"No, thank you, but it was very good."

Eliza took the cup and set it on the table. She poured water from an iron pot into a wooden bowl and laid out some linen cloths and a square bar of soap. "While you take a good wash, I'll go tell Lester we have company. I don't s'pose you have any clean clothes in your chest, so I'll lay out one of my nightgowns. A good sleep will do wonders for you." She fastened shutters over the two small windows, which left the room in semidarkness, and pointed to a white sheet hanging on a rope beside the bed. "Pull that curtain when you get into bed."

Tears shimmered in Susanna's eyes when Eliza hugged her again and kissed her forehead. "Since God didn't favor us with any children, it will be wonderful to have some of my own kindred to share our bed and board."

As she washed away the stench of the long sea voyage, tears streamed down Susanna's face. The kindness of Joshua Deane and the obvious pleasure of Aunt Eliza to have her visit had made her arrival in Jamestown more pleasant than she could have imagined.

She wrapped her body in the voluminous nightgown, climbed into the high bedstead, and pulled the curtain. She tucked the bag of coins under the pillow. The mattress was filled with straw, but it was more comfortable than the damp cot she'd been sleeping on. It seemed strange to lie down without the shifting motion of the ship beneath her, but her eyelids felt heavy.

Susanna's last conscious thought was about Joshua, wondering if she would see him again before she left Virginia. . . .

Susanna sat up in bed and yawned, happy to be feeling like her old self again. She opened the curtain. Sunrays filtered into the room through the windows covered with oiled paper. She swung her feet over the side of the bed.

Eliza sat on a stool by the fireplace, sewing, and she turned at the movement.

"Good morning," she said pleasantly. "You look better."

"I feel like a human again, and I'm even hungry. I don't remember much about the past day or two, but I think I went through the motions of eating."

"You've been here two days, and you've been out of bed a few times. But you would eat a small amount and fall asleep at the table," Eliza said, her face crinkling into a smile. "But you've been drinking a lot of water, and I thought that was better for you than food."

Susanna made a face. "After the first month, the water on board tasted terrible." Noticing her trunks beside the bed, Susanna said, "Good. I can have clean garments now."

"I washed the ones you were wearing when you arrived."

"You shouldn't have done that," Susanna protested. "I don't want to make extra work for you."

Lester, a large man with a full-moon face, stepped into the room. His blue eyes brightened when he saw that Susanna was awake. "Welcome to Jamestown and our home, niece. We talked a bit yesterday, but I don't think you were alert enough to know what we were saying."

31

Laughing, she said, "No . . . Everything is hazy, so we'll have to start over."

"Wrap a blanket around you and come to the table," Eliza said. "We'll have breakfast so Lester can go to work."

Breakfast consisted of porridge made from peas and beans, a hunk of dark wheaten bread, and sassafras tea. The food tasted strange to Susanna, but she could have eaten more than she did. Hesitating to risk more sickness by overeating, she settled for small portions.

While Susanna changed into fresh garments behind the curtain, Eliza washed the breakfast utensils. "You should unpack your trunk today and hang your clothes on the pegs behind the bed. But before you do that, we might as well discuss what Mother had to say in her letter."

Susanna sat in the only chair in the room before the fireplace, while Eliza settled down on a nearby bench. "Mother writes that she's expecting you to stay with me, yet you said when you arrived that you intend to return to England on the *Warwick*. As you must realize, this places me in a predicament."

"I know, and I'm sorry, but although Grandmother is my guardian, I'm not content to let her dominate my life completely. What exactly did she write?"

"She asked me to give you a home until I could arrange a suitable marriage for you. But what puzzles me — if you intend to go back to England, why did you come in the first place?"

"Because Uncle Felton was in Scotland, and I had no one else to go to. Living with Grandmother had become impossible. Besides, I wouldn't insist on staying with her when she wanted me to leave. I believe I'm courageous, but not to the extent of trying to live on my own in London."

"God forbid that you would have tried that! But unless you step beyond the pale of society, what else can you do except marry? So why not marry and settle down here?"

Susanna shook her head, and she couldn't hide the discouragement that overwhelmed her. "It's not that I object to marriage so much . . . I'd just like to feel some emotion for the man I marry. Grandmother's only concern was that I marry someone with money and prestige. I don't believe that's the kind of marriage God had in mind when He said that a man should leave his parents and stay close to his wife, and that the two of them would be as one."

Eliza's eyebrows lifted and her mouth twisted humorously. "Well, well! I hadn't expected such biblical insight from someone reared in my mother's home."

Susanna felt her face flushing. "My last tutor was a devout Christian. He studied at Oxford University where he had an opportunity to read a Geneva Bible. He copied passages from that Bible, and he had me memorize them. Grandmother didn't know or she probably would have let him go, for she seldom went to worship. I'm thankful that God worked through my tutor to teach me how important faith is in my life. If I hadn't already trusted God as my protector, I wouldn't have lived through this voyage."

"We, too, have become more dedicated in our faith since we came to America," Eliza said. "We face danger every day, never knowing when the Indians will attack our settlement. And there's so much disease! Lester and I turn each day over to God. Otherwise, we couldn't bear the frustration. The first preacher who came to Jamestown brought a Geneva Bible with him, and it's still in the meetinghouse. But now there's a copy of the King James Bible, which the preacher uses most often in his sermons."

"Yes, that's the translation used in most English churches now. My tutor thought the day would come when every home would have a copy of the Bible. Wouldn't that be wonderful?"

"It would, indeed," Eliza agreed. "But we've strayed from the subject. I wish I could persuade you to forget about returning to England with Captain Trent. Several ships come to Jamestown each year now — you can always go home later if you don't like it here. So why not give the colony a chance?"

Susanna shook her head. "There's nothing here for me."

"But what is there for you in England? Have you considered that it might have been God's will for you to come to America? I know it takes courage to carve a new home out of the wilderness. But an eighteen-year-old girl who would set out on a sea voyage to an unknown land rather than bow to her grandmother's wishes has to be courageous. Jamestown needs people like you."

Susanna didn't answer, but as Eliza turned toward the fireplace to check a simmering pot, she considered her decision. *Should* she take a look at Jamestown before she made up her mind?

CHAPTER 3

Within a week, Susanna had walked with Eliza several times around the settlement. Despite an agitated protest from her aunt, Susanna had moved into the storeroom to sleep. The room was cold, but after she made her bed there, Eliza kept the door open all of the time so heat from the fireplace could penetrate the room. The first night she slept on the floor on a pile of blankets was a miserable experience, but Lester solved that problem by building a wooden cot for her.

Although minus a few pounds, her health had improved remarkably, and she was barraged with suitors. As soon as the unattached men of the colony learned that she was no longer ill, there was a steady stream of callers at the Wilde home.

Uncle Lester had turned out to be quite a tease, and he thought it hilarious that Susanna was besieged with eligible men.

Finally, she accused, "I believe you're inviting these men to see me."

He laughed uproariously. "I'll admit it. I want you to stay with us."

"I warn you, Uncle Lester. When the next man shows up, I'm going to lock myself in the storeroom and you can entertain him."

"It's cold in there."

"Nonetheless, I mean it."

"I agree with Susanna, husband," Eliza said. "I want to keep her with us, too, but if she doesn't have a little peace, we'll drive her away."

Lester threw up his hands. "All right, I'll discourage any more visitors. But be honest with me, girl — haven't you seen one man that has stirred your heart a little?"

Susanna lowered her eyelids. How could she answer? None of the men who had called at the Wilde home had touched her heart, but she couldn't forget Joshua, and she wondered why he hadn't come to see her. She chose her words thoughtfully so she wouldn't be lying but would still prevent a statement that would make Uncle Lester suspect her feelings for Joshua.

"All of the men who've come this week have seemed nice enough, but marriage is for life, Uncle. I don't know any of these men, but you do. Which one do *you* think would make a suitable husband for me?"

Eliza seemed amused at Susanna's statement. "There!" she crowed. "She's put you on the spot. Serves you right for meddling."

Lester stirred in his chair, and his face flushed.

Hoping to add to his discomfiture, Susanna teased, "I really think you're tired of having me in the house, and like my grandmother, you want to get rid of me."

He jumped as if he'd been stung. "That's not it a'tall!" He looked reproachfully at his wife when she joined in Susanna's laughter. "There are several settlers who might make you a good man, but I'll mention two. Aaron Waller is probably your best choice — or Philemon Sommer."

Lester stared defiantly at Eliza, as if expecting her to disagree with him.

"Aaron Waller?" Susanna had seen so many strangers that it was hard to put faces and names together. But she finally placed Waller as a well-dressed man with a lean face, long, prominent nose, and wavy blond hair. "Isn't he that *old* man?"

"He's not as old as I am! Besides, he's a nobleman with some wealth. He has a nice home on his plantation and even has servants, so you wouldn't have to do the housework."

With a frown in his direction, Eliza said, "And he also has two grown children who are almost as old as our niece. Besides, he talks continuously about how rich he is and what famous ancestors he has."

Irritated, Lester said, "Well, if you don't like him, what's wrong with Philemon Sommer?"

"I remember him," Susanna said. "He's a very shy young man, but he seems like a good sort of fellow."

"Everybody likes him, for he's trustworthy and easy to get along with. He's a cooper and works hard. I think he'll be going a long way in the colony. You could do worse."

"No doubt you're right, but I won't marry him. And although I don't appreciate your matchmaking, I would like for you to do a favor for me. Will you find out who Ada Beemer married? She was one of the brides on the ship with me, and I'd like to see her. I hope she found a good husband."

"I'll ask around," Lester promised. "But it could be that she married someone who lives away from town."

Because Susanna knew that many of the settlers had taken up land outside the settlement, she didn't expect any immediate news, so she was surprised when Lester came in for supper that evening and said, "I found the lady. She's living in the settlement, married to Eli Derby. He's a good man — never misses Sunday meeting. He makes a decent living by cutting trees and shaping them into fairly good lumber."

"Ada will probably be at church tomorrow," Eliza said. "Do you feel able to attend? I should warn you that the preacher gets carried away sometimes, and we could be there a few hours."

"I want to go. I feel as healthy as I ever did. It was the rough seas that caused all the trouble."

"Another reason for you to stay in Jamestown," Lester said. "Why would you take another sea voyage and be sick again? I was seasick most of the time when I came over, and when I set my feet on the solid earth again, I vowed I was staying in America, either dead or alive."

He stared hopefully at Susanna, but when she didn't encourage him, he shrugged his shoulders in defeat and promised, "I won't meddle anymore."

The building was crowded. The benches were uncomfortable. The room was cold. But when Susanna lifted her voice with the other worshipers in the meetinghouse on Sunday morning, she sang as fervently as she had when she'd joined her tutor and the housekeeper as they worshiped in London's Chapel of St. John.

"Thou the all-holy, Thou supreme in might.
Thou dost give peace, Thy presence
    maketh right;
Thou with Thy favor all things dost enfold,
With Thine all-kindness free from harm wilt
    hold."

As she continued singing the hymn that had been used in worship since the twelfth century, Susanna's troubled spirit found peace. While all heads were bowed in prayer, she whispered, "God, flood my soul with the assurance that Your presence does make everything right. It doesn't matter whether I'm in England or in Virginia; You can keep me safe from harm. Father, increase my faith and help me make the right decision. Should I stay in Jamestown or go home?"

Susanna raised her eyes to find Joshua Deane watching her. He was leaning against the wall, and she wondered if he had placed himself so he could watch her. One corner of his mouth lifted into a slight smile. He smiled with his lips, but not his eyes, but still she sensed that the attraction she felt for him was not one-sided. Unlike those other men whom she'd met the past few days, she wanted to see more of Joshua. All through the long sermon, her thoughts kept returning to him.

After the benediction, Susanna leaned close to her aunt. "Joshua Deane is here. Why don't you ask him to eat with us?"

Eliza regarded her niece with an appraising glance, whispering, "I'll invite him, but you're barking up the wrong tree."

Not wanting Joshua to suspect that she had initiated the invitation, Susanna didn't accompany her aunt when she approached Joshua. Instead, she searched the congregation to see if Ada was present. Susanna spotted her friend several feet away and waved to her.

With a word to the man at her side, Ada hurried toward Susanna. They clasped hands, and Ada said, "You look so much better. I've been worried about you."

"My health is almost back to normal." Looking deep into Ada's eyes, Susanna asked, "How are things with you?"

"Good! I've got a lot to learn about living here, but I'm sure I have a good husband. Come and meet him."

Susanna walked beside Ada to her companion, a small man with a pleasant countenance, gentle brown eyes, and long, black hair tied back with a leather thong. "Eli, this is my friend, Susanna. I told you about meeting her on the ship."

He bowed slightly. "It's a pleasure to meet you, ma'am. I didn't have an easy time on my voyage over either, so I know what you went through. Welcome to the colony."

"Are you going to sail home with Captain Trent?" Ada asked quietly as the congregation filed out of the building.

"I don't know. My aunt and uncle are eager to have me stay here. If only everyone would stop trying to find a husband for me, I wouldn't mind waiting for the next ship so I could be sure I'm strong enough to start another ocean journey."

A smile trembled on Ada's lips, and she said softly, "Come to see us. I'll not do any matchmaking."

"Where do you live?"

"I'll show you." They walked outside the stockade, and Ada pointed to a small house at the edge of the forest. "That's our home," she said, and Susanna noted the pride in her voice.

"I'll come sometime this week."

Ada and Eli walked away, and Susanna waited for her family. As the churchgoers passed by, she recognized a few of the women she had met on the ship, most of them with men noticeably older than they were. Eliza had explained that the mortality rate among women was extremely high in the colonies, especially during childbirth, and that some of the settlers were widowers with children who needed a mother.

Before Eliza joined her, Susanna saw Joshua mounting his horse and riding away. Her gaze followed him.

"Turned me down," Eliza whispered when she stepped to Susanna's side. "I'm not surprised. I need to talk with you about Mr. Deane."

Someone called her name, and Susanna turned to see Aaron Waller approaching with a girl and a boy, probably in their late teens. Although most of the people in Jamestown wore drab garments without any ornamentation, the Waller children were dressed in the latest London fashions. Obviously, when he bragged about his wealth, Aaron was telling the truth.

Acting as if he were doing her a favor, Aaron said, "I want you to meet my daughter, Margaret, and my son, Abraham." Susanna shook hands with them, but hostility blazed from their eyes. Even if she had been interested in their father, their attitudes would have discouraged her.

"You're invited to be a guest in our home

44

whenever it's convenient for you," Aaron said, but Susanna was spared an answer when Captain Trent hailed her. She turned toward him.

"Miss Trent, it's a pleasure to see you in such fine fettle."

"I'm feeling much better. When will you start back to England?"

"I wanted to talk to you about that. There's a leak in the hold that has to be repaired which will delay our departure. Are you still considering a return to England, or has one of the settlers persuaded you to stay here?"

Aaron, who had overheard their conversation, said, "What's this? You're returning to England?"

Although annoyed, Susanna said, "That's my intention, and nothing so far has happened to make me change my mind."

Ignoring Waller, the captain said, "Since we've waited this long, I may delay our departure until after Christmas."

"But you must come to my plantation for a weekend visit before you return to England," Waller insisted.

"Thank you, but my future is unsettled, and I can't accept the invitation."

Eliza, who had silently witnessed this exchange said, "Gentlemen, please excuse

45

us. My niece is still recuperating, and it's time she went home for a rest."

Riding away from the settlement, Joshua was angry with himself for turning down Eliza's invitation. Instead of saying a blunt, "No, thank you," he should have answered civilly. He could have offered the excuse of another engagement, which was true, for he intended to stop at a sick neighbor's to take care of his animals and cut some wood. But he could have done that after they had eaten.

Since the day he had seen Susanna on the ship, Joshua had thought of her often. And judging from the look of gladness he'd seen in her eyes when she looked at him during worship, he was foolish enough to believe she had thought of him, too. Was it possible that she had asked Eliza to invite him to eat with them? He groaned aloud. If so, what must she think of him?

Many times during the past years, as he'd worked hard to claim his plantation from the wilderness and had built a comfortable home, he wondered why he had bothered. He intended to remain single, so why did it matter whether or not he made a success of this New World venture? Only to himself did Joshua ever admit that he was lonely.

Because his first marriage had ended in such a disaster didn't mean that it would happen again. Why should he deny himself the pleasures of a wife and family because of fear?

When he had set out for the Virginia colony, he had compared himself to Abraham — the biblical patriarch who had made several long journeys before he arrived in the land God had promised him. Abraham had had plenty of problems, but his faith in God hadn't wavered, believing that what God had promised He would fulfill. Joshua had that kind of faith once, but he had lost it. Was God speaking to him again? Calling him to put the past behind him and step out in faith to start another life? His decision would be easier if he knew whether God was also preparing Susanna Carter to share his life.

CHAPTER 4

Plodding the short distance from the meetinghouse to the Wilde home, Susanna's
heart seemed as heavy as her feet. She had
been exhilarated when the worship service
ended, but now weariness had overcome
her.

She glanced upward and noticed that
Eliza watched her with concern in her eyes.

"Did he give any reason for refusing?"

"He said, 'No, thank you,' and walked
away."

When they entered the house, Susanna
said, "I'm going to rest awhile." She picked
up a quilt from the bed, saying, "I'll lie
down in the storeroom. You and Uncle
Lester go ahead and eat. I'll have something
later."

When a knock sounded on the outside
door, Susanna said, "I'll see who it is."

Susanna took a sharp breath when she
opened the heavy door. Joshua stood on the

threshold. She stared at him, speechless.

"Who is it?" Eliza asked, tying an apron around her waist.

Susanna stepped backward and motioned for Joshua to enter.

"Mrs. Wilde," he said, "I was too hasty in turning down your invitation. I'm committed to stop at a neighbor's and help with his work, but I decided I could do that after dinner. That is, if the invitation still stands."

"Of course it does. I'm just ready to set the food on the table. Take his coat, Susanna."

Distracted by his presence, Susanna remained tongue-tied as she laid the quilt on the bed and hung Joshua's coat on a wooden peg. She was thankful when Lester entered the cabin.

Ending an uncomfortable moment, he said, "Glad to have you share our food and drink, Joshua. Wife, if we've got time, I'll take him to the shop and show him the progress I'm making on his furniture."

Eliza nodded assent. "I'll be dishing up the food while Susanna sets the table, so don't take long."

"Let's go out the back door," Lester said, and the two men left the house.

Susanna went to the cupboard and lifted out the pewter plates and spoons. "Why do you think he came back?" she asked.

With a deep sigh, Eliza said, "It's beyond me to figure out how a man's mind works. Does it matter a lot to you that he did return?"

"It doesn't matter so much that he *did* return, but I would like to know *why* he changed his mind."

Susanna had gotten her emotions under control when the men returned, and she entered the conversation, hoping that she wasn't betraying the confused thoughts and feelings that still surged through her. The roast duck, sweet potatoes, and corn bread her aunt had prepared could have been tasteless for all she knew. She found Joshua's presence across the table disturbing, although she occasionally forced herself to meet his eyes. Most of the time she observed him through lowered lashes, keenly aware that he watched her with a clear, unfaltering gaze.

They were almost finished when someone pounded on the door. "Come in," Lester shouted.

A boy opened the door and stepped inside. "Mrs. Wilde, my pa's got a fever and he's thrashin' around in bed. Ma wants you to help."

"Right away," Eliza said, getting up from

the table and taking off her apron. "You come with me, Lester. I may need your help. Joshua, please excuse us for a short time. You and Susanna finish your meal. We'll be at the house across the street."

With some unease, Susanna watched her aunt and uncle leave the house. A tense silence seemed to envelop the room until she said, "Would you like another serving of sweet potatoes?"

"No, thank you. I'll finish this piece of corn bread and that will be all I need."

She sipped on a noggin of milk until Joshua laid his spoon aside and pushed his plate away from him. "This was a fine meal. Eliza is a better cook than I am," he added, a humorous glint in his eyes.

"Why don't you take a seat closer to the fire? I'll put the plates and spoons in a pan of water and wash them later." But he helped her carry the utensils to the basin, and she spread a cloth over the food on the table.

She pointed to a rough straight-back chair, covered with one of Eliza's quilts. "In spite of all the pretty furniture Uncle Lester makes now, he won't give up that chair. It was the first one he made when they came to the colony, and he's attached to it. I think you'll find it comfortable."

He waited until she was seated on a three-legged stool with her back to the fireplace before he sat down. "You look very well. You must be over your illness," he said, as his eyes swept over her approvingly.

"As soon as I got off the ship, the nausea stopped. I slept for a few days then started eating Aunt Eliza's nourishing food. I regained my strength rapidly."

He eyed her speculatively. "The day you arrived, you indicated you might sail with Captain Trent when he returns to England."

With a slight smile, she said, "From what he said this morning, that may not be for a few weeks. I haven't made definite plans. My aunt and uncle are urging me to stay in Virginia."

"Perhaps I shouldn't ask, but why did you make the trip in the first place if you're going back so soon?"

She explained briefly that her grandmother had forced her into coming to Jamestown. "She had her own social life, and I was a hindrance to her." Susanna stopped short of mentioning that the biggest argument was because she wouldn't get married. To forestall further questions, she queried, "I'm interested in hearing about your plantation."

"When I first came to Virginia, I rented

land from the Virginia Company, but two years ago, a provision was made whereby the company would give a man fifty acres for each person he brought to Virginia. I imported enough indentured servants to be awarded three hundred acres, but I've only had time to clear a hundred acres or so. My major crop is tobacco. Part of my land lies along the James River, and I bring my tobacco to Jamestown on a barge where it's transferred to ships and shipped to England. I exchange it for supplies or livestock to improve my holdings."

"And you prefer living here rather than in England?"

"Yes, I do. I was the youngest of four sons, and I didn't think I could move forward at home. The New World gave me a chance and I took it." He stood up, with what appeared briefly to be a reluctant look on his face. "It's been a pleasure to visit with you, but I must leave now. My neighbor may have several things to be done."

"I'm pleased that you could share a meal with us. I think often of how you helped me on the day I arrived in Jamestown."

"I've thought of it, too," he said. "It was an unusual meeting."

Flustered by the gentle softness of his voice, Susanna took his coat from the peg, and Joshua shrugged into it.

He paused before retrieving his hat. "I live about fifteen miles from the village. If you would be interested in seeing my plantation, I could bring my cart and take you for a visit. Or would you prefer to go on horseback?"

"Horseback would be fine, although I haven't ridden much since I had a pony as a child."

"I'll bring a gentle horse."

Without any idea what the social customs were in the colony, Susanna hesitated for a moment. "Then I would like to visit your plantation, with Aunt Eliza's permission, of course."

"I'll come into Jamestown Tuesday morning and bring an extra horse and ask your aunt's approval. I have two families living on the plantation — one of the women cooks for me sometimes. I'm sure she will prepare a meal for us."

"I'll look forward to it."

Joshua picked up his hat from a bench as the door opened and Eliza entered. Shivering, she rushed to the fireplace. "The wind is cold. Even if the house is just across the street, I should have worn a shawl."

"How is your neighbor?" Joshua inquired.

"His condition isn't critical. He's had a

high fever for several days and started talking out of his head this morning, which alarmed his wife. After he drank some herbal tea, he settled down, but Lester is staying until he goes to sleep. Must you leave so soon?"

"Yes. But I would like to come back Tuesday morning and escort Miss Susanna to see my plantation. With your permission, of course."

Eliza's eyebrows pulled together, and perhaps trying to assess Susanna's wishes, she scanned her niece's face with keenly observant eyes. "You're sure you're up to a long ride in the cold weather?"

"Yes. I'll rest most of the day tomorrow."

"Then, by all means, go. I want you to learn more about our colony." With a hearty laugh, she said to Joshua, "You see, Lester and I are trying to persuade her to stay with us."

"So she told me." He stepped out on the porch and pulled his wide-brimmed hat low over his ears. "I'll be here Tuesday."

After closing the door behind Joshua, Eliza stirred the coals, added more wood, backed up to the blaze, and lifted her skirts.

Susanna sat on the stool she'd occupied earlier. "What did you mean this morning when you said you'd have to talk to me about Joshua?"

Eliza pulled a bench closer to the fire and sat down. A thoughtful smile curving her mouth, she questioned, "Why, of all the men you've seen, have you fixed your interest on Joshua Deane?"

"I don't have the least idea," she answered, with a trace of laughter in her voice. "I suppose Grandmother would call it contrariness. And really, I can't say I've fixed my interest on him, but I've thought of him often since our eyes first connected at the wharf. Don't you approve of Joshua?"

"Of course — there's not a finer man in this whole colony. But he's not interested in getting married. He's a widower, and before you get any further involved, you need to know how his wife died."

Terrible images built in Susanna's mind. Her concern must have shown in her expression, for Eliza hurried to explain, "Oh, Joshua didn't have anything to do with her death, except he may blame himself for not being more watchful of her. You see, about two years after they moved to Virginia, both she and their son were killed in a native uprising while Joshua was away overnight. All of their buildings were destroyed. Joshua was heard to say after their deaths that he would never sacrifice another family to the rigors of colonial life. I didn't hear him say that, mind you, but I believe it's his opinion, for I've not known him to be attracted to any woman — that is, until you came."

"My interest in him probably stems from the help he gave me when I was so sick, but there is some spark between us. Enough attraction, at least, that I'd be foolish not to explore its possibilities."

"I agree that you should see more of him, but I wanted you to know the obstacles you face. Nothing would please me more than to see you wed to Joshua."

"I'm glad you approve. Let me help you wash the plates and utensils. I haven't done any work since I've been here."

Grinning, Eliza said, "Have you ever done any housework?"

She shook her head. "You know we had servants, and Grandmother would have been appalled if I'd offered to help. But I don't intend for you to wait on me, so you can teach me how to be a housekeeper."

"Which you'll need to know if you stay in the colony. But as long as you're a guest, you don't have to work." She picked up a long piece of wood and made another notch on it to indicate the passing of another day. "This year has gone by fast. It's only a short time until Christmas and the beginning of a new year."

"How do you celebrate Christmas in Jamestown?"

"There's not many festivities that day. We have a service at the meetinghouse, and I prepare a big meal. But on New Year's Day, there's a lot of revelry — shooting contests, races, and things like that. I do hope you will at least be here for all of the fun."

Susanna found herself hoping that she might still be in Jamestown at that time, also, but the celebration had little to do with her reason why.

CHAPTER 5

Susanna had never given much thought to choosing clothing because her maid usually laid out her garments each morning. Since she'd arrived in Jamestown, she had chosen the simple dresses and petticoats she'd worn on shipboard. But considering the ride with Joshua to be a special occasion, she searched through her trunks. She'd been so opposed to coming to Virginia that she hadn't paid any attention to what her maid had packed.

The first trunk she opened contained summer garments, so she pushed it aside. From the other trunk, she selected a cotton petticoat, a linen chemise, and a rust-red dress with an open-fronted skirt which exposed an underskirt of dark gray. For warmth she chose a black cloak and a matching hood.

Unaccustomed to styling her own hair, Susanna asked Eliza to help her. Her aunt brushed Susanna's auburn hair briskly and pulled it back tightly from the forehead to the back of her head, leaving a fringe of bunched curls along the sides.

Although the air was still cold when Joshua called for Susanna, the sun was shining and Uncle Lester predicted a fair day. The horse Joshua brought for her was a small, dapple-gray mount. As he helped her into the sidesaddle, Susanna wondered if the saddle had belonged to his wife. As if he was reading her mind, Joshua said, "I borrowed the saddle from my tenant's wife. She rides this horse when she and her husband come into the settlement, so the horse is accustomed to ladies' skirts. You'll be perfectly safe."

Riding side by side, they followed a narrow, northwest trail out of the settlement. Numerous acres had been cleared for the village, but only a small portion of the area had buildings. The rest of the clearing had been planted with corn and other grain and vegetables, for the stalks were still standing. Soon the forest closed in around them, and with Joshua leading the way, they rode single file.

Most of the trees had lost their leaves, but the barren limbs spread out over the trail blocking the sunlight. In midsummer when foliage was on the trees, Susanna imagined that the trail would be semidark throughout the day. Recalling tales she'd heard of native uprisings and how they attacked from the forest, a nervous tingle spread through her body. But Joshua looked back from time to time and smiled, which was reassuring. Had there been any danger, she was confident he wouldn't have invited her to go with him.

After a few miles, the trail widened, and Joshua slowed his horse so she could ride beside him. "I've never seen so many trees in my life," Susanna said.

"Thick forests cover most of this peninsula, and we don't have the kind of tools we need to clear acres of land. We girdle the trees, and when they die, we plant around them. The forest soil is fertile and produces good crops."

"I don't know what you mean by girdling."

"It's a method used in England. We cut a notch about a foot wide in the bark all around the tree and peel off the bark. This causes the trees to die, and even though the trunks continue to stand for a few years, it doesn't hinder growth. After they completely decay, we dig the roots from the ground and burn them. It's a slow process, but there isn't any easier way to clear the land."

"I can understand now why the explorers called America a *new land.* At home, so many people have lost hope, but in spite of the difficulties they've had, everyone I've met in Jamestown is optimistic about the future. Has Virginia lived up to what you expected? Are you sorry you emigrated?"

The moment the words escaped her lips, Susanna wished she could recall them. A bleak expression crossed his face.

"I'm sorry — I shouldn't have asked that."

His eyes were speculative when he looked at her. "Eliza has told you about my family?"

"Not much, but enough to know that you may have regrets."

"For months after they were killed, I was miserable, blaming myself for their deaths, wishing I had never brought them to this dangerous place. But I eventually realized that people die young in England, too. I left home because I thought I could make a better life for my family in Virginia. My wife was willing to come with me — it isn't as though I forced her to do so. After several miserable months, I finally realized I had to put their deaths behind me and continue to do what I'd come to this country to achieve. I've been satisfied, but not particularly happy. Still, I haven't let that stand in my way of creating a home in the wilderness." Joshua spoke with the certainty of a man who would never be content with an unfulfilled dream.

"I'm torn between conflicting emotions, too," Susanna said. "I lost my parents several years ago, and I've felt as if I'm a nuisance to my grandmother. My aunt and uncle want me to stay here. I like much of what I hear about the New World, but it's a big choice to make."

The trail narrowed again, which made conversation difficult, and when Susanna's eyes grew weary of the wide expanse of barren trees and the leaf-littered trail, she concentrated on her companion. His powerful shoulders were covered with a black woolen coat, he wore a wide-brimmed hat, and his knee-high boots came to the cuffs of his breeches. He glanced often from side to side, and she knew that he was alert to any kind of danger they might encounter. She felt safe with Joshua — a security she hadn't experienced since her parents had died. But was this reason enough to stay in the New World, especially if Joshua didn't want her to stay?

As they neared his home, Joshua was beset with a nervous tension that was not habitual for him. Why was it so important for Susanna to like his home?

When they left the main trail and turned toward the area where his holdings were located, he slowed his horse until she rode beside him. They climbed a small hill, and he said, "We're almost there. I hope the ride hasn't been tiring for you."

"A little," she admitted, "because I probably haven't ridden for a year or more. But everything has been interesting — so unlike anything I've ever seen at home."

"You can rest before we start back. I told Eliza we wouldn't return until late afternoon."

They came out into a clearing, and Joshua halted his horse to give Susanna an overall view of his home. He watched her expression anxiously, as she surveyed the ten-acre clearing marked by trunks of girdled trees, two tenant houses, a barn and stable, fields of tobacco stubble, pasture fields for his horses and cattle, the rail fence that kept his livestock out of the cultivated fields, and lastly his home that overlooked the James River two miles away. To add to the pastoral scene, a herd of white-tailed deer grazed at the edge of the forest.

After several minutes, she turned and looked directly at him, and her eyes glowed with enjoyment and pleasure. "I have never seen a more beautiful place. Most of my life has been spent in London. I didn't know such natural beauty could be found anywhere."

Because of her pleasure in his home, Joshua experienced an air of calm and self-confidence, knowing for certain that he had reached the place to which God had directed him. Like Abraham, he had followed God's leading into the Promised Land.

He briefly touched Susanna's gloved hands as they rested on the pommel of her saddle. "Your approval means a lot to me. Let's go on to the house, so you can rest."

As they neared the buildings, Susanna said, "This is the first brick home I've seen in Virginia."

"My first house, similar to those in Jamestown, was destroyed by fire. The local kiln turns out good bricks, so I decided to build a more durable structure than my first home had been."

Stopping in front of the one-story house, which faced the river, he lifted her down from the saddle and tied the horses to a hitching post. "I built only one large room at first, but I've recently added a bedchamber. Lester is making the furniture for that room."

He opened a wide, heavy door and ushered her into the interior of his home, which was similar in size and furnishings to the Wilde dwelling. A woman, who was working at the fireplace, turned to face them.

"This is Mary Stevens. Mary, meet Miss Susanna Carter from London."

A stocky woman with a ruddy complexion and graying hair, Mary dipped into a slight curtsy. "Pleased to meet you, ma'am. Would you like some refreshment now? I have some mint tea ready."

"Yes, please. I am thirsty."

Joshua helped remove her coat and shawl and laid them on a bed built into the wall. "Sit and enjoy your tea while I take the horses to the stable. They'll get their food before we do. I'll return soon."

Mary brought a mug of tea to the table and a small piece of cake. "I'd not want to spoil your appetite, but a cup of tea goes better with a little something sweet. We pick the leaves from native plants in summer and dry them. Be there anything else I can fetch you?"

"Nothing more. Do you do all of Mr. Deane's cooking?"

"No, ma'am. He fixes most of his vittles. I just help out when he has company."

"How long have you been in Virginia?"

"Two years. My man and me, we be indentured servants."

"What are your terms?"

"Mr. Deane paid to bring us over — two hundred pounds of tobacco for the both of us. But we had to promise to work for him seven years to pay back our fare. When that time is up, we're free to take up land of our own."

"That seems like a fair arrangement."

"I guess so, but the time seems to pass immortal slow. It's almost like being a slave."

"Except that you have hope of being free."

"Yes'um — that's why we took the chance. Mr. Deane is good to us. Though it's smaller, our house is as good as this one. And he gives my man a day each week to work on a field of his own. The sale of our tobacco so far has brought enough to buy a pig, and by the time we're free, we'll have some more livestock to take to the fifty acres of land we're supposed to be given. We could have done worse."

"I pray that you'll continue to prosper."

"Thank you."

A blast of cold air heralded Joshua's return. He hung his coat and hat on a peg behind the door and held his hands toward the warmth of the fireplace. "What have you prepared for us?"

"A pot of succotash, corn bread, and a squash pie. Ought I to serve it now?"

"If Miss Carter is ready."

"I'm hungry, and the food smells good."

"You can put the food on the table," Joshua said, "and we can serve ourselves."

Thoughtfully, Susanna watched as Mary dipped the mixture of corn and beans into a large wooden bowl and cut the corn bread from an iron skillet and placed it on a trencher. She carried the two containers to the table, then took a pewter platter from the mantel and put the pie on it. Susanna had already learned that there were few servants in Jamestown — the woman of the house took care of the household chores. Unmarried men usually did their own housework, as Joshua had done since his wife's death. Prior to coming to Jamestown, Susanna had never done any work in the kitchen. Could she ever learn to be a house-wife?

"If that's all, Mr. Deane, I'll go home," Mary said.

He nodded. "Thanks for helping."

Joshua pulled out a bench for Susanna, sat to her left, and bowed his head in a brief prayer of thanks for the food.

Dipping the succotash into pewter bowls,

he explained, "Mary has two little ones, but her husband, John, watched them while she prepared our food."

"Is hiring indentured servants satisfactory?"

"It has been for me because I hired men with families, who are likely to stay put. Sometimes single men will run away to live with the natives."

"That surprises me. I thought they were hostile."

"There are always a few renegades who hate the English and are dangerous. But if it hadn't been for the help of the natives, the first group of settlers in Virginia thirteen years ago would all have died. This area was populated by thousands of Algonquin Indians, who lived in two hundred villages governed by Chief Powhatan. They taught the settlers how to farm."

"When I knew I was being exiled to America, I talked to my tutor about the colony. He explained that most of the first group of settlers perished because none of them were farmers, and that was about the only way to make a living here."

"All of them would have died if the natives hadn't provided food. Later, when John Rolfe married an Algonquin maiden, a pact was made with her father, Powhatan, and we've had peace for a few years. But it's an uneasy truce because the natives don't like Europeans taking their land. I can't say that I blame them. We have about a thousand settlers in Virginia now and less than a hundred live in Jamestown — we keep taking land that the natives claim. I'm always alert for an Indian attack."

"Uncle Lester said that many of the men who came in 1607 expected to find gold just as the Spanish had farther south."

Nodding, Joshua said, "That's true, but there is no gold in this region, which disappointed the men who weren't willing to do manual labor."

After they finished their meal, Susanna insisted on helping Joshua wash their utensils. Although she tried to put into practice the few things she'd learned from Eliza, her hands were soon smarting from the strong soap, and she handled the bowls and spoons awkwardly. Embarrassed at her ineptness, she wondered if Joshua realized how inexperienced she was as a homemaker.

"We'll start back to Jamestown soon," he said when they'd finished. "But let me show you the bedchamber I've added. One of my servants has some carpentry skill, and he did most of the building."

Almost as big as the main room, the bedchamber had no furniture. There was one window with a glass pane, which Joshua explained was made in Jamestown. "It's not high-quality glass but preferable to the oiled paper over the windows in the other room."

He pointed out the beamed ceilings that had been carved from trees cut on his own property. "Instead of attaching a bed to the wall, I'm having Lester make a bedstead, as well as some other furniture." He noticed when Susanna shivered slightly, and he pointed to a small fireplace in one corner of the room. "I'll keep a fire going when I start to sleep in here."

"You have a very comfortable house. It seems to me you've done very well."

He closed the door behind them as they went into the other room. "It's a slow process, though, and I'm not a patient man," he admitted with a slow smile. "It seems as if I've been struggling for years to build a house. My plans are to have an even larger home before I'm an old man."

"How old are you now?"

"Thirty, my last birthday." Susanna quickly calculated that there was a twelve-year difference in their ages.

"Perhaps we should start back now, so I can escort you into Jamestown and have time to return before nightfall." He held her

71

coat. "You can wait here in the house while I bring the horses or walk with me to the stable."

After buttoning the coat, she put on her hood. "The walk will be good. My joints are already a bit stiff from the morning ride."

As they walked, she commented on the vast clearing, and Joshua explained, "We have to provide a broad expanse so we won't be subject to a surprise attack. The natives prefer to do their fighting from the protection of the forest."

She shivered, knowing that it wasn't caused by the cold wind wafting upward from the river. Rather, she was startled to think how frightening to be inside the buildings and have enemies attacking from all sides.

Although Susanna didn't know a whit about farming, she sensed that Joshua was a good husbandman of his property as he proudly showed her around his land. Her respect for him had increased greatly during this visit.

She was tired, and the trail seemed endless before they reached Jamestown. When they arrived at the Wildes', she invited him to come inside.

But he said, "Not today. Make my excuses

to Eliza."

"Thanks for sharing this day with me," she said simply. "I had a wonderful time."

He took her hand and pressed his lips against her gloved fingers. "No more than I did. Your approval of my plantation caused me to like it even more. I hope you decide to stay in Jamestown so this won't be your last visit."

Susanna stood on the porch and watched him ride away until he was out of sight. This day had left her with much to think about. Did she have a future in Jamestown?

Joshua's mind was made up. Since his wife's death, he'd had no desire to marry, but spending a day with Susanna had made him conscious of how fond he'd become of her. He didn't doubt that their mutual attraction to one another was of God. Should he speak to Lester, or should he allow some time to pass before he made a move? But if Captain Trent should make a sudden decision to return to England, she might go out of his life as quickly as she had come into it.

Thinking that Susanna might leave the colony before he saw her again unnerved Joshua, and he knew he must move quickly. But how soon? If her feelings weren't as involved as his, he didn't want to scare her away.

CHAPTER 6

Curious about the kind of furniture her uncle was making for Joshua, the next morning Susanna wrapped a shawl around her shoulders and ran across the short distance to his shop. He was smoothing a large board with a plane, and he didn't see her immediately.

When he looked up, he said, "You've come for a visit, have you? Better be careful or I'll put you to work."

"I'd like that. I'm not much help to Aunt Eliza. What can I do?"

He peered curiously at her. "Do you mean it?"

"Yes."

"This is dirty work, and we don't want your pretty brown dress to be soiled. Wear an old dress tomorrow, and I'll find something for you to do."

"Do you have time to explain what you're making now?"

Pleased, he said, "I'll take time. I'm making a bed, chest, and night table for Joshua Deane. I bought a big log from Eli Derby. He sawed it into lumber for me, and I've done the smoothing and shaping myself."

"Joshua mentioned that you were making some furniture for him. I'd like to see it."

"This chest is his. It's finished except for putting oil on it. It's a pretty piece, if I do say so myself." He ran his hands over the smooth surface of a plain chest made with six cedar boards nailed together, secured with a latch and wooden pegs. A long drawer at the bottom of the chest opened with knobs which were shaped like claws. "The top part is four feet by twenty inches, and it's two feet deep. It has an eight-inch drawer."

He pointed out the headboard, footboard, and railings of the bed, also in cedar, which had already been oiled, giving Susanna an idea of what the finished product would look like. She sniffed the clean, aromatic scent of the cedar, thinking how pleasant Joshua's bedchamber would be.

"I'll finish the chest today. Then I'll start on the night table. It's the smallest, but it will take more time."

"Maybe I could put oil on the chest."

"That would be a help, but it's a hard

job," he warned. Holding up a wide slab of lumber, he added, "I'll make the table tomorrow out of cedar, but I'll use small oak limbs for the legs — they're sturdier than sawed lumber."

Lester showed her some tops he was making for the kids in the settlement for Christmas. "You can oil these, too, if you want to."

"I'll plan on doing that tomorrow. I'm going to see Ada Derby this afternoon."

"Have a nice visit, and I look forward to having you work with me tomorrow."

Susanna noticed the big smile on his face as she turned to leave. She was pleased that she had been able to bring her uncle a little pleasure for all he and Aunt Eliza had done for her.

The custom in Jamestown was to eat only two meals daily, so Susanna figured that midday was a good time to pay a visit. Marveling that she could move around the little settlement without a chaperone, she walked toward the fort and found the house Ada had pointed out to her.

"Oh, come in," Ada said when she came to the door. "I'm so happy to see you. I've been lonely today. Let's sit close to the fire."

Ada's home wasn't as big as the Wilde

house, nor was it furnished as well. Except for a few benches, the table, and a bed, furniture was nonexistent. Pots and pans hung from the rafters. Only one window, covered with oil paper, provided light in the room. A large fireplace covered one wall of the dwelling, however, and it was cozy.

"I've been baking this morning," Ada said. She put a bran muffin on a wooden plate and gave it to Susanna.

Susanna nibbled off a section of the pastry and complimented Ada on being a good cook. As she continued to enjoy the muffin, Susanna asked, "Why have you been lonely?"

Ada sat beside her on the bench. "Thinking about home. My mother and father were happy together, and we had such jolly times. That is, until my father inherited some money and gambled it all away. Although I knew when I left that I'd never see any of them again, it seems so final now that I'm actually settled in Virginia."

Hesitantly, Susanna asked, "Are you sorry you came?"

Blushing, Ada said, "I miss my family, but I'm not sorry I've become Eli's wife. I'm sure I couldn't have found a better man in England. He's a hard worker, and he has great plans for the future. I'm fond of him," she added, and her face reddened.

"Then you believe it's possible to love a person after such a short time?"

Ada nodded. "It happened to us — there was an immediate attraction when we first met. You can't imagine how much I dreaded marrying someone I didn't know, but I'm sure we'll have a happy marriage." She looked curiously at Susanna. "Why do you ask? I hear you've had lots of men calling on you. Do you have a fondness for one of them?"

"I'm not sure. I'm not ready to name him, but there is one who interests me. He's a fine man, and my aunt speaks highly of him. But I don't know if I think enough of him to give up my ties to England. And I don't know if he would want me to stay."

"You said you'd lived with your grand-mother. Is she your only relative?"

"I have some aunts and uncles in England, but I've always liked Aunt Eliza best."

"Then it would work out all right for you to live here."

Since she was unsure of her feelings for Joshua, Susanna tried to think of another subject. She noticed a lute hanging on the wall. "Does your husband play the lute?"

"He plays every evening. It rests him after a long day at work."

"According to Aunt Eliza, there isn't much celebration of Christmas here except a church service. But wouldn't it be nice if we could have some special music? Maybe you and I could sing while Eli plays for us."

"He's shy, but I'll ask him."

"Come by for a visit and let me know."

When Susanna returned to the Wilde house, Aunt Eliza was entertaining Aaron Waller. Susanna wasn't glad to see him, but she displayed the good manners she'd been taught.

He stayed for a long time, and before he left, he again issued another invitation for Susanna to visit his home. She turned him down firmly, hoping to avoid other invitations.

After she closed the door behind Aaron, she turned toward Eliza in distress. "Do you think I'm wrong to discourage him so firmly?"

"No, I don't. I feel sorry for the unmarried men of the settlement, for I know they're lonely, but that's no reason for you to sacrifice yourself by marrying someone you don't even like."

"That's the way I feel about it," Susanna said, relieved that her aunt shared her opinion. "No one except Joshua has stirred one bit of emotion in my heart, and I won't lead other men on by flirting with them."

"And you —" Eliza stopped abruptly in the middle of the sentence and rushed to open the door. The church bell was ringing. "Oh, my!" Eliza exclaimed, her hand at her throat.

"What is it?"

"When the bell rings like that, it's either very good news or very bad news. A ship could have been sighted, or it could be that the Indians are attacking." She threw a coat around her shoulders. "Get your coat. We'll go see."

As they ran down the street, a man stuck his head out of the door of his house, shouting, "Indians! Indians! Get to the fort."

"You rustle on inside," Eliza urged. "I'm not going without Lester. His hearing's none too good, and he might not have heard the warning."

Susanna obeyed her aunt, but she stopped at the fort's entrance and watched until she saw Eliza and Lester hurrying toward safety.

Inside the fort was chaos. Frightened women huddled in the middle of the area, clutching their children, most of whom were crying or looking around wildly, fear in their eyes. Men huddled in groups, some waving their arms excitedly, a few of them talking and shouting, others seemed stunned into silence.

Pulling at the collar of her dress, Susanna struggled to catch her breath. She wondered how long she would have to stay inside this place. She had never liked being in crowds. She was thankful that her grandmother had arranged a private cabin for her on the *War-wick* and spared her from spending weeks in constant company of a large group of women.

"Susanna!"

She turned at the sound of her name and spied Ada hurrying toward her.

"Do you know what's going on?"

Susanna shook her head. "Aunt Eliza and I headed this way as soon as she heard the bell ringing. A man said that the natives are attacking but that's all we heard."

"Eli is circulating among the men, and he'll let me know when he can."

Eliza joined them. "Don't worry until we find out what has happened. We've had false alarms before. Some people are just naturally skittish and see an Indian behind every bush. Let's find a place to sit down — maybe inside the church. We need to be praying anyway."

"I'll tell Eli where we are, so he won't worry about me," Ada said.

As they watched her approach Eli, Susanna said, "I'm happy her marriage is working out so well."

Smiling, Eliza said, "Eli is a good man, and I'm pleased he and Ada got together. Not all of the marriages work out. One woman stabbed her husband to death a few nights ago, and the leaders of the colony have put her in irons to send her back to England when the *Warwick* sails. Another man has been beating his wife, so he's been locked up."

"Then this wife experiment hasn't been successful?"

"Oh, I think it has, but you can't expect 100 percent success. God's own Word said that man shouldn't live alone. It's His plan for us to live together in families. It's my opinion that the colony wouldn't have survived if the women hadn't come."

Several men and women were inside the church, but unlike the tension that had prevailed outside, Susanna sensed a calmness of spirit among those who had gathered for prayer. She sat beside Eliza on a bench near the back of the small building, clasped her hands, and looked toward the front of the church, where a crude wooden cross hung from the arched ceiling.

Looking at the cross and remembering what had happened on a similar cross hundreds of years before, Susanna had the overwhelming conviction that she was in the place God wanted her to be. She bowed her head, first asking God to forgive the ill feelings she had harbored against her grandmother. Silently she prayed, *God, maybe she did me a favor to send me to this unknown land. If You have a purpose for my life here, guide me to know what it is.* Her thoughts turned to Joshua. Although she had looked over the crowd of men inside the palisade, she hadn't seen him and that concerned her. *God, protect him if he's in danger.*

When Susanna raised her head, Ada, who had sat down beside Susanna while she had prayed, whispered, "Eli said the preacher will make an announcement as soon as they can sort out truth from rumor. He'll call us if the preacher speaks outside, but he thinks he'll come inside the church."

In the front of the room a man started softly singing a song that English children particularly liked, and soon others joined in. As they sang about the ships sailing to Bethlehem, Susanna said quietly to Eliza, "Is there room in this fort for all the inhabitants of Jamestown?"

Grimly, she answered, "During an Indian attack, you'd be surprised how many people can crowd in here. Not only the people in the village but from the outlying plantations, too. It's bedlam. Usually, we're forted up only a short time, but once we were sequestered for a week, and I thought I'd lose my mind. I told Lester then that I'd not come inside again, but whenever there's a scare, we always head this way."

"I've been wondering about Joshua. Will he take refuge in the village?"

"Not likely. He's got a brick house, hasn't he?" When Susanna nodded, Eliza continued, "He was living in a daub-and-wattle house when his family was killed. I figure that's the reason he built a sturdier home."

"His tenant houses are made out of brick, too, and his house *is* sturdy. I'll try not to worry about him."

The preacher came into the building, followed by others, until all the seats were filled and men stood around the walls. He didn't have to call for silence, for everyone seemed tense and eager to know what to expect.

"We've ruled out a general attack by the natives, but there is some bad news," he said. "A family who lived on the edge of the wilderness has been killed, but it apparently occurred a few days ago. This seems to be an isolated incident, for which we're thankful."

Susanna held her breath until he gave the name of the family.

"Let's thank God for our safety. The leaders of the colony have already dispatched some soldiers and other citizens to investigate what has happened."

After the pastor prayed, a man asked, "Then it's safe for us to return to our homes?"

"The head of each household can make that decision. If you want my opinion, I'd say that those who live in the village would be as safe at home as you have been. Those who live outside on plantations may want to stay here until the search party returns with a definite answer about what has happened."

Joshua was unaware of the Indian scare until the soldiers stopped by his plantation to learn if he'd had any trouble. He volunteered to go with them, leaving his tenants to guard his property.

When they arrived at the small clearing and saw the mass slaughter of the family, Joshua's mind flashed to the scene on his property when he had returned from an overnight hunting trip and found his wife and son dead and his buildings burned. His stomach roiled, he felt dizzy, his ears rang, and he staggered toward a tree and leaned against it for support. He forced himself to open his eyes and look at the destruction around him. The house had been burned, and the man, his wife, and three children had been slaughtered.

One of the soldiers came to Joshua and placed his hand on his shoulder. "If I'd known what we would find here, I wouldn't have asked you to come with us. Why don't you go back home, Joshua? We'll take care of this."

Joshua straightened his shoulders and shook his head. "I'll stay. Everyone here has had someone die in this colony. I suppose it's the price we pay to settle a new world. But it's a bitter price, my friend."

"I know. If you think you're up to it, come and look over the victims. I don't think the natives are responsible."

"What?"

Steeling himself to look at the bodies of the slain where they were lying, Joshua walked around the area. "I see what you mean. They've been killed in Indian fashion, but there are no moccasin tracks."

"The outbuildings were burned, and the cattle driven off, but the house is still standing and none of the furnishings taken."

"So it's Englishmen who have done this."

"That's my opinion," the soldier said. "There has been some stealing in other places, and I'm laying the deed to a couple of runaway servants. As soon as we bury the dead, we're going after them. I figure they're not far away and probably saved the house to live in it at night."

"I'll help bury the dead and then go back to my home to tell my servants that the crisis is apparently over. We will be on our guard, because those men are liable to attack again."

As Joshua helped bury the five victims, he felt as if he were digging a grave for his own dreams and aspirations. Again he had been reminded that this country was too harsh for gentlewomen, especially one like Susanna. His hopes of bringing her to the plantation as his wife were as dead as this slaughtered family.

CHAPTER 7

When Lester came in for supper on the third day after the scare, he immediately said, "This crisis is over. The Benson family was murdered, but no one else."

"Thank God for that," Eliza said. "But who's to know when the Indians will strike again?"

As he washed his hands, Lester said, "It wasn't natives, but a couple of runaway servants. The soldiers discovered them and hanged them. I am thankful the matter is over and we are all safe."

As they bowed their heads and Lester prayed a blessing over their food, Susanna added her own silent thanks that Joshua had been spared. She had missed seeing him, but to convince herself that all was well with him, she had spent the days of waiting embroidering monogrammed handkerchiefs to give him for Christmas.

While she helped Lester in the shop, putting oil on the furniture he had made for Joshua, she had looked up expectantly whenever the door opened, but two days passed and Joshua didn't come.

She made plans with Ada and Eli to practice the music to sing at the Christmas service. Susanna had asked to borrow a hymnal from the preacher at the church. Although he refused to let her have a good hymnal, he loaned her a few sheets from an old book.

When Ada and Eli arrived for their first practice, Susanna invited them to sit around the table, and she spread the pages out so they could see them.

"Eli can't sing and play, too, and I'm not very brave," Ada said. "I don't think I can stand before the congregation and sing unless there's more than the two of us." She glanced toward Eliza. "Why don't you sing, too?"

"Lester is a better singer than I am, and I don't see any reason why we can't help out. That is, if we know the songs."

"I looked through these sheets and found a few familiar songs," Susanna said. "We can probably find one or two that we all know."

"I'll sing with you in the meetinghouse," Lester said, "if you'll promise to go caroling with me afterward. One of the highlights of my boyhood was when the carolers came on Christmas Day. My mother always had a treat of shortbread or some other pastry for them. As I got older, I joined the singers. It would bring back good memories to do that again."

"We could go caroling as soon as the meeting ends," Eli said, as he plucked the eleven strings of his lute with the thumb and fingers of his right hand.

Susanna read the titles of the hymns she'd found, and they finally agreed on two that all of them knew. "Let's try 'Good Christian Men, Rejoice' first and then 'The Coventry Carol.' "

After they had practiced for a long while, Eli pulled out his watch. "We'd better be getting home, wife. I have a lot of work to do tomorrow."

"We only have two more evenings to practice, but we'll make it," Eliza said.

The following day, Susanna couldn't seem to concentrate on any task. When her aunt asked repeatedly if anything was wrong, Susanna just shrugged her shoulders. She realized, however, that she wasn't hiding her unhappiness from Eliza, for she often found her aunt looking at her with sympathy.

Finally, Eliza sighed loudly and said, "I'm sorry, Susanna, but I tried to warn you against Joshua. He buried his heart with his wife and son."

Susanna could hold back her feelings no longer. "But he's seemed interested in me."

"I know he has. I may be wrong."

"Perhaps he's afraid to leave the plantation after what happened to the Benson family." Eliza didn't reply but continued to knit, the clacking needles blending with the crackling coals in the fireplace.

Susanna finally added, "Apparently you don't believe that's the reason."

"No, I don't, but I'm willing to be proven wrong. Lester is taking Joshua's furniture to him tomorrow morning. Why don't you go with him?"

"Wouldn't that seem a little forward?"

Eliza laid aside her knitting and walked toward the fireplace, saying matter-of-factly, "In England, it wouldn't be acceptable, but we aren't as restricted in our behavior in Virginia. If you want to know why he has stopped seeing you, go and ask him."

"Very well, I'll do that . . . if Uncle Lester doesn't mind."

"He'll welcome your company. I'll send Joshua a loaf of my bread, which will bake overnight in the oven and be ready by morning."

As Lester drove the cart pulled by two horses toward their destination, the trail through the forest seemed even smaller than it had on Susanna's first journey to Joshua's home. She shuddered in the crisp, frosty air, and she could see her breath like fog before her face, but after a few miles the sun shone through the leafless trees. She sat on a narrow seat, rubbing shoulders with her uncle, who took up more than half of the room. She repeatedly looked over her shoulder to be sure that the canvas still covered Joshua's furniture.

"Ho, the house!" Lester called when he pulled the horses to a halt as they arrived at their destination.

Joshua opened the door and stepped out. He smiled with what appeared to be pleasure when he saw Susanna, but his expression immediately stilled and grew serious.

"Brought your furniture," Lester said. "I thought it could be your Christmas present, even if you are paying for it."

"Good day, Susanna," Joshua said, extending his arms to help her from the cart. But after that first pleased glance, he hadn't looked directly at her. "Go on inside to the fire while I help Lester unload."

Without answering, Susanna went into the house to open and close the door as they carried in the furniture. When they brought in the last piece, Susanna followed them into the bedroom. The pinkish cedar furniture blended with the white oak wall paneling. Briefly, she contemplated little touches that would make the room more homelike. She decided upon a coverlet for the bed with a bright cushion or two, a bowl on the chest, and a tiered candlestick holder on the table beside the bed. But given the coolness of Joshua's reception, she didn't think she would ever have the opportunity to decorate this room. However, she wanted to know one way or another.

The bedroom was cold, and Joshua shut the door behind them when all the furniture was in place. They returned to the main room. "I'll drive your horses to the stable and feed them some grain," he said to Lester.

"Thank you," Lester said, "but I brought grain along with me. You can wait inside, niece, until the horses have eaten."

Joshua started to follow Lester outdoors, but Susanna said, "Could you stay a minute?"

He closed the door and turned to face her. His eyes met hers for a moment and they darkened with emotion, but he looked away.

"I've missed seeing you," she said.

"Yes, I've missed you, too."

She waited.

"But I've been busy working the plantation."

"Along with a loaf of bread, Aunt Eliza sent an invitation for you to share Christmas dinner with us."

He paused, and Susanna's heart hammered in her chest. Would he ever answer?

"Thank her for the invitation, but I won't be able to come."

Fighting back tears, she buttoned her coat and tied her hood more securely. As she brushed by him on her way to the door, Joshua caught her arm. "I have a reason for refusing. I've already invited my tenants and their families to share the holiday with me in this house."

"I'll tell Aunt Eliza." She tried to free her arm, but he still held her.

"I think you know how I feel about you, and I thought I had put the past behind me. But when I saw the slaughter of the Benson family, the past became the present, and I knew I couldn't risk another family. It isn't that I don't care!"

She shrugged off his detaining hand, smothered a sob, and answered him in a cold voice that reminded Susanna of her grandmother. "It's your decision. Aunt Eliza told me that you'd buried your heart with your family, and I believe it. But I wanted to find out for myself."

"Susanna," he pleaded, but she swept by him and out the door. Although she had humbled herself to come here today and confront him, she still had enough pride left that she wouldn't let him see how much his words had hurt.

Lester was checking the harnesses on the horses, but he gave her a hand into the cart. While Joshua paid him for the furniture he'd built, Susanna kept her eyes ahead. She didn't want him to see her tears, and she didn't look back as they drove away. Had she been wrong in thinking it was God's will for her to come to Virginia?

Joshua watched until Lester and Susanna were out of sight, wondering why any man in his right mind would turn down a future with her. He had been devoted to his wife, but theirs had been an arranged marriage, and he had never sensed the emotional feelings for her he had experienced when he held Susanna in his arms and carried her to the Wilde house.

After completing the day's tasks, Joshua

sat before the fire for a long time. Over and over in his mind he seemed to hear the words of Jesus to His disciples, "O ye of little faith." If Jesus were sitting with him now, would He be saying the same thing to him?

Joshua acknowledged that he lacked the faith to trust God for the future. Regardless of what happened to him *or* Susanna, if she became his wife, they could be happy during the time God gave them together. He knew he loved her, and he believed she loved him, too. And he would like to have a family. Each day as he worked long hours in the fields, he often wondered why he worked so hard. It seemed futile to build up a plantation when he had no progeny to inherit it.

He rehearsed in his mind several Bible references concerning marriage, and two in particular seemed to speak to him. In the beginning of time, *"The LORD God said, It is not good that the man should be alone; I will make him an help meet for him."* And the writer of the book of Hebrews had asserted that *"Marriage is honourable in all."*

When he retired to the bedroom and went to sleep for the first time in his new bed, Joshua's mind was made up. He would spend the holidays with his tenants and their families as planned, but the day after Christmas would find him in Jamestown, on his knees, asking Susanna to marry him.

The next day Susanna went looking for Captain Trent and found him in his tiny office on the *Warwick.* "Have you set a sailing date yet?" she asked.

"The day after Christmas."

"Uncle Lester thought the weather might keep you here all winter."

"It might have if I took a northerly route, but I aim to head south and hope to avoid stormy weather. I don't anticipate any problems." He peered keenly at her, his brown eyes speculative and concerned. "You aimin' to sail with me?"

The moneybag hanging around her waist felt as if it weighed a ton — it weighed on her conscience more than that. She had been angry with her grandmother when she'd stolen the coins, and it hadn't bothered her conscience, for she considered it part of the inheritance from her father, which her grandmother controlled. But she couldn't use the stolen money for her fare. She would take it back to Grandmother and ask forgiveness.

Realizing that the captain was peering at her with troubled eyes, she said, "Yes, I want to sail with you, but I don't have any money." From her pocket, she took her mother's gold brooch and a diamond-studded gold ring that had belonged to her father. "I know they're worth more than one hundred and twenty pounds of tobacco, and that's the price the settlers paid to bring their brides. Is this enough to pay my fare?"

Captain Trent bent his head and scanned the two items. "Money enough and to spare. But, Miss Susanna, I don't like to take your valuables."

"I don't want to lose them, either," she said, putting them back in her pocket, "but I must leave Jamestown, and I have nothing else to barter. I'll be ready to go on the twenty-sixth of December. That is, if there will be other women on the boat."

"The two chaperones are returning on the ship. You'll be safe enough."

Susanna's steps lagged as she left the riverbank and walked to the Wilde home. As always, her aunt was busy with household chores, and Susanna fleetingly wondered why she'd ever considered becoming a colonial housewife. At best, it was a life of drudgery. No doubt her uncle would arrange a suitable marriage for her in England, and she could live a life of ease. But why did this thought leave her with an inexplicable feeling of emptiness?

Unable to think of any easy way to break the news, Susanna squared her shoulders and entered the house. When Eliza looked up from her mending, Susanna said, "I've made arrangements to leave with Captain Trent the day after Christmas."

Eliza stared at her as if the words didn't register for a moment. Then she gave a cry of despair and said, "Don't leave us. You were made for the New World."

Cynically, Susanna answered, "No. If I stay here, I'll eventually give up and marry one of the colonists — for I can't continue to live in your home indefinitely."

Perhaps it was obvious to Eliza that her mind was made up, for her eyes filled with tears of frustration. "So be it."

"I'll not be using Grandmother's money. I'll take it back to her."

"But — but how will you pay your fare?"

Susanna took the jewelry from her pocket. "Captain Trent will take these in exchange for my passage."

"Susanna! Those are family heirlooms. You should keep them."

"I have no other way to pay my fare."

Shaking her head, Eliza said, "I pray that you won't live to regret this decision."

CHAPTER 8

Christmas Day dawned much like one would have in England. There was a slight mist in the air, a cold wind blew off the river, and fog hovered so low that it seemed as if the clouds had descended on the village. Walking to church with her aunt and uncle, the dampness penetrated Susanna's whole body and she shivered. Her mood was as dreary as the weather. Since the day her grandmother had given the ultimatum that she had to immigrate to Virginia, Susanna had planned her return to England. Tomorrow morning, she would finally have her way when she boarded the *Warwick.*

She knelt with the others when the service began, but although she prayed earnestly for God's guidance in her life, she received no satisfactory relief for her troubled spirit.

Perhaps knowing that the worshipers wanted to seek their own hearths during the raw weather, the preacher's message was shorter than usual. When the quartet prepared to sing, Lester said, "These songs are familiar ones, so join in with us if you know the words."

Eli plucked the strings of the lute to introduce their songs, and Susanna's spirits lifted during their presentation as her thoughts were transported to the little village of Bethlehem the night Jesus was born.

They sang the first lines of "Good Christian Men, Rejoice" before the congregation joined in. Susanna was pleased that they'd chosen songs that were meaningful to all of them.

When the service was over, they strolled through the village, singing songs that spoke of the coming of Jesus into the world to save all mankind. Despite her breaking heart, as she raised her voice in praise, Susanna received the assurance that God would work His will in her life — in His time, not hers.

The day that Susanna had looked to and dreaded finally arrived. Hoping until the last minute that she would see Joshua to give him the six monogrammed handkerchiefs she had made, before she left the Wilde home, she handed them to Eliza. "Please give these to Joshua the next time you see him. He may not want them," she said bitterly, "but I don't want them either."

"I feel in my heart that you're making a mistake to leave. Please wait for another ship. Some men are slow to change their minds. Joshua may come around yet."

Lester had tied Susanna's trunks on his wheelbarrow, and he waited outside. Opening the door, he said, "We should leave. The captain won't want to be delayed."

Susanna took one sweeping glance, trying to memorize every detail of the room where she had felt so much warmth and welcome. Then, with Eliza weeping beside her, they started toward the wharf. Captain Trent had announced his intention to leave by mid-morning, and when they arrived at the riverbank, Susanna decided that all of the colonists must have turned out to watch the ship leave.

Ada and Eli detached themselves from the larger group and hurried toward her. "I just can't believe you're leaving," Ada said. "I'll miss you."

"I've been proud to know you, miss," Eli said. "It would have been a pleasure to have you for a neighbor."

Susanna shook her head and swallowed the lump in her throat. "It wasn't meant to be."

"You didn't stay long enough to find out,"

Eliza hissed in her ear, even yet unwilling to accept her niece's departure.

But Susanna didn't believe she had much choice. She didn't want anyone except Joshua, and he wouldn't marry her. Maybe when she returned to England and went to live with Uncle Felton, she would find someone who would fill the void in her heart.

A wagon approached hauling several barrels of tobacco, and Captain Trent called, "Stand aside, ladies and gents, until we get these barrels aboard, and then we'll set sail."

Obviously he was jubilant at the prospect of going to sea. Noticing Susanna, he stepped to her side. "Then you've decided to travel with me?"

She nodded and handed him a small bag holding the jewels for her fare. Two sailors shouldered her trunks and carried them onto the ship.

A bugle sounded and soldiers marched from the fort with the woman prisoner, who walked along with her head held high as if she felt no remorse for the crime she'd committed. Susanna felt sorry for the woman, because life was difficult for the people who lived in London's hovels — most of them didn't have an opportunity to live decent lives. Too bad this woman, too, couldn't have found a home in Virginia.

Everybody had boarded except Susanna, and Captain Trent said, "Are you ready, miss?"

She nodded assent, for her throat was too tight for words. She threw herself into Eliza's arms, and Lester put his big arms around both of them.

"It is still not too late to change your mind," he said. "You can have a home with us as long as you want to stay."

"I know," she murmured. Not since her parents died had Susanna experienced such love as she'd received from her aunt and uncle. It was hard to leave them. She turned from them, blinking away her tears and trying to smile.

"Wait!"

Susanna heard the shout and turned toward the sound of a horse galloping down the bank. It was Joshua!

"Praise God from whom all blessings flow!" Lester shouted, taking off his wide-brimmed hat and tossing it high in the air.

Just before he reached the gangplank, Joshua threw the reins to a bystander, leaped from the saddle, and ran toward the ship, his arms outstretched. With a glad cry, Susanna ran to meet him.

He hugged her tightly for a few moments,

then held her away from him and searched her face. "Surely you aren't leaving!"

"I have no reason to stay."

"You soon will have," he said. Dropping to one knee before her, Joshua kissed her hand. "I love you, Susanna Carter. I want to marry you. Please stay and be my helpmeet. We can build a beautiful life together in Virginia. I know we can."

Her eyes very bright and with a tender expression on her face, Susanna caressed his uplifted face. "I know we can, too, for I love you, Joshua. I've known for many days that you were my reason for coming to Virginia."

She tugged on his hand, and he stood beside her. To the cheers of the settlers, Joshua gathered Susanna into his arms and kissed her.

Flustered, Susanna pulled away from him. "I thought you didn't want me," she murmured.

He reached for her again but turned when Lester and Eliza crowded close to them.

Lester pumped Joshua's hand. "Boy," he said, chuckling, "you just about missed the boat."

Eliza tucked her moist handkerchief into her coat, and her smile was tender as she bent over to kiss Susanna.

"Hey!" Captain Trent shouted as he bounded down the gangplank. "Does this mean I'm going to lose a passenger?"

Susanna turned in his direction. "Yes, Captain. Joshua said the words to keep me here. I'm going to marry him."

The captain handed her the leather bag holding her jewelry. "Then you don't owe me any passage fare. I hate to lose the money, but I'm happy you're staying. You two were made for each other."

Quietly, she said, "And will you do a favor for me?" She unfastened the bag of coins from her waist. "Will you see that my grandmother gets this? It's a bag of coins I took from her, intending to use the money to pay my way home."

He pointed to the bag of jewelry she held. "But why did you give me these jewels?"

"The jewelry was mine, but even though the coins could have been taken from my inheritance, when it came right down to it, I couldn't steal from her. I pray that she'll forgive me."

"I'll have a word with Lady Carter and tell her what a fine man you're getting."

"Thank you. I'll write a letter to her eventually, but I don't want to delay your departure. May God be with you as you journey!"

Susanna placed her hand in Joshua's and smiled at him. "I have found my home here in Virginia — the one God planned for me."

EPILOGUE

A week later, Susanna and Joshua stood hand in hand in front of the fireplace in the Wilde home. Ada and Eli stood beside them. Eliza and Lester sat on a nearby bench, holding hands, looking as happy as if the wedding were their own. The room was crowded with as many well-wishers as the room could hold.

Susanna wore a white wool dress she had brought with her from England. It had a long pointed bodice with full short sleeves and a voluminous skirt gathered at the back. She fingered the pearl chain with an ivory cross pendant that had belonged to Joshua's mother. Eliza had placed a lace cap on her head.

Susanna slid a sideways glance toward Joshua, who looked handsome in a dark blue doublet and a white shirt with a lace ruff at his neck. His gray breeches met his white stockings at the knees, and he wore a pair of buckled shoes he'd recently imported from England.

The smell of pine branches permeated the room and mingled with the scent of food Eliza had worked for days to prepare for the wedding feast. The church bell pealed for several minutes to mark the beginning of the ceremony.

The minister stood before them, and in a reverent tone began the traditional service accepted by the church. After a short prayer, he read passages from the Bible dealing with marriage.

The ceremony was short, but Susanna was breathless with joy and awe when she took her vows. It was inconceivable that after such a short time in Virginia, she was actually getting married. She remembered her arrival at Jamestown and how miserable she had been until she had met Joshua. Her life hadn't been the same since, and she silently thanked God that it wasn't her grandmother's dominance but His will and wisdom that had brought her to the New World.

Their vows taken, smiling broadly, the minister declared them man and wife.

Susanna's lips found their way instinctively to Joshua's, and when their lips met, she felt transported on a soft and wispy cloud of emotion. "I love you," she whispered softly through half-parted lips. His grasp tightened, and he kissed her again to seal the vows they had made for eternity.

■ ■ ■ ■

Angel of
Jamestown

BY LAURALEE BLISS

■ ■ ■ ■

To Sherry Davis.
Thanks so much for your prayers
and encouragement over the years.

As we have therefore opportunity, let us
do good unto all men, especially unto
them who are of the household of faith.

GALATIANS 6:10

CHAPTER 1

Jamestown, Virginia Colony, 1676

"Fire! We are all on fire! Help us! Dear God, save us!"

Paul Dodson leaped from the ground at the voices that filled his dream. His face was drenched, his heart beating rapidly, his hands trembling. He looked wildly around, only to see his fellow men on the ground nearby, wrapped in their blankets. Several of them opened their eyes and growled at him. Some told him to be still or be gone. He wiped away the sweat from his face and stared at the fire before him. It was a small fire kindled to ward off the night chill but a fire all the same. Angry orange tongues licked the air. The sharp scent of smoke stung his nostrils. He wiped his face once more. Just then he caught sight of his hand. Ugly skin now covered his flesh, like the leathery hide of some animal. The fire had burned him when he tried to rescue his

117

prized possessions, leaving him scarred in both his body and his heart.

Paul collapsed to the ground, too tired to do anything. The memory of that time was seared in his mind as much as the flames had burned his hand. He could still see it — the burning homes in Jamestown and then his blacksmith shop, his joy and refuge and the place he called home, consumed by flames. It all erupted into a fiery inferno reminiscent of something from the burning fires of scripture. He shuddered as he raced to his dwelling that night, trying in vain to retrieve the family Bible he had brought from England, along with a painting of his mother and a few clothes. The scorching flames drove him back. He then saw the fire move to engulf his blacksmith business. Like a huge mouth filled with flaming teeth, the fiery beast swallowed his dreams whole.

Paul should be accustomed to hardship in this land but not like this. Many had faced losses since coming to Virginia to seek a new life. And many had lost all they owned but still managed to go on with their lives. He could not go on. Instead he felt his shock turn to anger over his circumstances. The need for revenge burned as hot as the fire itself.

He tried to fall back asleep but knew it

was useless. Instead he watched the stars begin to fade with the coming of a new dawn. And what did the day bring but bitter memories of all he had lost in a land that was supposed to give him a new start. A land and the people that had betrayed him. He had been unwittingly caught up in other people's battles, their own personal rebellion against authority, and now his livelihood had been reduced to ashes because of it.

Paul stood to his feet and grabbed for his blanket. Likewise, the other homeless ones who had gathered around the fire took up their possessions. Where they disappeared to at the beginning of each new day, Paul did not know. Nor did he care. The only thing he cared about was trying to see the governor once again about his circumstances. Every day he ventured to see him, and every day he was turned back. *But today would be different,* he vowed. He would see the governor and demand to know how the man intended to assist in this crisis — if England would spill its coffers in aid, if soldiers would be dispatched to help rebuild homes, if the broken pieces of his life could be patched back together.

Paul found a water barrel and threw water on his face. It did little to douse the anger burning inside of him. He adjusted the hat he wore, not caring that his clothes looked as if he had dipped them in an ash barrel. They were as black as the ruined forge and burned-out bellows. He shrugged. *What does it matter?*

Paul began the journey by foot, as he had on previous occasions, toward the place where the governor had taken up temporary residence since the burning of Jamestown. He kept moving until a wagon came along and a man offered him a ride.

"Where are you off to this day, friend?" the man inquired.

"To see Governor Berkeley." Paul was surprised at how coarse his voice sounded, as if he had been among the smoke and flames that very day. In a way he had — the smoke and flames of despair.

"And why is that?"

Paul snorted. "Are you blind? Jamestown is still smoldering in its devastation, even months after the fire. And our grand governor has done nothing. He ignores the pleas for help."

The man stared at him in silence, no doubt looking at him and his apparel as if wondering how Paul dare present himself before such an important figure as the royal governor. Paul took little notice of the man's reaction. He had one thing on his mind, and today he would make certain his voice was heard.

"We are here," the man said, pausing at a road with a fine mansion set back on a hill. "May it go well with you."

Paul thanked him for the ride and immediately began walking the road. He had not gone but thirty paces or so when several of the governor's guard detail intercepted him, brandishing their gleaming bayonets from the rims of muskets.

"You again!" one shouted. "The governor will not see you. Be gone from here."

"Yes, he will see me," Paul said through clenched teeth. "I am a citizen of this colony whose home and business were destroyed and looted. I will see the governor and plead my case."

"He can do nothing," another of the soldiers said. "The governor is already besieged with difficulties since Jamestown was burned. He is most distressed, but there is nothing he can do. Now be gone, I say, before we feed you to the lions."

"I have no home to go to," Paul declared. "If the governor is so distressed over our plight, why then does he not allow citizens to dwell inside this fine plantation home of his? Or at least offer money from his purse?"

The soldier bristled. "That is enough! If you do not leave these premises at once, we will arrest you for trespassing on royal grounds. And where we send you, there is no return."

"Arrest me then!" Paul shouted. "What else have I to live for anyway? You may as well have my life, too, for I have nothing else."

To his astonishment the men stepped back as if they had confronted some heavenly witness. Paul could not believe his words would have that effect on them. He marveled until he turned to see a beautiful woman flanking him. He was startled by her presence. He had not even heard her come up behind him.

She smiled and curtsied before the awestruck soldiers. "Please excuse the gentleman. He is most distressed, as we all are over our great losses these many weeks."

"Yes, madam, we know," a soldier said. "But the governor cannot see him or anyone else."

Paul stared as the woman reached out and gently took hold of his arm to guide him back down the road. He could not react, let alone speak.

At last he was able to find his voice. "Madam, what are you doing? I have business here."

"I'm trying to save you, sir, if you will allow me."

"Save me from what, pray tell?"

"Do you think for a moment the governor cares for your loss? You are but one of many. He has no reason to help you. He would rather cast you aside."

"He must help. He is the governor."

"He is only here to help himself and the crown he serves. He can do nothing."

Paul bristled. "He will if I have anything to say about it."

"Calm yourself, sir. You know that only God alone can bear your loss. No man will ever be able to, and no governor either. In your heart you must know this."

Paul was speechless. When they came to the road, he saw a carriage waiting for the lady. It was rare to even see carriages within the colony. The grandeur of the sight nearly took his breath away, especially after the depravity he had witnessed in Jamestown with its gutted buildings and masses of hopeless faces. "Ah, I see why you believe the way you do," he sneered. "A carriage such as yours could build many fine homes."

"If that is the price for your happiness, sir, then you may take it and do with it as you wish."

Paul's mouth fell open. He felt the warmth enter his cheeks. "Madam . . . I . . ."

"But I think once you have it in your possession, you will feel no better than when you first arrived at this place, ready to confront the governor. Possessions cannot grant peace to a troubled soul." She paused. "Now, do you wish to have the carriage? I will say I do find a horse more comfortable on a rocky road such as this."

He shook his head, taken aback by the woman who talked so brashly, if not honestly.

"Then I wish you good day, sir." She entered the carriage with the help of a servant and quickly rode away. Paul stood where he was, still stunned by the encounter. Never in his life did he expect to witness such a thing or to have so beautiful a woman intervene on his behalf. "She must be an angel," he said softly. "One sent from heaven above."

Paul began the long walk back to Jamestown. Even if nothing remained for him, somehow his steps felt lighter and not so downtrodden. He did not know what he would do or where he would go, but hope burst forth in his heart. And though the journey was very long, exhaustion was far from him.

When he entered the town to see the remains of burned buildings and a few hardy souls trying to rebuild makeshift dwellings by the light of a few lanterns, he sensed peace for the future.

Paul immediately went to the place he once called home. All that remained were blackened timbers, broken glass, and burned books.

He picked up one such book written by Shakespeare, sent to him from his father, who had passed away just last year. Paul loved to read and was grateful for the barrel of books that his father sent him. Now little of them remained. He opened the blackened cover to find most of the pages scorched. He would have searched more but let it all go. Darkness was rapidly falling. He would need to go to where the other vagabonds gathered, around the makeshift fire, trying to stay warm and live through another long night . . . although he did not sense the hopelessness as he had on previous nights.

Paul took his ragged blanket and went to seek the warming fires. He heard the people murmur at his arrival. "The man who has lost his senses," they called out to him.

"I hope you will not keep me awake again," a burly man grumbled. "We are ready to cast you aside."

"Have you no mercy for your fellow man?" Paul asked.

"Only if you have mercy to allow a fellow man his rest and not take to ranting like one who has lost his senses. Find your rest this night and allow us a measure of rest, too."

Paul said no more. He had no will left to fight. The beautiful lady had driven the anger out of him, along with the long journey back to Jamestown.

He took off his worn leather shoes to see his feet covered by sores. A chilling wind made him put the shoes back on. He did not know where he would get the coins for new shoes. He had no trade anymore. He had nothing. Nothing but what the woman said — he had God. God was with him. He was glad she had reminded him of that fact, that faith had not likewise been burned away.

Paul wondered where the lady lived. She must be quite wealthy to own such a carriage and fine dress. Maybe she had been on her way to see the governor, too, and somehow felt compassion for a ruffian such as he. She did possess great faith. And she was willing to part with her wealth if he so asked. She was different from any other woman he had ever met.

Paul tried to relax on the cold ground with only a bed of straw to provide warmth. The wind began to stir. Others groaned and shivered. Some drew closer to the fire that once burned their homes but now provided the warmth they needed. They would have to think of homes soon. Winter's chill was calling with a vengeance. They would need dwellings to keep out the cold and even the snow that sometimes came to grace the land.

Paul wrapped the blanket tighter about him. He stared at the flickering flames, but instead of anger for what the fire had done, he thought about the beautiful lady with a smile on her face. *I wish I knew who you are,* he thought. *I would like to know your name. And why you helped someone like me when there are so many others.*

He looked up into the clear night and the multitude of stars. How was it that he was thought of among all the heavens? He was but one mortal and needy man out of many. Many had likewise suffered as he did. Could it be that God was trying to whisper something to him? That he mattered? That God knew of his losses? That he was not alone, even if he felt alone? That God could send an angel of sorts, even in the form of this woman, to help him in his time of need?

"Thank You, most holy God," he murmured. "Thank You for Your divine care this day that would have surely seen me imprisoned with the vermin if not for Your protection. And show me, I pray, what my future is to be. And who this woman is that You sent to help me." He wanted very much to discover her identity. He must thank her for her small act of kindness that brought more hope than any he had seen since the day of calamity.

Paul lay down then, exhausted from life itself. But his dreams were filled with visions of the angelic beauty on the road, the one who had led him to safety, the one with pale, soft skin; an enchanting smile; and a heart open to the woes of others.

CHAPTER 2

Alice Wells breathed a sigh of relief. Paul Dodson had not known who she was! *And why would he, after all this time?* she admonished herself. They had not laid eyes on each other for many years — since she was a young girl of twelve. He was a man of eighteen, new to this land of Virginia, but with a strong will to make his life worthy. And she was the daughter of an aristocratic family who had made their home by the James River.

She shivered then as the breeze blew over her from the open fields where her father grew the crops that brought in their income. It was good the harvest had been plentiful that fall, especially after the devastation wrought from the recent rebellion. Alice sighed. If only Paul knew that many had suffered, and not just the people inside Jamestown. While he indeed lost everything, Alice had suffered, too, though certainly not at such high cost. It was trivial things, really — some fine china, her father's horses, a prized necklace. Some things were broken, also, when the marauders came running through their home. The kitchen had been emptied of its provisions. The flocks and herds were scattered. But they had a home still and many of their possessions. Not like Paul, who had seen it all taken away by both fire and the hand of plundering.

Alice inhaled the fresh air scented with the damp mist from the river beyond. After the rebellion, she'd made inquiries about the fire that scorched Jamestown. Through others she learned of the devastation and the loss of Paul's blacksmithing business. Little did he know, but she had kept herself acquainted with all manner of his life. She must, after all. She owed him her life.

Alice shivered once more. She did not want to revisit that time where peace left her for fear. At times the memories would awaken her in the night. The angry faces of the Indians. The glint of the tomahawk raised above her head. And then the strong hands that tore it away before she saw the face of God.

"Oh, Paul, if only you could know," she said softly. "If only you would remember." But he did not, even though the image of his concerned face was burned forever into her mind. The face of her benefactor. The one who had kept her from the hand of death that day in the woods.

"How wonderful it is," she had said that day, recalling the very words she spoke. "All this marvelous corn. How glad Papa will be to have it. We will have our fields, and I will have my new tea set!" The find had been a marvelous discovery for a twelve-year-old girl — a large basket of seed corn abandoned in the woods. She felt certain God had sent it as a gift from the new land of Virginia after they had arrived from England. Papa needed the seed corn to plant his crops. And Alice wanted a new tea set after hers was broken during the long voyage. Papa told her that when they had enough money from a seed crop, he would send away to England for a new set.

With all her strength she had tugged and pulled on that basket of corn seed. She did not know how she would bring it to her father, but she was determined to do it. All she could see from this great find was her porcelain teapot and cups, and she would have them.

Suddenly there came a strange shout from the woods. Alice recalled the shivers and then the cold fear that swept over her. Was it an animal? She forced away the thought and again tugged on the basket.

Then they came. Two of them. Strange men with dark skin. They shouted at her, pointing at the corn. She was her father's daughter, and she was determined to keep it. "No, this is mine. I found it. I need it so I can have a new tea set. Go find your own."

Suddenly she saw the gleaming edge of the tomahawk. She screamed. Her life was about to be taken away.

At that moment in her dream, the quiver of a "No!" escaped from her lips. Alice flung her hand over her mouth. The day seemed so real to her, as if it were only yesterday. And so, too, was the image of Paul. She didn't know why he was there, but he was. He rose to challenge the two Indians. He stripped them of their weapon of death before it found its way to her skull.

"No," he said to them. "No kill. Foolish girl. Very sorry. *Netoppews,* yes?" He held out his hand in a gesture of friendship.

The Indians spoke back in angry words. Despite the differences in their language, Paul convinced the Indians that this was a mistake, that Alice was young and foolish, and that he wanted the Indians to be his friends. At last the Indians took up the basket and left, only after Paul gave them something of value. What, she didn't know.

He then turned to her after it was all over. "You were very foolish to do such a thing," he scolded. "Their seed corn is not for your taking."

"I only wanted a tea set," Alice had grumbled.

"And you would have tasted a tomahawk instead. Foolish girl. Now go home, and do not come to these woods alone again."

At the time Alice was angry over his words, but she knew now the man had saved her life. Whenever she breathed the fresh air of a new day, she thanked the Lord above for Paul Dodson, who had been there in her time of need.

Just as I now intend to be there for him and help him during his time of need, whether he wants it or not. She knew deep inside he was crying for help and hope amid his losses. And what better way to spawn such hope than for friends to do things when one least expected it. And that is what she intended to do.

Alice walked off the steps leading to the main house and came to the huge barn where the family blacksmith, Charles, kept the forge burning hot. She watched him at work, thinking of Paul. How she would love to give Paul a job here, tending to the blacksmithing. Charles, though, had been with the family for many years. Papa would never hear of letting him go. But she had another idea how to reestablish Paul's trade.

"Miss Wells," Charles said, wiping the sooty sweat from his brow. "What can I do for you?"

"I'm curious. You seem to have an abundance of tools here."

"Why, yes. I made them myself."

"Likely more than you will ever need."

He nodded. "Yes, indeed. It would do well for me to go through the tools I have and sell them."

"Wonderful. Set aside the tools you no longer require. Just put them in a crate, please."

He stared at her. "Miss Wells?"

"I would like whatever tools you find unnecessary but may be of help to someone in your trade. As it is, I'm certain Papa would be glad to see the shop looking tidier. And with the joy of the Yuletide season soon upon us, a tidy shop would make him in a much fonder spirit for the celebration of giving. Especially since our harvest was so great — if you understand what I say."

His eyes widened. "Why, yes, indeed. I will gladly go through my stock of tools and put aside anything I don't need."

Alice smiled, curtsied slightly, and left, delighting in the fresh air after the sooty smell of the shop. She cared little for the work of the blacksmith as it was dirty and hot, with the floors caked in black cinders and the smell of molten metal tainting the air. But it was the work Paul loved, and Alice was determined that he do it once again.

She met her father on the steps of their home, the curiosity clearly written in his blue eyes, the same eye color they both shared. "Is there trouble, daughter? I see you have come from the blacksmith."

"I only suggested it might be good for Charles to tidy up the shop, Papa. He has so many useless tools lying about."

"And do what with them, pray tell?" It was almost as if her father could sense her plan.

"To give to those who have nothing," she said, "as the Lord would have us do with everything we own." She brushed by him and went inside the house, where a servant stood ready to take her cloak.

"You can't help everyone, daughter," Papa admonished, following her. "I know there is a great deal of suffering everywhere after the events this fall. . . ."

"No, I can't help everyone, Papa. But I can help the one the Lord puts on my heart.

Is this not the reason we have a time of giving and celebration? To ask God where we might give of the excesses we have? Certainly Charles has a great deal of excesses when it comes to his tools. The shop is cluttered with them. Oh, and I did promise him that you would remember him at the Twelfth Night celebration this year."

"Aha. So you have left nothing undone, have you, daughter?"

She planted a kiss on his rough cheek. "I only wish to give where the need is greatest."

"And what about your need? What about a young man for your lonely heart?"

Alice could not help but flush at the comment. How could she tell him that love was the furthest thing from her mind at the moment? Not when there were duties of the heart to perform. "I have no need for a man right now, Papa," she stated most emphatically. "Nor will I bargain for love either. Love must come from the heart, brought forth by God alone. My desire right now is to help those in need."

The smile he offered made her wonder if he believed her. She went off to the sitting room where the servants had kindled a fire to warm the chilly day. She thought of her reason for doing this. Certainly it was not out of some romantic interest. She didn't think of Paul in that way. Yes, he was a man. And yes, when she did see him that day, standing on the road that led to the governor's home, he did appear handsome, even if distress distorted his fine features. But she didn't think of Mr. Dodson as a man to marry. He had been her rescuer after all, and she was only reciprocating.

"I didn't mean to anger you," Papa said. His voice startled her out of her thoughts. "I see that again I've disturbed some musing."

"I was listening to my heart, Papa," she told him.

"And a good heart you have, Alice. Just like your mother."

Alice sighed, wondering how Papa could believe that. If that were so, why hadn't Mother followed them here from England? Instead, she'd stayed behind. While they were apart, Papa wrote Mother faithfully, sending her messages by way of the ships that came into Jamestown. They received replies from her, asking that they return to England. When Papa declined and, instead, sent money for her to come join them, Mother did not write back. And one day they heard of her unexpected death from the fever.

"We are alone," Papa told Alice that day when she was fourteen. "Your mother has gone to be with our Lord."

His tears moved her unlike anything else. Alice shed tears along with him and collected flowers of remembrance. Papa asked if Alice wanted to return to England. Alice shook her head. Her home was here. Since then her existence had been filled by life in Virginia — helping her father whenever she could, along with trying to help him overcome the loss. And when she heard of other families who had loved ones still in England, she could sympathize with them and help them when tragedy arose. She could not have gone through the trials herself without hoping God would use her to help another. As it now was with Paul Dodson.

"I see I have again caused you distress, but I'm uncertain why," said Papa.

"I was only thinking of Mother, wondering why she never came here . . . and why you never went back to see her. Why you both chose to stay apart."

Papa sighed, staring at the fire that reflected in his eyes. " 'Tis difficult to speak of, Alice. I have needed to forgive myself for leaving her in England. We should have been one in our decision. But she was so against it. And I knew it would do well for our liveli-

138

hood that had waned in England. All our neighbors and friends had taken up roots and come to this place. But her heart was in England. And now her body rests there, too, as she would have wanted." He sighed again. "But I do have regrets. Regrets that I didn't at least go back and try to make her come." He gazed back at Alice with his crystal blue eyes. "Never leave your loved one behind, whoever he might be, Alice. Never be separated. Be there for each other always. Ask God to knit your hearts together as one. And always be willing to serve each other."

Alice offered her father a swift embrace, watching the slow tears collect in his weary eyes. How she loved him. She would take his words to heart, planting them deep inside where they would grow and bear fruit.

The next day, Charles filled a large wooden crate with tools he'd gathered from inside his shop. He showed her the tongs, hammers, and other implements, even an extra apron. "What will you do with it?" he asked.

Alice fetched some parchment and a quill. "I must have them delivered."

"Delivered to whom?"

"Someone in great need. A gift of the

heart to bring hope. Certainly you've known the need for such blessing in your life, Charles."

"Why, yes indeed, Miss Wells. The skill the Lord gives me is a great gift. With it I can feed my family during the coming winter."

Alice smiled as she wrote out the note with long strokes of the quill and then used a bit of sand to dry the ink. She folded the parchment carefully and sealed it with hot wax and a seal. "Deliver this note to Jamestown, Charles, along with the crate. Place it by the gate. He is sure to see it when he comes by the gate in the evening."

"Whom may I ask is it for?"

"A Mr. Dodson. If he or anyone asks, though, tell no one who this is from." She centered her gaze on him. "That is of the utmost importance."

"Why, yes, I understand."

Alice sighed as Charles asked another servant to help him carry the heavy crate to a wagon. How she wished she could be there to watch Paul receive the crate and see the startled expression on his face. Such a sight would delight her soul. All at once she took to her feet and raced after Charles. "Never mind. I will accompany you to Jamestown."

"Madam?"

"That way I'm certain he will receive it." She thought of alerting Papa of the plan, but he had gone off to see their neighbor for the day. She would certainly be back before he realized her departure.

"You should go by carriage, madam."

" 'Tis not an unpleasant ride on the road. I will be fine in the wagon." She allowed the man to assist her onto the rugged seat. "We must see that this is delivered to the proper person and that no vagabonds make off with it."

"As you wish." Charles took up the reins as the horses bobbed their heads.

Along the way to Jamestown, Alice could still see signs of the rebellion that autumn with stark images of burned buildings on many of the farms. But she knew nothing would compare to the devastation within Jamestown itself. She inhaled a breath to steady herself. It had been several months since the affair. Certainly rebuilding must be taking place. The town would be revived with God's blessing and neighbors helping each other. She glanced back at the crate. And Paul would be able to help others as well with the tools they carried.

The ride turned chilly in the brisk December day. She tried not to shiver while Charles talked about his family. A wide grin spread across his face. "And my wife tells me we will soon have another little one come late summer."

"Why, what news!"

"Yes, six children, Miss Wells. I'm very thankful for the job your father gives me. And my wife thanks you, too, for the squashes from the garden."

"You must bring your children to the main house one day soon. I should like to see them. And I will have the cook bake them gingerbread."

"They grow quickly, for certain," he said with a chuckle.

Soon they entered the outskirts of what had once been the bustling capital of the Virginia colony. Little remained of the city of Jamestown. The fire had been thorough, taking with it homes and people's livelihood. Alice was glad to see some buildings being restored. But for the most part, the town seemed to slumber as if admitting defeat to a more powerful foe. She sensed the place would never rise to what it once was. The mere fact saddened her greatly.

Suddenly she caught sight of him — Paul Dodson, she was certain. She wasn't certain how she knew. Perhaps because the man was standing in front of the darkened remains of his blacksmith shop.

Alice whispered to Charles for him to leave the wagon near the remains of another small building and seek out the man to whom the tools now belonged. "But you are not to say who they are from," she warned.

"I understand, madam," Charles said.

Alice hurried to hide behind the rear of a building as Charles walked over to address Paul. She could not hear the words they exchanged, but from where she stood, she saw Paul stare at Charles and then at the wagon. He nodded when Charles inquired of his identity. When they came closer, she could make out his words.

"This is kind of you," he said.

"Oh, 'tis not from my hand, sir," Charles said. Alice bit her lip and shook her head, praying with all her might that Charles would not reveal her identity to Paul. "I am only the deliverer."

Paul peered inside the crate, taking out the tools one by one. "Why, these are for blacksmithing," he marveled in disbelief.

"Yes, indeed. I made them myself."

Paul stared at him in confusion. "Then how can you say they aren't from you? Who is your master?"

"Please ask me no more. I only do as I'm bid. I hope you can make use of them."

The men lifted the heavy crate to the ground. Alice continued to watch Paul sift through the tools then glance around, as if expecting to find the one who had bestowed such a gift. "Thank you very much for this. Please . . . tell whoever sent this that 'tis an answer to my prayer."

"Indeed. I will help you carry it to your shop."

"Little of the shop remains," Paul said. Alice followed at a distance, straining to hear his words. "What was not burned men came and stole. Why they would steal blacksmith tools goes beyond my will to understand. Perhaps to keep the town from rising again. They may have succeeded, sadly enough."

"The forge is still intact," Charles was saying. "You will need to rebuild the bellow system. I can help with that task when next I come."

"Thank you. At least tell me your name."

Charles opened his mouth to reply, then shook his head. "It would be better if I say no more."

Again Paul thanked him for bringing the tools. Alice returned to the wagon, joy welling up within her. "Thank you, Charles," she said to the blacksmith. "Truly we have given Mr. Dodson a great gift."

"But you left him quite puzzled, madam. And curious."

" 'Tis fine that I do. We do not always need to know who it is that blesses us. 'Let not thy left hand know what thy right hand doeth.' Our God rewards what is done in secret." Charles nodded even as she took a seat, a sigh of content on her lips. *Dear Paul, I hope someday you will know how grateful I am. You are a wonderful man. . . .*

She caught herself with these thoughts. A wonderful man? How can that be? Was she thinking on things to fill a lonely heart, just as Papa had said? She glanced back, even as Jamestown disappeared in the distance, and with it, the man who had already begun to draw upon her heart. She could do nothing more but wait and see.

CHAPTER 3

I must know, God. Is there is any way to discover this angel of Jamestown? He had seen but a glimpse of her sitting in the wagon beside the burly man who had given him the blacksmith tools. He wondered if she could be the same woman who averted calamity on the road to the governor's house. If so, who was she? And why did she care so much? Certainly she was a woman of means. He was nothing — only a lonely soul wondering about his future. Yet hope once again visited him. The angel had given him the means for a future. And a beautiful angel she was — too beautiful to even consider, especially for a man like he.

Paul sighed as he looked over the tools. There was plenty here to renew his trade once he had the forge and bellows operational. The people in town desperately needed a blacksmith. Pleas came forth for tools and nails to help with the massive reconstruction. With the money he could purchase what he needed and hire laborers to help him rebuild his house. A new beginning was written on every tool Paul examined. He owed it all to the delicate angel. He simply had to know who she was and why she cared. Why she had looked upon him out of so many suffering in the land.

Paul puzzled over it long and hard, trying to think who she might be. He had not known many people in his life, save for some of the single men like himself who had come here to Virginia looking for a new life. There had been few women to speak of. Certainly none of the aristocratic status like the one who had intervened on the road to the governor's residence and now bestowed on him this fine gift of tools.

Paul took up a dipper of water and drank deeply. In the water barrel he gazed at his reflection. His face was streaked with dirt, his once-fine shirt soiled, and his breeches were mere tatters. The leather soles of his shoes flapped. He had a worn coat and a blanket to ward off the coming winter chill. He had no worthy appearance, much like his Savior Christ. Nothing that should draw this woman's attention yet had done so on two different occasions.

He wondered then if there might be a way

to set a trap for this angel. To catch her in her act of kindness so he could thank her and then inquire as to the reason why. But how does one go about doing such a thing?

At least Paul did have a hint of sorts. The man who brought the tools knew the art of a blacksmith. While it could take a long time, he would find out who else in the colony possessed the skill. But should he be scouring the countryside looking for such a person when he needed to reestablish his trade? Should he not allow it rest with Almighty God, and when the time was right, the angel would be revealed?

Paul sighed, deciding at once to rebuild his work. It was the least he could do, especially given the tools to work with. He would have to find his angel another time.

Not many days later, a few colonists ventured forward, looking for him to make them tools. Paul was able to make the bellows work and kindled a fire to begin shaping carpentry tools and nails. When the first coins jingled in his pocket, his heart burst with joy. He never thought the sound would bring such gladness. And he owed everything to the angel, his own dear angel — if he dared to call her that.

"You seem in better spirits," a hearty voice

addressed him.

Paul turned to see the burly man who had once scolded him by the fires for his nightmarish dreams, the one who even called him mad. He now stood in the doorway, his arms folded, but a grin lighting his face. "So how did you come to possess such money?"

"Would you believe an angel sent it to me?"

The man raised an eyebrow before his mouth opened in loud laughter. "Ha! Now the man says he has angels at his beckoning call. Is this more madness?"

"There is nothing mad with believing that God shows mercy in times of need," Paul said smoothly. "And I do indeed have an angel, of a kind. I will show you." Paul pointed at the crate. "See the tools she brought me?"

His laughter continued. "*She,* is it? An angel of feminine light, eh?"

"I think I met her once before on the road to the governor's plantation. I was about to be arrested, and she intervened on my behalf."

"Hmm. An angel indeed. Who is she?"

Paul shrugged. "I don't know, but she has a blacksmith who works for her. They both came here the other day, bearing tools and a letter."

The man asked to see the parchment, which Paul produced. He scrutinized the seal. "You can see a symbol in the wax seal if you look closely. That might provide a clue to the author's identity."

Paul's heart began to beat rapidly. "What do you see? Can you tell?"

"The symbol is the letter *W.* You can be fairly certain the last name of your angel begins with that letter."

"Glory be. Thank you, Mr. . . ."

"Abel Crawford." He shook Paul's hand. "So now that you are here in your shop, you will no longer grace us with your presence at the gate at night?"

"No. I will remain in this place, even if I still need to build a roof. At least I have four good stone walls about me. You're welcome to stay, as well. With some of the money I've made, I can soon have a roof over our heads."

"Sooner than that, friend." Abel pounced on the invitation and offered to help Paul with his work, along with discovering the identity of his angel. Paul was glad for the companionship but even gladder of the clue in the wax seal that drew him ever closer to the one that set his feet on this new path.

The work went quickly, and in no time

Paul was able to build a makeshift roof over the shop. People came by regularly as he fired up the furnace and began pounding out all manner of tools for the colonists to use. Money trickled in, and with it his spirits rose.

If only he did not have the identity of his angel plaguing his waking moments. He wanted so much to know who she was. He thought several times of returning to the place where he had first laid eyes on her at the governor's home. Maybe he would see her again and discover if the letter *W* on the wax seal matched her name or any of her relations. But for now his work kept him occupied, leaving his curiosity unfulfilled.

Paul was fashioning nails one morning to fill a large order when he heard Abel hail him. The man's round face beamed. "Your angel has returned, sir." He heaved two crates onto a table. Paul set down the hammer and washed his blackened hands in a barrel of lukewarm water before venturing over. He stared in shock at the contents. Several gentlemen's coats were there, along with breeches and shirts made of the finest cloth. "And a note." Abel gave it to him. "It bears the same wax seal."

Paul examined the seal before carefully unrolling the parchment. The note was simple, hoping the clothes fit him and that God was watching over him. " 'Tis indeed the same angel," he murmured. "Abel, I must find out who she is."

"So sure you are that she's the lady you met that afternoon on the way to the governor's house?"

"No. But I do know 'tis the one I caught a glimpse of in the wagon when the first crate came with tools for the blacksmith shop. She accompanied the man who brought the crate. But they left in such haste, I could not see her clearly enough nor make any introductions." Paul lifted out the clothes. "There is plenty for both you and me. We will look like lords of the castle in these."

"Yes, indeed. It does make one believe there is a God in heaven."

Paul piled the clothes on the table. "Sir, you mean to say you are not a Christian?"

Abel's face reddened. "If you mean do I believe in God, perhaps. I do believe there is some manner of kindness in people's souls. Though it has been hard to see it, with the struggles here in Jamestown and the wounds men have inflicted upon their brethren. But after such an event, we have also come together to help in times of need. Like your angel delivering tools and clothes."

"Jesus Himself said in this life there would be trouble but be of good cheer, for He has overcome the world. We see that happening even now, bless God."

Abel chuckled. "I remember one moaning in despair not a week ago, wondering if such a God even looked upon his misfortune."

"Quite true. I've learned much after all this." Paul admitted his struggle with injustice. He'd had no part in the recent rebellion even if he was a so-named commoner, the very kind that had risen in anger to find justification in the colony. The anger then turned to revenge and the fire followed. And in a stroke of irony, it was his own business that was laid to waste while others made off with his possessions. Commoners had destroyed a commoner's business. He began to doubt after that, wondering why this had come upon him — why he must suffer like Job in these times. Hope teetered on the brink of despair.

Now hope had been rekindled by the kindness of a stranger — or rather the blessing of an angel. He liked calling her an angel. The woman with no name — now the angel of Jamestown.

"But she does have a name," he murmured aloud, his finger tracing the *W* on the seal.

"Abel, as soon as we finish this order of nails, you and I are going to ride to the James River plantations upward toward Henrico. If we must inquire at every plantation along the way, we will find out who is doing these deeds of kindness."

"That could take a great deal of time. And there's much work to be done here."

"It will only take a few hours, and then we will return. But my curiosity is about ready to drive me to the grave. I simply must know who this lady is."

Abel nodded, a grin lighting his face. "I have a friend I know who will allow us to use his horses. We will go speedily on our quest."

"Thank you, friend. May God guide us."

The cold was sharp with the wind blowing across their faces. Paul watched in alarm as clouds began to gather from the west, bringing with them the makings of a storm. With such cold, he wondered if he would witness the delicate lacy particles that sometimes fell from the skies. It did not snow often, but when it did, everyone came out to celebrate. Children would run about the streets of Jamestown, trying to catch the flakes in their hands, only to have them melt. Others would scoop up the flakes as best they could and throw them like balls or even catch them in their mouths as if swallowing manna from heaven.

Paul lowered his head to keep the wind from biting his face with its angry teeth and rode on. He considered the wisdom of trying to find his angel in weather like this. What could he be thinking? Why could he not let go and trust in Providence with these blessings? That God Himself would reveal the angel's identity in His own timing?

"We must turn back," Abel finally said, pointing to the darkening skies. "The storm is blowing up quickly. And 'tis getting colder."

Paul had to agree. He did not have a heavy enough coat to keep the wind from slicing through him like a knife. His fingers and toes were already turning numb. Even the horses snorted as if complaining about the weather. "We will go back," he decided. "There is always another day, God willing."

They had turned their horses for the trip back when a carriage came rattling down the road. Paul glanced up to find a face peering at them and a hearty voice addressing them. "Are you a long ways off?" a gentleman inquired.

"Jamestown, my lord."

"At least several hours' journey. I do

believe there is a storm coming."

At that moment icy pellets began falling in a vengeance, as if heaven had unleashed its own shot and shell from above.

"Come find shelter with me for the night," the man insisted.

Paul looked over at Abel, who nodded in enthusiasm. Another angel to their rescue! "Thank you indeed, sir. We're grateful."

The horses were tied to the back of the carriage, and the men took their places on the fine leather seats. Paul had never been in a carriage like this. Its elegance, similar to the one the young woman had ridden in, overwhelmed his senses. No doubt many of the inhabitants in this area were wealthy enough to own luxuries. He would have loathed such flagrant wealth only a few days before. Since the blessings bestowed upon him by his secret angel, Paul looked on it without any jealousy for his own circum-stances.

"Where are you going?" the man inquired. "To Henrico?"

"We are looking for someone who has a last name beginning with the letter *W*." Paul withdrew a parchment for the man to see. "Do you recognize the seal?"

"Indeed. I know this seal."

"What? You do?" Paul stared in shock, unable to believe his ears.

"This is the seal of my neighbor, Samuel Wells."

Paul and Abel exchanged glances. "Sir, can you take us there?"

The man looked at him. "You have business with Mr. Wells?"

"Yes, my lord. Very important business."

The man announced to the driver the change in direction. "The Wells are a fine family, too, and of good Christian faith."

"Does a young lady also dwell there?"

The man chuckled. "Ah, so is that your intention? Samuel Wells indeed has a daughter."

" 'Tis not what you think, my lord. The lady brought much comfort to those of us who lost possessions in the fire at Jamestown. If this is indeed her, I wish to thank her personally."

"It certainly may be. The Wells are a giving family."

Paul could not believe his fortune, or rather this blessing of God, even as he saw Abel grinning at him. When the carriage came to a stop, Paul looked upon the large manor home and fields that began to glisten with ice that fell from the skies. Several servants came to the carriage to assist them.

"Master Young," they greeted the man.

"I have two charges for you from Jamestown," the gentleman announced. "They wish to meet with your master. And bid him a good day for me. I would stay to visit, but I must tend to my affairs before the storm grows worse."

"Yes, indeed. Good day, sir."

When the carriage pulled away, Paul stood there with Abel, wondering what he was doing. He righted himself and followed the servants into the home. They stood in the foyer, waiting to be introduced. Paul tried not to stare at the rich surroundings. The tall ceilings. The carved staircase. The many paintings. At first it proved too much for him to take in after the depravity he had witnessed the past few months. Then he considered his recent blessings provided by the family and thanked the Lord for their wealth.

"The master bids you welcome," a servant said, showing them the way to the sitting room.

Paul entered, feeling a bit awkward in his present attire, with ice sticking to his coat. He bowed. "Paul Dodson from Jamestown, my lord."

"And Abel Crawford."

"Welcome to Southridge, Mr. Dodson and Mr. Crawford. I am Samuel Wells. What brings you here?"

Just then there came a rustle.

"Oh, daughter, you are just in time to meet some guests — a Mr. Dodson and a Mr. Crawford of Jamestown. This is my daughter, Alice Wells."

The young woman who walked in suddenly turned pale. Her hand grasped the doorway to steady herself. Paul thought he saw something pass in her eyes, though he couldn't be certain. "P–Pleased to meet you," she managed to say.

Is this my angel, standing before me? Paul tried to remember if she was the same woman he had seen on the road to the governor's home or the one in the wagon that day. Instead he noted how she trembled slightly, as if the meeting troubled her.

"I'm most curious to know why you sought me out," Mr. Wells stated, thanking the servant who brought them all refreshment in pewter goblets. "I don't believe we've met, have we?"

Paul slowly withdrew a parchment. "No, my lord. I came to show you this."

Alice gasped. The men turned in her direction. "Please excuse me," she said, quickly standing to her feet.

"Alice, do you know about this?" her father inquired. "Why does this man possess a parchment with our family seal?"

She sighed. "I do know, Papa. They are the notes I delivered along with the blacksmith tools and some garments. I didn't want our identity made known, but somehow it has."

Paul's heart burst with the news. He nearly laughed aloud. His angel had been discovered — and what a lovely angel at that.

"Ah!" A grin lit her father's face. "Very interesting. I was not told until later about Alice's wanderings. And so you both came seeking your benefactress?"

"Indeed, sir. Or as we have come to know your daughter's secret deeds, we came seeking 'the angel of Jamestown.' " Paul smiled at Alice, who returned a tremulous smile.

Mr. Wells chuckled. " 'Tis kind of you to say that, but Alice is only doing what her Christian beliefs would have her — to love thy neighbor as thyself."

"We are very grateful for it. Because of such kindness, we have been able to set up business once again. How can we thank you for all you've done?"

"There is no need, Mr. Dodson. We receive our thanks from God above. But you are most welcome."

A red flush now filled Alice's pale cheeks.

She tried to pick up the goblet with dignity, but her hand shook, nearly upsetting its contents. Again Paul watched her reaction in curiosity and interest. Surely this woman would have no reason in the world to feel nervous before him, would she? She was a lady of wealth who had everything. And what did he have? Only what she had brought to him. Her reactions puzzled him more now than when he first came seeking her identity. He wondered what it all meant.

CHAPTER 4

Alice could not believe Paul sat before her in the parlor of her home. After so many years, to look upon his face now was like something out of a dream. She had envisioned it, of course, the meeting they would one day have and how she would tell him of his rescue that fateful day in the woods. Since that day she had watched him from afar on infrequent occasions when she and Papa were in Jamestown. But now she could hardly bring herself to know what to say or do. Never had she been caught speechless, and the men around her seemed to sense it. She tried to put a smile on her face even as she fought to conceal her inward reaction. *Please, dear Lord, help me know what to say. I dare not speak of that day long ago, not here and now. But soon I must.*

She sipped from her goblet as the men conversed. Paul was even more handsome close up than the times she had seen him from afar. Though she knew well he had handsome features from the encounter on the road before the governor's home, even if those features were distorted by anger. Here in this place, relaxed and of good spirits, his face shone like the sun. She wondered if he had a lady. She knew he remained unmarried. Why would she even consider such a thing?

Even if he is unmarried, what business would you have with a humble blacksmith, Alice Wells? You have seen the work Charles does. Is that how you wish to live your life, in a shop stained black and scented with the odor of molten metal?

But he is not all that, she admonished herself. *He is much more.*

Just then she saw that day in the woods with Paul's face above hers, his hand forcing away the tomahawk before it was embedded in her flesh. He had saved her life. Was there not more to a man than his life's work? Like the noble characteristics of the one who had risked his life to save hers?

"I say, Alice, you've seen the destruction in Jamestown, haven't you?"

Alice looked up to find Papa addressing her with a look of consternation on his face. "Yes, yes indeed, Papa, I have seen it. Quite sad. But I know we are determined to survive. Didn't those who come before us possess such will? So also we must survive this test." She turned her gaze to Paul, who sent another smile her way. She smiled back. He then averted his gaze, though she noted the ruddy tint to his cheeks.

The men conversed for a while longer about business, trade, and the people that were arriving to the colony to make new lives for themselves. Papa spoke of his own livelihood in his crops and the timber on his land that fetched good prices in England. "And have you always done the work of a blacksmith, Mr. Dodson?"

"I learned the trade when I came here, my lord. I worked as an apprentice and then set up my own shop. It thrived well until the fire. It would have remained a profitable trade if men had not sought to steal what they could not burn. But thanks to your daughter," he said, his gaze again reverting to Alice, "it thrives again and even more so with all the building that is going on."

"Well, I'm glad we could be of help. But know, too, that others suffered in the rebellion. We also lost possessions. Our livestock. Other valuables. But by the grace of God, our crops were plentiful enough that we were able to replace our livestock."

"In this life we will have tribulation, sir.

But as I've seen so well, God is strong enough to overcome our worst lot."

Alice drew a breath. What a fine Christian man he seemed to be. How she would like to know more about him. If he would consider riding with her in her father's carriage, they could speak of many things — away from the curiosity of others.

"Daughter?" Papa asked. "Do you have a matter to discuss?"

Did her face betray her interest? *How I would like to go riding with Mr. Dodson? How I want to tell him what happened long ago? And how I would love to know everything about him?*

"I only wonder, Papa, with this storm, if the men should stay here rather than return to Jamestown."

"Yes, of course. You will stay the night, won't you?"

Paul and Abel again exchanged glances. Abel seemed eager to partake in anything they had to offer. Paul appeared more hesitant, weighing everything before nodding. "Thank you, my lord. With the storm, it would be a difficult ride in the coming darkness."

Papa nodded while Alice sighed and stared down at her folded hands, trying not to appear eager. Now if God would only grant her time alone with Paul during their stay . . .

The night turned blustery and cold. Limbs snapped from the ice and crashed against the side of the house. Alice awoke to the terrific sound. She huddled under the mass of blankets, watching the moving objects before the windows and hearing the constant sound of breaking branches. After a time, she knew she could no longer remain like this. She put on wraps and lit a candle. Maybe a cup of warm milk would soothe her. Yet even if the storm were not keeping her from sleep this night, thoughts of Paul Dodson would do the same. It amazed her that he had not found a fine lady to settle down with as many men had. Nor could Alice say she had found a suitable suitor. Could it be that God had kept them for this special reunion?

Alice quietly descended the stairs. She stopped when she saw flickering in the sitting room. A fire still burned in the fireplace, warming the room. She drew forward, only to find a figure sitting in a chair before it. She paused. "Papa?"

The figure came hurriedly to his feet. No, it was not Papa. He was taller and thinner. "Miss Wells, I hope I didn't disturb you."

166

"No, Mr. Dodson. I couldn't sleep."

"Neither could I. The storm." He pulled up a chair for her.

Alice smiled at his consideration. "Thank you." She set down the candle carefully on a small table.

"I must say, I was quite taken aback by all you've done for me."

" 'Tis nothing, really."

"No, 'twas everything. Because of your kindness, I'm now able to return to smithing and make money to repair my home. Not to mention the fine clothing you gave."

"I thought I recognized Papa's shirt," she said with a laugh. "Though he didn't seem to notice. His eyesight is rather poor. And he seems weary these days, more so than usual."

"I'm sorry to hear this."

"We all go through trials. And for certain you've been through serious trials yourself."

Paul shrugged. "I did lose my home and a good deal of my trade. But I grieve mostly for a family heirloom — a Bible that my mother gave to me for safekeeping. It had the births and deaths of our relatives from long ago. Now it is gone — burned to ash."

"I'm so sorry, Paul." Her face heated. "I mean . . . Mr. Dodson."

" 'Tis the only item of value I wish had

remained, though there are other family treasures, as well. A painting. Books." His finger traced the arm of the chair. "But I do wish I had the Bible." When he looked over at her, the firelight danced in his eyes. "If only my angel could deliver it to me."

"Dear Paul, how I wish I could!" Again she realized her foible and looked away, though she felt his gaze linger on her.

"Why?"

The question came with such suddenness, Alice trembled. "Why?" she repeated.

"Why are you doing this for me? Oh, I know the Christian command to help our neighbor in need. But why me, out of so many?"

"Why *not* you?"

"I . . ." He faltered. "I don't know. You're a lady of great means. I'm but a humble blacksmith."

"I hardly think one's trade should dictate whether one receives a blessing. God is no respecter of persons. And the trade you do is important to your fellow neighbor."

"I only ask because there are so many who are destitute. And you've brought me many things, almost as if . . ." He hesitated.

"Yes?"

"Almost as if you knew me. But you couldn't. We have never met, except on that road when I was nearly made a prisoner of the English crown." He laughed scornfully. "If you hadn't come, I would likely be decaying in some English prison. And I wouldn't have cared in the least for my lot. But there are heroines to be found, rescuers of both the heart and soul."

Oh, Paul, if you only knew our link to the past. She wanted so much to tell him what happened many years ago. She opened her mouth to do so when she heard the patter of footsteps. Papa appeared, holding a candle.

"And what is this?" he inquired. "I thought there were more guests entering my house."

" 'Tis only sleepless souls from the storm, Papa," Alice said. "I've been keeping Mr. Dodson company for a bit."

"A nasty storm indeed," Papa agreed. "You may need to remain another day with us, Mr. Dodson, unless you have matters of concern awaiting you in Jamestown."

Again Alice saw Paul regard her and then her father. "We will see what the dawn brings, my lord. But thank you for the invitation." He came to his feet, stifling a yawn. "Now I do believe I will find rest. I bid you all good night."

"Good night," Alice said. She watched him depart, then turned to find Papa studying her. He said nothing but led the way to the stairs. "Good night, Papa."

"Dream well, my daughter." He kissed her on the forehead.

Oh, I will, she thought. *My dreams will be filled with the face of Paul.*

When Alice awoke, she wondered if the encounter with Paul in the sitting room last night actually happened or was only part of a pleasant dream. She arose and looked out the window to see the tree limbs covered in ice, appearing like a work of art created by the finest glassblower. The sight of it drew a sharp breath of awe. How like the Lord to bring forth such beauty.

But what delighted her heart even more was the thought of Paul staying another day. What they would talk about, she didn't know. Perhaps she would find the time to confess to him about that day long ago when he saved her life. To tell him they had a bond that went beyond the years to the essence of life and maybe even love.

She dressed quickly so as not to grow too chilled and hurried downstairs. Despite the cheerfulness she felt, she was met with the grim face of her father. "We must pray, daughter," he told her.

"Papa? What is it?"

"Charles. He had gone out last night to discover what caused a terrible noise outside his home. A tree had fallen. As he stood there, another large tree branch fell, directly on his leg. The physician is caring for him, but they believe his leg is broken."

"Oh, Papa! Is he in pain?"

"Yes, he's most distressed. But his main concern is that he won't be able to help us. I told him not to worry, but he takes his work too much to heart."

Alice shook her head, even as she turned to see Paul standing quietly in the doorway, trying not to appear as if he were intruding.

The look in his eyes mirrored his concern. "Is everything well?"

"I fear not," Papa told him sadly. "Our blacksmith had a most unfortunate accident. His leg is broken."

"I'm sorry to hear that, my lord. What can I do?"

"There is nothing to be done unless you know smithing." He caught himself. "Why, you do know the trade, don't you, Mr. Dodson?"

"Of course he does, Papa," Alice reminded him. "We supplied him with the tools, remember? He has his own shop in Jamestown."

"Indeed, and I will gladly offer my as-

171

sistance while I'm here," Paul said.

"Charles was in the midst of shoeing my horses — and finishing a few other objects."

"I can help." Paul went to fetch his coat. "If you would show me where the shop is so I might begin?"

"I will show you." Alice dressed in a heavy wool cloak and drew woolen mittens over her hands. When she stepped outside, the beauty of the day surrounded her, though it was muted by the sad news they had received about their blacksmith. "I pray Charles will soon be well," she said softly.

"At least I can offer my help, especially after all you've done for me."

" 'Tis nothing, Mr. Dodson. If only you knew what . . ." She paused. Now was not the time to share in the past when they must confront the present. She led the way to Charles's shop. "You can see what he was working on. I know nothing about blacksmithing."

Paul nodded. "He keeps a very organized shop."

"Charles is a wonder in his trade." She watched Paul start the fire in the forge. "But you seem at home here."

" 'Tis what I know best."

"Is there nothing else?"

He gazed at her. "Not that I know of.

Though the work of a smithy is a lowly profession. And black as night."

"But very much in need within the colony. Charles is well known in this part of Virginia. Many come here to have their work done. You must be famous, too, Mr. Dodson, in Jamestown."

He chuckled. "I don't concern myself with titles but only that my work honors my Lord and Savior."

Alice sighed, watching her breath form a cloud in the frosty air, though her heart warmed with the fire of love. Paul was a godly and good man indeed. If only he did not see himself as a mere blacksmith. He was much more than his trade. And if he could see beyond this, perhaps other things would be ready to spring forth, like the bond of love. But she would be patient for now and wait.

CHAPTER 5

Alice Wells's attention was unmistakable, yet Paul did not know what to do about it. A fine woman like herself could have any man of her choosing. There were many Virginia gentlemen to be had. Why then would she pay him such interest? He had always been taught by his mother and by the Bible that God was no respecter of persons. It appeared Alice Wells wasn't either. Her admiration went beyond words. She spoke highly of him. She helped him in his time of need. Even when he had nothing of value to offer her, nothing that would entice her by any means, yet she was drawn to him and he to her.

When she brought him a cup of warm punch later that morning, he took it with grateful thanks. Her smile warmed his heart. She was so beautiful — ivory skin, blue eyes, and lips red like berries. And here he was — dark as night, his hands black as pitch from the forge, and his clothing singed with the smell of burning tinder. How could she stand this with such cheerfulness? There must be more to her than what he could see with his eyes.

Despite his thoughtful contemplation, the day had gone well. Paul managed to accomplish quite a bit in the shop. His friend, Abel, also helped wherever he could, tending to the stock in the barns and clearing the property of downed limbs. When they came in for dinner that evening, a sumptuous feast awaited them. The master of the house and his daughter were bursting with thanks for all Abel and he had done.

"But I know you must return to your own business in Jamestown, Mr. Dodson," Mr. Wells said.

Paul caught a pleading in the eyes of Alice Wells. "But there is still some work left for Mr. Dodson to do," she told her father.

"If you wish, I can go hither to Jamestown on the morrow and see to your shop, Paul," Abel added.

Paul looked over at his friend in gratefulness. "Thank you. As Miss Wells has said, I do have business to finish in the shop."

"Truly, 'tis no more your concern," said Mr. Wells. "Take your leave on the morrow, as well."

"But, Papa, 'tis a blessing that Mr. Crawford can return to Jamestown while Mr. Dodson finishes the work here," Alice said in earnest. "We must embrace God's will, Papa." She winked at Paul who drew back, startled.

He took a long drink from his cup. There was no mistaking now the attention of Alice Wells. Again his heart wrestled with the question of why. Why him? And again he heard her reply. *"Why* not *you?"* Maybe all this was just a dream conjured in his mind. Maybe inwardly he did crave her attention. To court and even marry such a fine lady would go beyond all his expectations. But he could not imagine it. It would be like the aristocracy forced to marry the servant. How could Alice Wells lower herself to such a state unless it was out of pity or some act of desperation? And he had no reason to think she would be desperate enough to marry him — unless there was more to this than meets the eye. But what, he could not begin to fathom.

Again he looked down at his teacup. When his gaze met hers, he saw once more a look of appreciation in Alice's eyes. If only he knew what she was thinking.

Later on, when he offered everyone a pleasant good night, Paul's puzzlement followed him to the bedroom where he retired. But sleep was far from coming. He gazed out the window instead, listening to the moan of the wind and thinking about his life. How glad he was to have fallen into company with the Wellses. Maybe he should act upon Alice's attention and ask her if she would like to go riding on her father's horses. Perhaps an early morning ride before they parted company and he returned with Abel forthright to Jamestown would help them both understand.

The next morning when Paul saw Alice, he inquired about the ride. She seemed taken aback but pleased.

"I would love to, but I fear there may be too much ice in the pastures for the horses to bear," she said sadly.

"You're right. That didn't occur to me." He tried to conceal his disappointment.

"But I do thank you for the invitation. If the weather does warm, I will gladly accompany you when next I come to Jamestown." She paused. "I heard from Papa that you're leaving today."

"I spoke to your father again, and he said plainly there was no reason for me to remain. He all but ordered me to go back so I might help the people of Jamestown."

"I hope you will return soon. You and your friend are also invited to our Twelfth Night celebration."

"A Twelfth Night celebration?" he repeated.

"Of course. You must know of it — a celebration of God's blessings. And to remember the coming of the Son of God. I know you're a believer, Mr. Dodson."

"Yes indeed, madam. I've never been invited to a Twelfth Night celebration, though."

"Then you must come." Her smile nearly took his breath away. For an instant he had a strange desire to kiss her if she were not standing inside her father's house. "Who knows, Mr. Dodson, but that night you might even receive the honor of being crowned king."

"I don't understand how that can be."

She only winked. "Come to Twelfth Night, and you will see."

Again Paul was taken aback by her attention. He wanted to pursue it further, to ask her outright what led to all this, when he heard a stirring on the stairs. Mr. Wells was descending the stairway. Paul turned instead and thanked the master of the house for his hospitality.

"We should be thanking you," said Mr.

Wells. "I am most grateful for the work you've done, both you and your friend. I hope you will return to celebrate the Twelfth Night with us. You're most welcome."

Paul chuckled. "Your daughter has already taken it upon herself to invite us."

He nodded. "Good. Then we will expect you at that time."

Paul smiled when again he caught Alice's look. The expression stayed with him throughout the morning meal and the time of his departure for Jamestown. She stood by as he slowly brought himself up and over the horse, righting himself in the saddle.

"I hope you will come again soon, Mr. Dodson."

"I have every intention, Miss Wells. Thank you." She smiled and nodded as he reined the horse around and, along with Abel, started for the road.

The sun had risen, igniting the icy fields so they glistened. The road itself had become a thoroughfare of mud. The horses slipped and stumbled in the thick mire. Still it was a beautiful day for the ride back to Jamestown, made even more interesting by the attention paid to him by Alice Wells. At the festivity he would inquire of her interest, if she had other beaus, or if she would consider him suitable for courting. If she agreed to a courtship, it would make everything in his life brighter than even the brightness of this day, accompanied by the icy display brought forth from the heavens.

Paul rode for a time with Abel, conversing about the tasks to be accomplished once they returned to Jamestown, the money they would make at blacksmithing, and the fine home he would build. Abel mentioned finding a lady to settle down with. Hearing this, Paul could not help but think of Alice. So many things about her moved his heart. If only he could force away the differences in their status. Maybe it was the fire of disagreement left over from the rebellion that still smoldered, that social differences must be overcome in the colonies if they were to survive as a country. For all he knew, maybe God had brought them together to show how two different people could fall in love and marry. Maybe such a union would help bring reconciliation and healing.

Presently he and Abel came upon a military contingent of soldiers on foot, flanked by officers on horseback, traveling swiftly up the road. Paul paused, bringing his horse to the side of the road as they passed by.

All at once they stopped and wheeled before him. Paul offered them a good day. To him this was a good day with thoughts of Alice Wells, even if he scorned the military presence. In his eyes they were a worthless lot. But from where he had come — the humble house of the Wells family — he had seen people of great worth and hope.

Several soldiers circled Paul as if studying him. The move unnerved him. He shifted in the saddle and inquired if anything was wrong.

Suddenly a soldier proclaimed, " 'Tis him, my lord! I'm certain. The rabble that lay siege to your home a fortnight ago! I never forget a face."

Paul stared, even as the soldiers prodded him from his horse with their muskets. "What is the meaning of this? I know nothing of what you speak."

"Where did you get such a fine animal?" the soldier pressed.

"We borrowed the horses from a friend in —" Paul began.

"Do you see, my lord governor?" the soldier shouted. "We know how the people here have lost their livestock to these ruffians. And I'm certain I've seen his face many times, trespassing on my lordship's land." The soldier whirled. "You have been there at the governor's residence, have you not?"

"To seek an audience, yes, but I —"

"Out of his own lips, my lord!"

The governor waved his hand. "Yes, yes. Detain him, then, if you feel you must. We cannot delay further."

Paul gasped. "But I've done nothing!"

"He speaks the truth, my lords," Abel added.

"Quiet!" the soldier snapped. "We know you rabbles. 'Tis you and your kind who have laid waste to the colony. And you just confessed to trespassing on the governor's land, ready to stir further trouble."

"I only came seeking justification after losing everything I own. Where is the help of the governor when the people cry out for mercy?"

"Do you see, my lord? He only wishes to cause mischief and mayhem, just like all from Bacon's den of traitors."

The governor sighed and shook his head. "I have no time for this rabble. Take him to the temporary gaol. His fate will be decided on the morn."

Paul could not believe his misfortune. He continued to argue, but the men rebuked him until a soldier jabbed him forcefully with the butt of a musket to silence him. *Dear God, why?* his heart cried out, even as he was prodded along.

He glanced back to see Abel still astride

his horse, looking after Paul in bewilderment. When Abel appeared as if he might try to intervene, Paul shook his head. Abel then quickly reined his horse about and galloped off from whence they came.

The contingent soon turned off the main road and onto some worn path. Paul had no idea where they were going. Footsore after several hours of travel, Paul wanted to stop, but they continued until they reached the outskirts of a small town the people had begun calling Williamsburg. He arrived thirsty and famished, but they only shoved him in an empty room in one of the outlying buildings without anything to eat or drink. Paul could not believe this was happening to him. It seemed his life was forever caught in the web of a curse.

When he tried to speak to the jailor, the man only told him to keep quiet. Yet he could not quell the injustice. "I must be allowed to speak to Governor Berkeley," Paul pleaded. "I've done nothing. I only wanted to see the governor about the devastation in Jamestown. I had no ill intentions whatsoever."

The jailor, a beefy man with a dark face, strode up to him. "We know rabble when we see them. 'Fore this day is out, we'll have all the rest of you locked up in here. And you would do well to join yer leader, Bacon, in the land of the dead. We've already hung a bunch of his followers." He laughed. "Though Bacon himself didn't even taste the noose. He died of the flux, he did, before we could string him up."

"I had nothing to do with the rebellion. I myself was a victim —"

"Quiet!" The jailor shoved his fist through the open door before slamming it shut.

Paul retreated to the rear of the dingy room that smelled like the inside of a necessary. He ran his fingers through his hair. *God, have mercy! Hear my prayer. I have done no wrong. You know I'm innocent, blessed Jesus.* But all he saw was hopelessness. He had lost everything he had. Now he would lose his life.

"I don't understand," Alice wailed when Abel came riding back to Southridge with news of Paul's predicament. "How can this be? How could they arrest him? And when he is the kindest man there is!"

"Calm yourself, my dear," her father said.

"You don't understand, Papa. You know if they hold but a notion that Paul . . . that is, Mr. Dodson is involved with the rebellion, he will be hanged without trial. We must seek his release immediately."

Papa turned slowly, and from what Alice could see, with far less vigor than she had seen in recent days. Oh, why didn't her father show more concern for this dire situation? Didn't he realize they must ride out this instant and save the man's life?

Instead Papa went to find a chair. "I'm not well," he confessed. "I cannot seek his release."

Alice stared. "Papa, why didn't you tell me you were feeling poorly?"

"I didn't want to concern you, daughter. I'm very sorry. The physician says 'tis my heart. 'Tis been weak for many months. But with everything that has happened, my heart has weakened further."

"Oh, Papa." Alice was beside herself to know what to do She could see her father was ailing, but the thought of Paul languishing in some dank gaol, ready to face the hangman's noose, stirred her as well. Both men she cared about seemed on the brink of death. She didn't know what to do or where to turn. Tears filled her eyes along with a sense of helplessness.

"I would try to help Paul," Abel said sadly, "but I fear they will just arrest me, too. The reason they didn't is that they seemed to recognize him. I suppose he made himself known at the governor's residence one too many times."

"I even helped him there once," Alice said. "But it may have made things worse for him." She sighed. "Oh, I must know what to do."

"Daughter, there's nothing you can do for me, if that is your concern," Papa said in a soft voice. "I've lived a good many years. Others need to live still. Like Mr. Dodson, whom I believe is a good man. Though I want no harm to come to you, I know you will do whatever your heart tells you to do, guided by the grace of Almighty God."

Alice knelt to give Papa a kiss on the cheek. "I do love you," she whispered. "Please do nothing to make yourself weaker. Rest while you can. I will return soon."

"I will worry every moment you're away," he said wearily, "but I know you're in God's hands. And setting this man free is the right thing to do."

Alice sensed it, as well. She had no choice as far as Paul was concerned. She had fallen in love with him. "We must make haste at once," she informed Abel.

"Can you ride, madam?" Abel inquired.

"I can do a great many things when I need to, sir. And I will do what I must this day." She sighed. "However, I don't wish to be made weary with a long ride. Taking the carriage would be better. And it would be better for those I must call on, as well."

"I can drive the carriage, madam."

"Then I will ready myself." Alice hurried away with a prayer on her lips. She selected one of her best dresses to wear. She rearranged her hair and set ribbons in it. "Oh, dearest God, I pray for Your wisdom this day and for the words to speak to my lords that will gain Paul's release." She paused then. "And, please, preserve my father to complete Your work here on earth. Amen."

When she slipped down the stairs, Papa was sitting in the parlor, staring listlessly at the fire. His face seemed to brighten at her entry. "You look so beautiful, Alice."

"Papa, I don't want to leave you, but I must for a short while."

"Of course you must. Set Mr. Dodson free, Alice, as he once freed you."

Alice stepped back. "What? Papa, I don't understand."

"Only that I've never seen you so happy, ever since the day your gaze rested on Mr. Dodson. I'm not certain why this man has brought a fire in your eyes and joy to your lips, but it must be for good."

"There's much more I have not yet said, Papa." She kissed him quickly. "I will tell you when I return."

Alice hastened to the carriage that Abel had brought to the front of the home. She placed her hand in his as he helped her into the seat. "Do you know where they've taken him?" Alice asked.

"No, madam."

"Then drive me to the governor's home. 'Tis the only place I know to go. And I pray someone there will tell us."

"May you be right," Abel murmured.

"And may the right prevail," Alice whispered, clasping her hands together to keep them from trembling as the carriage pulled away.

CHAPTER 6

Paul should have known Alice would come. She was his angel sent from God, after all, though she was not an angel of the spirit but of the flesh. She was always there for him. When she came before his makeshift cell, giving the jailor a paper ordering his release, he still couldn't help but be stunned. He then saw the smiling face of Abel, who greeted him with a firm embrace of friendship.

"I'm very glad to see you, I must say," Paul murmured to him.

"No happier than we are to see you — and before they sent you to the gallows."

Paul nodded, noticing how Alice Wells gazed at him with tears in her eyes. Again he was taken aback by her concern. Why had she done all this for him? Could it be that God was bringing them together as he so hoped?

"You look weary," she said softly, the

concern evident in her voice. "You must come back to Southridge to recover."

"I will go on to Jamestown to see about the shop," Abel added. "The governor was kind enough to return the horse which I must take back to my friend in Jamestown. If you are well enough to take the carriage, I will return the horses."

"Yes, of course," Paul agreed. "I would walk all the way if I must."

When Abel had taken his leave of them, Paul realized then he was alone with Alice Wells. She was not looking at him but rather at the carriage. "I can manage it quite well," she told him, as if seeking an answer to some unspoken question. "Hand me the reins."

"Certainly not, Miss Wells. I will do it. I'm well if just a bit weary. Prison is not a place where one can find refuge." He gave her his hand, helping her up. Her hand seemed to disappear in his. Only then did he see the scars from the burns on his hand and winced. Did she notice them, too — that he possessed not only the hands of a blacksmith but hands charred by fire?

She made no comment but settled herself on the seat, spreading a blanket across her lap.

"Whatever did you say to the governor?"

Paul inquired. "They gave no thought to anything I had to offer in my defense. They only claimed that I was part of Bacon's rebellion."

" 'Twas quite simple, really. I told the governor that he could not lock up the only excellent blacksmith Jamestown has left. The people need your skill to help them rebuild their homes. An outcry and even further unrest would surely follow if he didn't free you at once."

Paul shook his head, marveling at the wisdom of the woman beside him. What grandness God had bestowed. What blessing and honor. And beauty, as well. He thought then how he would love to kiss her, not for her outward beauty but for the beauty of her spirit, for her giving and merciful heart, for being strong and fearless, for everything. "I must ask you again, madam. Why me? I know you once replied with, 'Why *not* me?' But there are many with cries of injustice on their lips. Many are falsely imprisoned. Many need help."

She hesitated for a moment. "Because I know you personally. You once helped me. How can I not help you in return?"

He turned to see her eyes, but her glaze lingered elsewhere. When did he ever help her? He could not think of such a time except most recently. "If you mean the smithing done for your father . . ."

"I mean as a young girl, when you saved me from an Indian tomahawk."

Paul yanked on the reins, bringing the horses to a standstill. "You are the girl?" he said in disbelief.

She managed a small smile. "So you do remember."

"Yes, I remember. 'Twas the most frightening day of my life!"

Her eyes widened. "I could not tell that, sir. You were as brave as any man I've ever met. You eased the anger and saved my life."

Little did she know, but he had been frightened beyond comprehension. She was so close to death that day when he stumbled upon the scene in the woods. She sat huddled beside a basket of corn with Indians all around. He'd placed himself between her and the avenging Indians, not knowing if he would taste the deadly edge of the tomahawk. But God was with him. He had his own angels sent from above to intervene on his behalf. "It seems impossible to believe. And you've remembered me these past years, though I've never laid eyes on you until recently."

"At different times when Papa and I came to Jamestown, I would see you hard at work in your blacksmith shop. For many years I wondered how I could help you as you once helped me. Then the fire happened. I saw how it destroyed all you worked so hard to build. I knew then I could help you in small ways, though it can hardly compare to saving my life."

He stroked the leather of the reins. "You're wrong, Alice. The acts of kindness you have done saved a soul from despair. Depression might have been my lot, perhaps even stealing my life away, if you hadn't intervened. Though you needn't have repaid the kindness of long ago, I'm forever grateful."

"God does knit hearts together . . . to serve one another when trials come. To give another strength when one wanes and to offer aid when the other falls. This is why we are here."

He drew in a breath. Never did he consider his angel to be the young girl he had rescued, now a beautiful woman of privilege and wisdom, who had been watching him all these years. The mystery had been revealed, and with it, a bond remained. "Though I understand now, I never thought a woman of your means would wish to do all this for me."

"Dearest Paul, do you only see what is on the outside and not the inward soul? That if

I must dispense with my worldly possessions so that you no longer compare my outward appearance to what I believe, I would do so?"

"I'm only amazed," he said softly. He was even more amazed by the way her soft eyes regarded him. Without thinking, he leaned toward her and kissed her.

When he drew back, she looked at him in surprise. "Paul?"

" 'Tis but a kiss of thanks," he explained hastily. "While I don't deserve your generosity these past days and weeks, I'm grateful."

"And I told you that you deserved it and more. I would not be here were it not for you. But a kiss is also a conviction of the heart — a pledge that must be fulfilled. Is that why you kissed me?"

Paul looked at her. What was his heart saying? Could he find a matter of agreement between him? That while the past might have brought them together, could it preserve them? Even if he remained unsure, he knew he was falling in love with this beloved angel of mercy and giver of hope. He quickly turned aside and gathered up the reins.

"I hope you will consider staying at our home," Alice said. "Papa is not well, and we need the help."

"I'm sorry to hear he's ill. I pray 'tis nothing serious."

Alice sighed. "He says his heart is weak, that the physician told him nothing could be done. Today he seemed so pale and tired." He felt her hand suddenly slip around his arm as if searching for strength. "I'm afraid, Paul. Afraid I might lose him. What will I do? He means everything to me." Her hand shook as she heaved in distress.

He patted her hand. "I will pray for his recovery, Alice."

"What if the Lord decides his time is nigh? What will become of me, alone at Southridge? How can I manage such a place and the lands?"

Her head suddenly found rest on his shoulder. Love for her welled up within him. How he wanted to protect her and help her through life's unpredictability.

"There is no hope," she said softly.

"What? Pray tell, what talk is that, my angel? There is always hope." He chuckled at the words coming from his own mouth. "For me to say such things when only a short time ago I thought all hope had been abandoned shows a miracle indeed. But I found my hope renewed by the blessings of God. I assure you, Alice, that you will not be left alone to manage your home. His blessing will likewise fall upon you."

She righted herself as if the words imparted strength, and her lips uttered a soft amen.

When they arrived at Southridge, Paul and Alice found her father in his chair by the fire, reading a book.

He smiled at them. "Well, Mr. Dodson, I'm glad to see that my daughter was successful in her quest. Though I do wonder where she finds the will to do such things."

"She is successful in everything she does, sir. And she has a heart of gold, like her father. Not that I would say such things to bring about some manner of agreement, but I have something I would like to ask you."

"Yes?"

"If I might have permission to court your daughter."

Alice stepped back in surprise. Paul heard a sigh escape, and her gaze lingered on him in apparent awe and wonder.

Mr. Wells put down his book. "This is a surprise. So the rescue went that well?"

"Papa, 'tis more than that," Alice said. "I didn't tell you . . . but long ago when I was a young girl, Mr. Dodson rescued me from an Indian tomahawk. I was foolishly trying to steal corn to help replace my tea set I lost on the voyage here. Paul — I mean, Mr. Dodson — saw the Indians' anger before it was too late and saved me."

"Indeed. Is this what you meant when you said you had an important message to tell me?"

"And what has led to my happiness, Papa. How can one not be joyful when life is restored?"

He nodded. "Then I must ask, Mr. Dodson, if you have made the Lord Jesus ruler of your heart and soul?"

"Yes, sir."

"And you seek to put my daughter and her needs above your own, guiding her and guarding her from the trouble of this world?"

"Yes, indeed, sir. With my life."

"And that you will both take time in the Lord during this courtship to learn about each other and seek to discover if the covenant of marriage is what He favors for your lives?"

Alice came forward then, slipping her hand through the crook of Paul's arm. "We wouldn't want it any other way, Papa. His will be done."

"Very well. You have my blessing."

Paul felt like laughing and singing. Never did he imagine all these things in his life would culminate to courting the beautiful Alice Wells. "Now if you would permit me, my lord, I will take my leave and see to the blacksmith shop."

Alice followed Paul to the shop and the cold stone forge that he set about restoring to life. "I'm surprised you would agree to court a blacksmith," he remarked. " 'Tis dirty work indeed."

Alice laughed. " 'Twas you who asked my father, sir."

"I did sense, perhaps, that we do belong together. That somehow God has brought us to this place, even as He first did long ago. Though I can't help but think there are many better than I, that if another were to come along, I would be lost."

Alice shook her head. "Do you know what I see before me? I see a generous and giving man who helps in our time of need. And though I did help you in return, I'm grateful to God that we can share in our lives." She sighed. "Yes, I was surprised you asked Papa to court me, but I supposed you did take our kiss seriously."

His gaze locked with hers. "Very seriously. I knew I had fallen in love with my angel even before we set eyes on each other at your father's house. I only saw you from afar, yet I knew differently. An angel with a merciful heart — how can I not be the most blessed man there is?"

Alice looked away, clearly moved by his remarks. But they were true, and he would say them continually for all to hear.

The next day, Paul was out early at the blacksmith shop, tinkering with some projects Charles had left unfinished since the accident. Earlier that morning, Paul had gone to see the blacksmith to find the man's leg splinted with boards, his face downcast over his plight, until he learned of Paul's arrest and release. Charles had shaken his head in wonder. " 'Tis extraordinary, indeed, that you now return here at a time when the master needs you," Charles marveled.

"I will do all that I can to help. Tell me what needs to be done with your master's work."

After that, Paul set his sights on accomplishing the tasks given to him. He had just lifted a heavy metal rod out of the hot furnace when he heard a rustle in the doorway.

Alice stood there, dressed in her black wool cloak, her blue eyes regarding him. "When I couldn't find you, I knew you would be here and no other place."

Paul placed the hot iron in a cauldron of water, the sound of hissing and the sight of steam filling the air. He wiped his hands on the leather apron tied around his waist. "Charles told me there was still some work that needed to be done."

"You are like Charles in many ways. Perhaps that's the way of a blacksmith, working from the rising of the sun until it sets. I see why Charles had so many tools to give away. He buries his heart in his work." She tipped her head. "Are you likewise buried, sir?"

"No longer. I was set free by my angel."

Alice shook her head though a smile decorated her face. "Oh, Mr. Dodson, you do know how to brighten a day."

"I speak the truth." He took up the rod and placed it once more in the forge to heat it.

"Anyway, I'm here to request a special gift for Papa to be given at the Twelfth Night celebration. Can you make him a cross?"

Paul turned the rod. "A cross?"

"Such as one that can be stood on a table? Ours was taken during the raid."

"Why would anyone take a cross?" Paul took out the rod, positioned it on the anvil, and struck the tip with a sledge to form a hook.

"I don't know, but it's missing. Papa loved it very much. He says when he looks upon it he remembers all that our Savior Christ did for us. It gives him hope and joy." Her head lowered. "Especially now when he is so ill, I think he would take much pleasure in having it again."

Paul paused in his work. "He is no better?"

"I'm sending for the physician. Though he assures me there is nothing that can be done." At that moment he saw her wipe a stray tear from her face. "What will I do if anything happens to him?"

Paul gathered her in his arms. "I will be here for you," he promised. "On every occasion."

"And you will be here for Twelfth Night?"

"Of course. I've never celebrated the time with so loving a family or such a fine lady."

Again she wiped a tear away. "I'm glad you're here, Paul, but I wonder what will become of Southridge after all the eating and drinking is done. I wish I knew the future."

"Only God knows, Alice. We must trust Him with it, just as we trusted Him when we first came to this land. And even with the trials we have faced, He has been faithful. He will not allow you to bear anything beyond your strength."

"I'm grateful for you, Paul," she said, her voice wavering. "Even if you hadn't saved me that day in the woods, I would have still hoped and prayed for a man of your strength and faith to be a part of my life."

Paul stepped back. "We do have a great deal to learn about each other."

"But we know the things that are important — that we will be there for each other."

"I will work immediately on the cross." Paul nodded as Alice prepared to return to the house. "And what would you like, dear Alice, for the celebration?"

"I have no need."

"But there must be something on your heart."

Alice hesitated. "Just to have you here is a gift, Paul. Thank you."

Paul watched her walk away, wondering if there was something he could do for her that went beyond the work in the shop. Something that might show his affection as he now set to work heating metal to fashion the cross. He prayed God would provide the answer to what lay in secret on his sweet angel's heart.

CHAPTER 7

Never did Paul experience so joyous a time as he did with Alice Wells during the weeks leading up to the Twelfth Night celebration. While he accomplished what needed to be done at the blacksmith shop, he took it upon himself to learn everything he could about the fair young woman as they rode throughout the Virginia countryside, meeting neighbors and the few friends he had in Jamestown. When they arrived one day at his humble blacksmith shop in town, he discovered that Abel had turned it into a bustling trade.

"When are you coming back?" Abel inquired. "I can do little else unless I have another to help me."

Paul looked at Alice questioningly. He had stayed within her father's house to help in their time of need and to court Alice. He didn't know if he should take his leave and return to Jamestown. Were he and Alice in one mind and accord for him to even consider the next step in their courting — the covenant of marriage? If so, should they continue to dwell at Southridge or remove themselves to this place?

"I think Mr. Crawford has earned his place in your establishment, don't you agree, Paul?" Alice inquired.

"Certainly. You may remain, Mr. Crawford, and hire an apprentice if you wish."

"Thank you, but you must return yourself."

Paul gazed at Alice. He could see the look in her eye but could not discern her heart in these matters. To Abel he said, "Continue as you have done, sir, and we will allow the future to rest with Almighty God."

Abel nodded, thanking Paul once more for placing his confidence in him.

"Don't forget, you are also invited to the Twelfth Night celebration at our home," Alice added. "Invite your friends, if you wish. It will be a grand time."

Abel bowed, thanking her for the invitation and saying he would not miss it. As they walked out into the center of town, Paul felt Alice's hand slowly slip into the crook of his elbow. "Are you having difficulty coming to a decision about the future?" she asked.

"I'm only listening to what God would have me do," he told her in all honesty.

"And what is He saying?"

"It's still not clear. But I know I've very much enjoyed our time together. 'Tis been the joy of my life. If only your father's health would improve."

Alice sighed. "He seems to be growing weaker. I do pray he will be well enough to enjoy the festivities. He loves Twelfth Night so. For him, 'tis a way to celebrate with the neighbors, to give of himself to others as Jesus did when He came to this world. Papa feels it fitting that we be of a merry heart with the gladness of God during this season."

"I'm eager to be a part, as well. I know festivities have happened in Jamestown other years, but since the fire, 'tis difficult to make merry."

Her fingers tightened around his arm. "If I could, I would invite them all," she murmured, as they watched townsfolk still in the midst of repairing their homes. "But at least I can help a few."

He patted her hand. "And that you have, my lovely angel. We have helped Abel and some of his friends. There will be others, as well, as time goes by." He paused, turning toward her and grasping her hands in his.

"You're so lovely. I'm a blessed man, in-deed." *More than mere words can say,* Paul thought. More than he could hope or dream. And how well he would make merry on Twelfth Night in celebration to God for all His blessings and pray he might come to a decision about the future.

A great many people gathered at Southridge for the Twelfth Night festivity. Beyond the main home in a wide-open field, a large bonfire had been kindled, warming the cold winter's night. Everyone laughed and sang songs in celebration as the servants bustled about, filling pewter cups with apple drink sweetened with sugar and honey. People toasted each other with the fond word of "Wassail!" — *Be well!* On a large table a feast of roast turkey, corn, squash, apple pastries, and jumballs — sweet cookies containing a variety of spices — had been laid out. And in the center stood the main delicacy of the night — the decorated Twelfth Night cake.

"When do we cut it?" Abel asked, gestur-ing toward the cake with his pewter mug before downing the mug's contents.

"Very soon," Alice said, "when my father comes to join us."

"He will come?" Paul inquired. "I thought

he was ill in bed."

"He will come, even if he is ill. Papa would not miss this. So tell me, Mr. Crawford, what will you do if you are crowned king this night?"

"Dare I say that I would oblige Governor Berkeley to return to England?" He laughed loudly as did several of his friends who joined them.

"If I were king, I would see that everyone has a home," Paul said. "And perhaps their own angel sent from above." He smiled as Alice's eyes shown in the light of the bonfire. She looked beautiful, even dressed in her woolen cloak, though he believed Alice Wells would look beautiful no matter the place or the dress.

Paul stepped aside then, gesturing to Abel.

"Your gift to Miss Wells is ready," Abel whispered.

"You're a good friend, Mr. Crawford."

"Paul, I know you speak of angels, but I believe I've seen the kindness of men. And I'm beginning to believe your words that speak of God's kindness. I know I'm not a Christian like you, but I hope in the days ahead you will teach me what that means."

"Tell me, can you read, friend?"

"Not very well," Abel admitted.

"Then we will begin with reading lessons.

And when spring comes, you will be reading the Bible and all the promises the Almighty has to offer."

Abel nodded, his hand slapping Paul's shoulder, and raised his mug. "I will toast to that."

All at once a bell sounded. Everyone took their leave of the bonfire, slowly making their way to the grand ballroom of the manor home. Paul carefully helped Alice out of her cloak, appreciating at once the pretty dress she wore, with matching ribbons decorating her hair.

A servant carried the Twelfth Night cake into the main room and set it on a table. Presently Mr. Wells appeared, flanked by another of the servants, who helped him to a chair. He smiled at the gathering. "I welcome you all to Southridge. This is a grand night indeed, but a night I think of most humbly when I consider our Lord coming as a wee babe to dwell among men. 'Tis good and right that we take this night to think on this and offer Him thanks. Would you bow your heads with me as I pray?"

Paul bowed his head along with Alice, listening to the thoughtful prayer from Mr. Wells that could stir any soul. He glanced over at Abel and saw the large man praying along with everyone else. Joy filled his heart at the reverence coming forth from his friend. A celebration of Christ's birth had also birthed a new believer for His Name's sake. No other joy could be so great on a night such as this.

"Amen!" Mr. Wells pronounced. "And now we will cut the Twelfth Night cake. As tradition holds, whoever finds the jewel within his or her piece is to be crowned 'king' of our festivity."

Everyone eagerly stepped forward to receive a piece of cake. Paul obtained cake for both he and Alice, but neither of them found the treasure.

"I thought surely you would be crowned king," Alice said in dismay. "But do not fear, Paul. You will always be a king in my eyes."

A commotion suddenly arose among the guests. "He has it! Look!"

Everyone strained to see who had found the revered jewel piece. Just then Paul saw the look of surprise on the face of Charles, the injured blacksmith. His family all shouted for joy, crowding around him when Charles held up the glimmering trinket for all to see.

"Papa is now a king!" a little boy said, climbing up onto his father's lap.

Charles didn't seem to know what to do.

He looked to Mr. Wells for help.

"Congratulations," Mr. Wells offered. "My blacksmith, Charles, has won the honors this night. I think it interesting how our Lord rewards us. 'Tis not in possessions or the land that makes us rich but in how we help each other in times of need. And in that we are all kings. But since we do have a king for this night of nights, what is your command, sir?"

Charles looked over at Alice as if searching for a direction. "Perhaps the king would allow us to give gifts to one another?" she suggested.

"Yes, yes." A concert of agreement filled the room. Charles then uttered a proclamation, to the joy of the assembly.

"Papa, here is your gift," Alice said, handing him a package.

The elderly man slowly unwrapped the gift to find the metal cross Paul had fashioned. Tears immediately filled the older man's tired eyes. "My cross. Thank you, my dear. 'Tis beautiful, indeed."

"Mr. Dodson made it, Papa."

"Thank you, sir. And thank you, too, for everything you've done for my household and my family."

Paul couldn't help the words that flowed from his lips. "No, sir, the thanks must go to you. For this is not just another house in all the colonies but a humble home that hails the love of Christ. And I do pray, sir, that you will likewise bless what I'm about to say." He turned then and picked up Alice's hands in his own. "I ask in the presence of all these witnesses, dear Alice, if you will do me the honor of becoming my wife."

"Oh, yes," she answered without hesitation to the cheers that erupted throughout the room.

Abel came forward at that moment with a package in his hand. "And now my gift to you," Paul said to Alice.

Alice took the somewhat large package from Abel with a look of puzzlement in her eyes. Slowly she undid the brown paper and gasped as it fell away. "Oh, Paul. My — my tea set. The set I once lost, the one I wanted that day in the woods when you saved me." Tears trickled down her cheeks. "I don't know what to say."

"You have already said it, my love," he whispered, "when you said 'yes' to me."

She wiped away the tears. "You must have your gift. Mr. Crawford, if you please."

Once more Abel came forward, handing a package to Paul. He opened it to reveal a Bible. "Why, how beautiful, my love."

"Open the cover," she said.

He did so to find other pages, some torn and blackened but still intact, carefully placed inside. "Mr. Crawford was able to find remnants of your family Bible, Paul. He took what he could from the original and put it in here. Do you see — there are still some of your family's writings, also? Not all of them, I fear, but enough for you to remember them by."

Paul could say nothing, so overcome he was at the sight. "I thought it had all been burned to ash," he finally said.

"There was enough left to spare, Paul," Abel added. "In fact, I have other pages as well that are not here. 'Tis not the complete Bible of your family, but . . ."

"But still a miracle from heaven. Thank you."

"What was once lost, God has found," Alice said softly.

Paul could not deny those words. He thought he had lost so much — yes, his personal possessions but other things more devastating, like hope. Yet when Alice Wells entered his life, he could see so clearly how God was the Heavenly Restorer. He gave the oil of gladness and love for the spirit of despair.

As the assembly ate their cake and continued to celebrate Twelfth Night, Paul stole

Alice away for a quiet time by the bonfire that continued to burn, lighting up the fields and beyond. "I once hated fire," he confessed, staring into the flames. He then regarded her. "But now it illuminates your beauty."

"Thank you for the tea set," she said softly.

"Thank you for my Bible. And for being my dear, sweet angel sent from above."

"Paul, I am only flesh and no one in particular."

"Quite true, but you are also going to be my wife. And that in itself is my royal crown, as the Bible says." With the firelight igniting her face, Paul drew her into his arms and kissed her, welcoming the healing of his heart and a cold Twelfth Night warmed by the fire of love.

■ ■ ■ ■

RAVEN'S CHRISTMAS
BY IRENE B. BRAND

■ ■ ■ ■

To my nieces,
Catherine Yauger
and Nannette Sowards

CHAPTER 1

Williamsburg, Virginia Colony, 1757

In her twenty years, Raven Maury had never had such a difficult decision to make. Should she marry a man she didn't love — a man fifty years her senior? Or should she allow Uncle Peter to steal her inheritance?

"I could do a better job fixin' your hair, Miss Raven, if you'd set still and stop scrunchin' your face into such a pucker." Mattie's words jolted Raven out of her reverie.

"Sorry! But I'm worried. If I don't marry Mr. Wharton by the first of the year, Uncle Peter will take Pleasant Hill away from me."

"Maybe Mr. William will come home 'fore then."

"I've been praying for months for his return, but it's been almost two years since he marched away with General Braddock and we left home to come to Williamsburg to live with Grandmother."

219

"And nigh onto a year since the last straggler from that big fight got home," Mattie answered with a sigh.

Mattie, who had been Raven's maid for as long as she could remember, brushed her mistress's thick brown hair away from her forehead, twisted it into a roll in the back, and arranged several ringlets to dangle over her shoulders.

Mattie handed Raven a mirror, and she turned sideways in her chair to look at the back of her head. Rather than wear a wig as most of the women in Williamsburg did, Raven preferred her own hair. Occasionally she let Mattie powder it, but not today, because she and her grandmother intended to spend the day at home.

"Thanks, Mattie. What gown have you picked out for me?"

"You want your hoop today?" When Raven shook her head, Mattie said, "Then step into these two petticoats. It's cold out, and you'll want the extra warmth."

Mattie helped Raven put on the petticoats and a quilted underskirt of Indian cotton before she took an open-front gown of green damask from the wardrobe and fitted it around her shoulders. "You look purty, miss."

Giving Mattie an impulsive hug, Raven

said, "Thanks to you. You take good care of me."

After Mattie left to pursue other duties, Raven opened the blinds and surveyed the backyard. She closed her eyes, leaned against the window frame, and silently thanked God for Mattie. She would have had a dreary childhood if it hadn't been for her. After Raven's parents had been lost at sea seventeen years ago on their way home from a visit to England, Uncle William, her father's brother, had moved to Pleasant Hill as her guardian, placing her in Mattie's care. He had provided everything for her — a good education, spiritual training, and a secure home — but he had never married. If it hadn't been for Mattie, she wouldn't have experienced much maternal love.

Grandmother Thomasine lived in a timber-framed, one-and-a-half story house, roofed with clapboard shingles, along quiet Francis Street. She slept in a bedchamber on the first floor, and Raven had been given an upstairs room. Compared to her spacious bedchamber in the two-story brick house on Pleasant Hill plantation, Raven's room was tiny, but she was comfortable in the room with the slanted ceiling and the two dormered windows that overlooked the neat lawn and garden behind the house.

221

Raven watched as Mattie hurried along the covered walkway separating the kitchen from the main house. The kitchen was located in a smaller building similar to the main house, and the slaves' quarters were upstairs.

Raven walked downstairs, her long skirts fanning out over the steep steps. She stopped in the lower hall and peered out the window in the front door. Wind whipped fallen leaves around unpaved Francis Street. Seedpods of the catalpa trees on the lawn across the street shook like rattles in the blustery weather.

The street was deserted except for a man who strolled along, seemingly unmindful of the wind. He looked with interest at the houses and shops along the quiet street, bordered along the north and south by large estates. The man was tall and slender, and his movements were full of grace and self-confidence. Although he was dressed in a waistcoat and breeches similar to those worn by other Williamsburg gentlemen, his garments seemed a bit more elegant, causing Raven to wonder if he was visiting in town.

Unable to look away from the man, she watched him intently until he disappeared around the corner on Blair Street. His presence had filled her with a strange inner excitement — an emotion so totally new to her that she searched for a plausible explanation.

"Raven?" her grandmother called.

Startled, Raven turned toward the living room where Thomasine Gilmer sat in her favorite chair, her tiny feet propped on a wooden stool. A Bible lay open on her lap.

Raven entered the room, approached her grandmother, and leaned forward to kiss her wrinkled face. "Have I missed morning devotions?" She sat on the upholstered loveseat.

"No, I was searching for a place for today's reading when I heard you come downstairs. It's little more than a month before December 25, so I decided to start with the Christmas story."

"I would like that. I'm dreading Christmas this year, so perhaps hearing about Jesus' birth will help me remember the real meaning of the season, rather than focusing on my problems."

"Being mournful won't bring William back. We should celebrate the birth of the Savior. Don't forget the angels rejoiced when Jesus was born, as did the shepherds, so I'm sure our Lord expects us to be joyful during this season."

Thomasine turned to the book of Luke and started to read. " 'And it came to pass in those days, that there went out a decree from Caesar Augustus, that all the world should be taxed. . . .' "

Raven sat with closed eyes, listening to her grandmother's crisp, clear voice. She envisioned Roman soldiers as they entered with pomp and ceremony into the market square of Nazareth to read a decree that had originated in far-off Rome. She had often wondered why Mary's mother allowed her young daughter to travel the long distance to Bethlehem with Joseph. And for the first time Raven realized that since Mary's family, as well as Joseph, belonged to the tribe of Judah, Mary's father and mother, if still living, must have also gone to be taxed. And since it had been prophesied that God's Son would be born in Bethlehem, Mary *had* to take the journey.

As she had often done, Raven wished she knew more about what happened in Bethlehem that night. But she had to be satisfied with her own imagination. She saw Mary and Joseph turned away from the inn, and she envisioned the lowly shepherds hovering around a fire, which might have been for light rather than heat. Because the exact day of Jesus' birth was unknown, the rector had once suggested that the weather could have been warm at that time in Bethlehem. It wasn't difficult to imagine how startled the shepherds must have been when the majestic angel chorus appeared and told the shepherds about the birth of a child, who was to be Christ the Lord.

"And the shepherds returned, glorifying and praising God for all the things that they had heard and seen, as it was told unto them," Grandmother concluded.

Raven opened her eyes. "A beautiful story! It seems as if it's happening again every time we read it."

She took the Bible from her grandmother and laid it on the walnut table between the two windows facing Francis Street. She sat with downcast eyes, wanting to talk to Grandmother about the decision she must make soon but unwilling to further involve her in a family squabble.

"Tell me what's troubling you, my dear," Thomasine said, and the compassion in her voice brought tears to Raven's eyes. "I'll listen to whatever you want to say."

"I've about decided to accept Mr. Wharton's proposal . . ."

"Go on," Thomasine prompted when Raven's voice faded to a mere whisper.

"I will not let Uncle Peter steal Pleasant

Hill from me. If I marry Mr. Wharton, my uncle will no longer have guardianship."

"But it will break my heart to see you married to a man older than I am! Does Pleasant Hill mean more to you than your happiness?"

"I don't know, but I'm sure when Papa stipulated in his will that his brother would inherit if I married without my guardian's permission, he had Uncle William in mind — not Uncle Peter. He's always contended that he didn't receive enough when Grandfather Maury's estate was settled, and I suspect this is an attempt to regain what, in his opinion, is rightfully his. That's the reason he didn't choose someone eligible for me to marry — he was sure I would refuse Mr. Wharton and he'd get the plantation."

"You won't be the first girl to marry an old man, but I don't like it. Since I went to court and was successful in staying Peter's hand for a year, I've prayed daily for William's return. Just because God hasn't answered my prayer doesn't mean He won't. I will not give up until after Christmas. Please don't tell Peter that you'll marry Mr. Wharton until we're sure William isn't coming home."

Raven rushed to her grandmother and

hugged her tightly. "I won't. You've given me new hope. I had almost stopped praying, believing that God wasn't hearing my prayers. I feel so much better."

It was a relief to have some hope that she might still keep Pleasant Hill, the family plantation located several miles from Williamsburg, which had always been Raven's home. Although she often visited Grandmother Thomasine, she hadn't lived with her until William went off to fight with General Braddock in England's attempt to drive French settlers out of the Ohio River Valley. Her uncle believed it was his duty to help preserve English rights in the New World, but he wouldn't leave Raven on the plantation. Grandmother willingly agreed to look after her granddaughter until he returned, but none of them had expected him to be gone more than a few months.

"I'm glad we had our little talk," Thomasine said. "I knew you were worried, but I didn't want to bring up the subject. Let's go shopping this afternoon and buy new bonnets to wear to church tomorrow. I might even buy a new wig," Thomasine said.

"Grandmother!" Raven said in mock reproof. "You have more wigs now than you need."

Grinning, Thomasine said, "It won't cost

anything to see if the barber has made up some new ones. Besides, I need a haircut."

When they strolled past his shop on Duke of Gloucester Street a few hours later, the barber whom Thomasine relied on to trim her hair and supply new wigs wasn't in. But the milliner's shop was open. As excited as any girl, Thomasine tried on several new hats and bonnets. It took more than an hour for her to choose a bonnet, although in half that time, Raven had bought a black glazed-cotton bonnet lined with light blue satin, which she thought would complement her newest blue gown and brown hair.

While the proprietor wrapped their purchases in brown paper, she said, "Have you heard the exciting news about the new dancing master and musician who's come to town? He's an actor, too!"

"No, I hadn't heard, but it's welcome news," Thomasine answered. "I've missed the programs we used to have at the theater. Has he been here long?"

"No, just a few days. He's staying at the Raleigh Tavern, but I've heard he's looking for lodgings, which must mean he intends to stay for a while." Perhaps pleased that she had such exciting news to relate, the woman lifted her eyebrows. "*And* he's studied music in Paris. I understand he plays several instruments."

"Have you met him?" Thomasine asked.

"Not face-to-face," the woman admitted, "but I have seen him walking around town several times."

"What does he look like?" Raven inquired, suddenly interested, wondering if the woman was talking about the man she'd seen earlier in the day.

"He's tall and well-favored, but he appears rather young to have all the knowledge and skills credited to him."

Raven's heart skipped a beat, but she turned away, fingering some lace on a rack. She remembered her emotional reaction to the stranger, wondering what she would think of him if she actually met him in person. In her heart, she thought she would like to make his acquaintance. Why did she sense that there was some significance in his arrival in Williamsburg at this particular time?

CHAPTER 2

The pealing of the Bruton Parish Church bell wakened Raven the next morning. She stretched languidly, turned on her right side, closed her eyes, and burrowed deeper under the heavy quilt. The room was cold, but she knew Mattie would be in soon to stir the coals in the fireplace. After the first bell, worshipers had a few hours to prepare. A second bell would eventually peal a warning to laggards. The third bell rang a half hour before worship started.

Mattie slipped in quietly, and apparently thinking Raven was asleep, she stirred the coals, put on two more chunks of wood, and left, softly closing the door behind her. The crackling of the fire and the faint scent of wood smoke, which was a homey smell, normally made Raven feel peaceful, but her mind was troubled this morning.

Her dreams had been worrisome. She'd dreamed that she stood in front of the rector, taking her wedding vows. In one dream, Mr. Wharton, leaning on his cane, stood beside her. She'd awakened with a start, only to go back to sleep and dream again of her wedding, but this time the prospective groom had the slender form of Williamsburg's newest visitor. Raven knew there was no way to control her dreams, but how irritating to dream of a man she hadn't even met!

The room was warm by the time Mattie came with a tray holding breakfast. Raven sat up in bed and took the tray while Mattie wrapped a shawl around her shoulders.

"It's still a mite chilly in here, but the hot tea will soon warm you." Mattie removed the cloth. "Bacon, biscuits, and taters," she said, as she sliced the biscuits in two, buttered them, and spread them generously with damson plum jam. "Eat it all. If the reverend's sermon is long, you'll be hungry before we get home from church."

While Raven ate, Mattie scurried around the room, laying out Raven's clothes for the day and chatting about the weather and interesting tidbits of gossip that the slaves always seemed to know first. When she removed the tray after Raven finished eating, she peered closely at her mistress.

"You're kinda peaked this mornin', honey.

Are you sick?"

Raven didn't meet Mattie's perceptive gaze. She feigned a yawn. "No, I'm not sick. I didn't get enough sleep last night."

"You can take a little nap this afternoon. We're supposed to rest on the Lord's Day anyway." Heading for the stairs with the tray, she said, "I'll be back soon with your bathwater."

When the church bell rang the third time, Raven knew it was nearing eleven o'clock, when the services would start. Her grandmother called from the foot of the stairs, "Are you ready?"

"Yes. I was trying to decide whether to wear my new bonnet or a shawl over my head. What do you think?"

"The weather has moderated since yesterday. Your new bonnet will be suitable."

"I'll be down soon."

Raven sat in front of the mirror to put on the bonnet. Deciding her face looked too pale, she dabbed a cloth in her cosmetic bowl and added a touch of color to her cheeks and lips.

She joined her grandmother and went outside where the chaise waited for them. Ezekiel opened the door of the closed carriage and helped Thomasine and Raven up the steps. Bruton Parish Church was located on Duke of Gloucester Street, which was within walking distance, but Thomasine preferred to ride on Sunday mornings when they wore their finest garments. They passed Mattie and the cook before they reached the church, and Raven waved to them. Ezekiel tied the horses and hurried to help his ladies alight from the carriage.

Before they entered the church, following the cobblestone walkway, Thomasine turned aside into the churchyard and stood for a few moments with bowed head beside the grave of her husband and her infant daughter. Raven knew her grandmother also mourned her oldest daughter — Raven's mother — who had perished at sea, leaving George as her only surviving child. Raven waited beside the brick wall for her grandmother and smiled at the slaves as they entered the church to take their place in the north gallery on the second floor.

The soft strains of the organ greeted Raven and Thomasine as they entered the building. Raven recognized the musical selection, for the organist played it often, one composed by Bach especially for the organ. Silently lifting their hands to greet their neighbors who were already seated, they moved toward the high-backed Gilmer family pew. An usher opened and closed the door for them, and they knelt in silent prayer before they sat down. The church was cold, and Raven welcomed the warmth from the little stove at their feet.

Raven took a moment to appreciate the beauty of the building designed by Governor Alexander Spotswood many years ago. The canopy-covered governor's pew was located to the right of the altar. She wondered if Governor Dinwiddie would attend worship today. He had never been a popular governor, and since he had been harshly criticized for promoting Braddock's disastrous campaign, in which many Virginians were killed, the governor rarely attended public functions.

The rector, appearing regal in his familiar black robe, took his place behind the lectern. Thomasine and Raven took copies of the *Book of Common Prayer* from their reticules and joined the congregation in reading a selection designated for the first Sunday in Advent.

" 'Almighty God, give us grace that we may cast away the works of darkness, and put upon us the armor of light, now in the time of this mortal life, in which thy Son Jesus Christ came to visit us in great humility; that in the last day, when He shall come again in His glorious majesty, to judge both the quick and the dead, we may rise to the life immortal; through Him who liveth and reigneth with Thee and the Holy Ghost, now and ever. Amen.' "

After the conclusion of the short sermon which followed, the rector said, "We have a special guest with us this morning, and for our closing benediction, we will depart from the customary order of service. Andrew Faulkner, newly arrived in Virginia and a relation of Mr. William Byrd, also comes to us with a recommendation from my brother in London. Mr. Faulkner is a musician, as well as an actor, and he is going to sing for us this morning."

A twitter of excitement passed among the worshipers, and Raven stole a glance at her grandmother, who gave her an amused wink. There wasn't a ban against acting in Virginia, but because some unsavory characters had appeared on stage, many Williamsburg residents were skeptical of the profession. Fortunately Uncle William was not among them, and he'd taken Raven to the theater since she was a child.

A tall man with a sharp and confident profile took his position on the steps leading to the altar. He *was* the man she'd seen walking on the street yesterday, and although his features had been obscure, Raven knew he was also the man of her dreams. Dark brown hair flowed from his high forehead to the base of his neck. When he thanked the rector for the invitation, his lips parted to display straight, white teeth. His handsome face spread in a warm smile, and as his brown eyes swept the congregation, for a moment, they caught and held Raven's.

She was filled with a strange inner excitement, sensing that there was something special about this man. But feeling other eyes upon her, she looked sideways into the devious, sneering face of Uncle Peter. Had he noticed her reaction to the handsome stranger and was contemplating how he could use her interest in Mr. Faulkner to gain his own purposes?

"Because we are entering the Nativity season," Andrew explained in a resonant voice, "I've chosen to sing a hymn written by Charles Wesley, brother to John, both ministers in the Church of England. He wrote this hymn more than fifteen years ago, but your rector says you haven't heard the song in your parish. I pray that the words will bless you this morning." He paused slightly and unaccompanied by music sang, "Hark, how all the welkin rings, 'Glory to the King of Kings; peace on earth, and mercy mild, God and sinners reconciled!' "

As he continued through several verses of the song, Raven was caught up in the message of the song, as well as the skill of Andrew's delivery. She held her breath in awe, as most of the congregation must have done. The last mellow note of the song faded away, and a collective sigh circulated throughout the nave of the building.

The rector gestured for his guest to walk down the aisle with him, and when Raven and her grandmother left their pew, the rector was introducing Andrew to the worshipers. Her hands felt clammy and she had difficulty breathing, but when they neared the door, she had her emotions under control.

"Mr. Faulkner," the rector said, "it's a pleasure to introduce you to one of our most faithful members, Thomasine Gilmer."

Andrew bowed and took Thomasine's gloved hand when she extended it.

"And this is Raven Maury, Mrs. Gilmer's granddaughter," the rector continued.

Raven gave a slight curtsy and smiled at him.

Andrew bowed slightly. "It's a pleasure to meet both of you."

"Rector," Thomasine said, "I would like for you and Mr. Faulkner to take dinner with us today."

Looking sincerely disappointed, the rector replied, "I would like that above all things, but I must visit a sick parishioner in the country this afternoon." He turned to Andrew. "If you aren't committed else-where, I urge you to accept the invitation. Thomasine's cook is one of the best in Virginia."

Andrew's generous mouth widened into a smile. "I've only been in Williamsburg a few days, and I haven't met many people, so I have no previous commitment. I'd consider it an honor to visit in your home. What time should I arrive?"

"Two hours from now. We live on Francis Street in a frame story-and-a-half house with brown shutters. My name is on a post beside the steps."

Andrew pulled a watch from the pocket of his waistcoat to check the time. "I'll be there."

Raven made an effort to keep her features deceptively composed, but when Andrew turned to look directly at her and smiled again, she felt a blush spread over her face. She looked away, hoping that the brim of her bonnet kept him from noting her obvi-ous joy that he had accepted the invitation.

When they turned from greeting Andrew,

Peter Maury stood in their path. "Good day, ladies." From his smiling countenance no one would have suspected what a menace he was to Raven.

"Good Lord's Day," Raven said pleasantly, for she didn't intend to air her dissatisfaction with her uncle in a house of worship.

In a low voice, Peter said to Raven, "Remember that the marriage banns must be published during next Sunday's service if the wedding is held before the first of the year. Or have you decided to refuse Mr. Wharton's offer?"

Hearing his words, Thomasine said curtly, "You'll have your answer in due time, Mr. Maury, but not this morning."

Taking Raven's arm, she swept by him toward their carriage where Ezekiel waited. When the carriage door closed, Thomasine said angrily, "The nerve of the man! To approach you in front of our neighbors! It's unheard-of behavior."

On the verge of tears, Raven said, "I don't know what to do."

"The Bible tells us not to worry about tomorrow — that tomorrow will take care of itself. So let's rely on the promises of the Word of God and enjoy our guest this afternoon. Try not to cry, dear. You don't want red eyes when Mr. Faulkner arrives."

CHAPTER 3

When they reached the house, Thomasine said, "Take a little nap before dinner, as I intend to do. I'll notify the staff that we're having a guest."

Andrew arrived punctually, and Raven knew that was appreciated by her grandmother, who was a stickler for being on time. He wore a maroon waistcoat, gray breeches, and a lacy white cravat, the same garments he'd worn in morning worship — but she'd been too flustered then to appreciate his fine appearance.

Soon after his arrival, Mattie announced that dinner was served. They went into the dining room where Thomasine sat in her customary seat at the head of the table. She placed Andrew on her right and Raven on her left, so every time Raven lifted her head, she encountered his thoughtful gaze.

Steaming crab soup and a platter of biscuits was already on the table, and after that course was finished, Mattie and the cook brought in platters of roast pork and rice pudding and a bowl of mixed vegetables grown in the garden behind the kitchen and canned for winter use. They ate leisurely, visiting as they enjoyed the food.

"May I be so bold to ask how long you plan to visit in Williamsburg?" Thomasine questioned.

"I really don't know, ma'am. I suppose until it strikes my fancy to move on. In every generation, some Faulkner takes off for unknown parts, and I seem to have inherited the trait. I had a great-grandfather who went to the Orient. My grandfather became a sailor. My father moved from Scotland to London. And after my father's death, I decided to see the world. I've spent the past year on the European continent, studying and visiting the wonders of ancient cities. I kept hearing tales of the New World, so I joined a traveling troupe of actors and came to New York a few months back. When the group disbanded, I decided to visit my cousin, Mr. Byrd, and see the southern colonies before I returned home. I like Virginia better than any place I've seen so far. I may settle here."

As they talked, Raven lost some of the timidity she'd felt in Andrew's presence, and she said, "I've always lived here, so perhaps I'm not a good judge, but I think Virginia is a good place to live."

He beamed a smile in her direction. "I'm sure you're right."

"I prefer to live on the family plantation, Pleasant Hill, but my guardian had to go away, and I came to live with Grandmother."

"Raven's parents were lost at sea on a return voyage from England when she was only a child," Thomasine explained. "Her father's brother, William, became her guardian, and he went to the western frontier on a military expedition and hasn't returned. It's a joy to have Raven living with me, but her uncle's return is long overdue and we're worried about him."

For dessert, Mattie served a tart made with egg whites, hickory nuts, and black walnuts. While they ate, remembering her grandmother's words, Raven started thinking of her trouble with Uncle Peter. She was startled when Andrew said, "Raven is an unusual name, but a very pretty one."

"It's traditional for Maury daughters to be given the name. My first ancestor in Virginia owed his life to an Algonquian woman, whose name was Raven. She nursed him and his family back to health, and he called his next daughter Raven. There isn't a Raven in *every* generation, but my papa chose to give me the name."

"I like it."

Grinning, Raven said, "I've grown used to it, but when I was a child, I didn't like the name, for the neighbor boys called me 'Crow.'"

This admission seemed to amuse Andrew for he laughed — a deep, warm sound that struck a vibrant response in Raven's heart.

Smothering a smile, Thomasine stood. "I think that remark is a good way to conclude our meal. Let's go to the parlor and give the servants time to clean the table so they can have free time the rest of the day."

After they moved to the parlor, Mattie brought in a porcelain teapot and matching cups. Thomasine fixed Andrew's tea to suit his preference and filled a cup for Raven with a drop of milk and a spoonful of sugar.

"The director of the local theater has asked me to appear on the stage here," Andrew said. "I'm a Shakespearian, and he would like for me to recite from Shakespeare's works and give musical entertainments a few nights each week. When I came to Virginia, I thought I might like to travel into the wilderness, but my cousin, as well as a few other men I've met, advised against it. But I'm restless if I'm not busy, so I think I'll appear in the theater and perhaps give music lessons. Is there already a music teacher in Williamsburg?"

"We have had one from time to time but not now. At least, not to my knowledge," Thomasine said.

"I don't have many musical instruments with me, of course, but I generally go into homes to give lessons anyway."

"I can name a dozen or so families right now who have instruments and no one in the family to play them." Thomasine pointed to the harpsichord near the door. "I could play a few tunes when I was young, but I've forgotten them. Raven has expressed the desire to learn to play." Looking directly at Raven, she said, "Would you like to learn to play the harpsichord?"

"Yes, I would, but I don't know if I have the touch. I tried to play the one at Pleasant Hill. Uncle William wasn't impressed with my efforts, and he didn't suggest any lessons."

Andrew surveyed her kindly. "That's because you didn't have a teacher. I'm sure you could learn to play."

"Then you can count on one prospective pupil," Thomasine said. "And I'll circulate the news among my friends. You won't lack for pupils, I can assure you. Where can we contact you?"

"I've been living at the Raleigh, but it's rather noisy there, and I may move to private lodgings. However, I'll contact you if I move." He put his cup on the table and stood. "I must go now. Thank you for a wonderful afternoon."

As he prepared to leave, Raven found herself already looking forward to her music lessons, as she would get to spend more time with the enigmatic Andrew Faulkner.

Upon leaving the Gilmer home, Andrew wandered aimlessly around the town. After being in the happy, relaxed company of Raven and her grandmother, he didn't look forward to spending the rest of the day in a tavern room.

He'd been wandering for three years — from country to country, city to city — and although his fortune was far from depleted, he suddenly decided that it was time to take root. Now that his parents were dead, he had no binding ties to England, and much of what he had seen in the New World pleased him.

With a self-conscious snort, he derided his sudden decision. During his travels, he hadn't experienced more than a passing interest in any woman, but one afternoon in the company of Raven Maury, inhaling her gentle nature and overwhelming beauty, and he was actually contemplating settling down in a small village he had never heard of six months ago. Andrew shook his head in bewilderment. What had happened to his common sense?

Prior to his father's death, he had depended upon his guidance, but since then Andrew had learned to rely on God for direction. When he reached Bruton Parish Church, on impulse Andrew walked into the graveyard surrounded by a brick wall. As part of his acting repertoire, Andrew had committed large portions of the Bible to memory. He sat on one of the table tombs, trying to recall a portion of scripture that would speak to his present concern.

With head bowed, he waited for God to speak. His mind turned to Psalm 139. " 'O Lord, thou hast searched me, and known me,' " he said quietly, recalling verse by verse the psalm until he came to verse seven, knowing he had part of his answer. " 'Whither shall I go from thy spirit? or whither shall I flee from thy presence?' "

He had God's assurance of protection and guidance in Virginia as if he were in the heart of his native London. He repeated the rest of the psalm quietly, his only audience a pair of trim, sleek, light gray breasted birds, with dark gray feathers covering the rest of their bodies, peering at him from the branch of an evergreen tree. He left the churchyard without a complete answer to his future but with the assurance that God was in control.

The proprietor at the Raleigh detained Andrew when he entered the building, and he stopped politely, although he desired nothing more than to go to his room and ponder the strange new emotions he had experienced.

"Are you enjoying your visit, Mr. Faulkner?"

"Very much, thank you."

"Have you heard that tomorrow is Fair Day? I'm sure you would find the activities interesting."

"I daresay I would," Andrew agreed. "We have fairs in England, and I suppose the local one is patterned after those. What kind of attractions do they offer?"

"There will be a variety of merchandise for sale, competitive games, puppet shows, and horse races. It's held in Market Square, which is located near the courthouse on Duke of Gloucester Street. It goes from sunup to sundown."

"Thanks for your information. I'll stop by."

CHAPTER 4

Raven awakened when Mattie entered the room and opened the blinds. She pulled the covers over her head to avoid the bright sunlight streaming through the windows.

"Get up, Miss Raven. It's gonna be a good day for the fair."

"You should have called me, Mattie. I don't want to miss the opening festivities. Is Grandmother getting ready?"

"No'um — it's just gonna be you and me. Miz Thomasine is a bit poorly this morning. She's got a touch of pleurisy. Her nose is runnin', and she's coughin'. But she didn't want you disappointed so she told me to go with you to the fair today."

"But you're supposed to have the day off."

"I wuz goin' to the fair anyway, so I can still keep my eye on you. 'Tain't fittin' for you to be walkin' around in that crowd by yoreself."

"I still think I should stay here," Raven

protested, although she *was* disappointed, because the fairs were a delightful break from the daily routine. "I'll take care of her."

Mattie shook her head. "No'um! She said you're not to come to her room for fear you'll catch it. All she wants is some hot tea and a slice of bread. She wants us to stop at the apothecary's and buy some more herbs."

Throwing back the covers, Raven stepped out on the floor, stood before the fireplace on her bare feet, and bathed quickly.

"What gown do you want today?"

"That blue one made from homespun fabric."

Lifting the gown from the wardrobe, Mattie said, "It's not as cold today as yesterday but still kinda breezy. You'll be warmer in the homespun than a fancy dress from England. Besides, when I was sweepin' off the sidewalk this mornin', some men walked by sayin' it's time the colonials stopped dependin' on England and started makin' their own things."

"I wouldn't put much dependence in comments like that."

"Slaves hear a lot of things not intended for their ears, and a lot of it is true."

When she and Mattie were ready to leave, Raven picked up her reticule and went downstairs. She gapped her grandmother's door about an inch. "Are you sure I can't help you?"

"Just stay away from me," Thomasine said in a raspy voice. "I have a sore throat and I don't want you to catch it. I've had two cups of herbal tea, with plenty of wood betony in it, and I'm going to sleep. Have a good time."

"I'll come home as soon as the puppet show is over."

Thomasine mumbled something behind her handkerchief, which Raven didn't understand, but it sounded as if she wanted her to stay longer. She turned toward the front hall where Mattie waited. Mattie picked up a large basket and followed Raven until they reached Duke of Gloucester Street. When they neared Market Square, Raven said, "I hear the drums already. Let's hurry."

A band of colonial militiamen, dressed in blue uniforms, were entering the square, stepping lively to the music of fife and drums. When they stopped, a drum roll indicated silence, and the chaplain of the group stepped forward and addressed the crowd. "Welcome to the December fair. Let's pray God's blessings on our events today."

As he prayed, the silence in the square

was broken only by the sound of a coach and horses' traveling at a fast gait along Nicholson Street. The chaplain closed his prayer with, "And God's blessings on all of you. Amen."

"What do you want to do first, Miss Raven? The missus told me last night that she wanted some fresh country butter and bread. And some headache powders and ointments, too."

"Let's buy those first, and then we'll get some spices and herbs at the apothecary's table. Cook can always use more seasonings."

Mingling with the crowd and greeting acquaintances, Raven soon filled Mattie's basket with their purchases. Ezekiel came by and volunteered to take the basket to the house so Mattie wouldn't have to bother with it during the day.

They returned to the exhibition area to watch the militiamen drilling and showing their skill in rapid loading and shooting. Colonial militiamen consisted of every free, able-bodied male British subject between sixteen and sixty, and a large group of them were on hand to engage in footraces and wrestling and cudgeling contests.

Mattie found a seat for Raven on the front row of spectator benches before she gathered with other slaves a short distance away. Sensing a presence at her side, Raven looked up. Andrew Faulkner stood near her.

"Do you mind if I join you, Miss Maury?"

The mystery in his eyes beckoned her with an irresistible appeal, and she was extremely conscious of her quickened pulse. She was flattered that Andrew wanted to sit with her, and she scooted farther along the bench to make room for him. "Sit down. I'm pleased you came to the fair."

"The innkeeper recommended it as a good place to gain an understanding of the colonial way of life."

"That's true." With Andrew sitting beside her, Raven found it difficult to concentrate on the competitive events, but she applauded at the proper time when prizes were awarded to the victors. She was puzzled by her response to Andrew, for every time his gaze met hers, his eyes communicated a message she didn't understand. Or did she understand his message and wasn't sure how to answer it?

While Raven's attention was focused on the physical prowess of the militiamen, Andrew watched her with a keenly observant eye. Never had he been as fascinated by a woman as he was by Raven Maury. He had sought her out this morning because she had been constantly in his thoughts since their eyes had met in Bruton Parish Church yesterday.

Glancing away often so she wouldn't realize he was staring at her, Andrew tried to analyze why she was different from other women. Why had she stirred his emotions? Of medium height, she was slender and willowy. Her smooth skin glowed with pale pink undertones. He admired her brown hair and gray eyes. She had a firm, silvery voice that fell softly on his ears. But he could have said the same of dozens of other women he had met. He had to look deeper to determine why Raven had unlocked his heart.

Although at times she seemed worried, her quick, pre-possessing smile came easily. He had noticed the regard with which she treated her slaves. He sensed in her a deep-seated faith in God and kindness toward others that seemed to be the very essence of her beauty and character. It was unusual to find all of these admirable qualities wrapped up in one person, and Andrew believed that he had finally found a woman he could cherish above all others.

Andrew was so deep in his contemplation that his face grew hot with embarrassment when Raven turned to him. He wondered if she was aware of how closely he had watched her.

"They will have the cockfights next, and I don't find them entertaining. If you'll excuse me, I'm going to walk around until it's time for the puppet show."

"May I escort you?"

"Yes, thank you."

When Raven stood, Mattie hurried to her side.

"Mr. Faulkner is going to keep me company until the puppet show starts. Take some time for yourself."

The maid nodded and went back to her friends. Because it was daylight and a public event, Andrew knew it was acceptable for him to escort Raven unattended, especially when they were in view of hundreds of people. He offered his arm, and she placed her hand lightly on it. Chatting amicably as they walked among the different booths, Raven seemed happy until they passed a bench where three elderly men sat. Her smile quickly faded, she took a deep breath, and her fingers tightened on his arm. She dropped a slight curtsy and passed on quickly without speaking.

Concerned at this sudden change, Andrew said, "I know I shouldn't presume on our short acquaintance, but I've noticed that in the midst of your smiles and laughter, sadness often comes into your eyes. Are you troubled about your uncle who hasn't returned?"

Raven didn't answer at first, but when they came to an unoccupied bench, she said, "Yes, but that isn't my main concern. Let's sit for a while, and I'll tell you."

They remained silent for several minutes, but it was a comfortable silence, which Andrew found he enjoyed. He was surprised, as he usually found such silences with people awkward. But with Raven, any time spent was pleasant. And he was glad that she felt she could confide in him. He truly wanted to know what troubled her, and he hoped he could somehow find a way to help.

Raven continued, "It's true that I'm distressed about the disappearance of my uncle. Not only has he taken the place of my father, but he's also a kind man and I love him. I sincerely pray for his safe return. But I'm especially anxious for him to come home before the first of the year. I wouldn't burden you with my problems, but since you've asked, I'll tell you what most of Williamsburg knows already."

Andrew listened intently as she related the

terms of her father's will and how Uncle Peter had declared Uncle William dead, had himself appointed as her guardian, and had chosen a man for her to marry.

"Although women don't have much influence in our law system, my grandmother was able to get a postponement of Uncle Peter's guardianship for a year. But if Uncle William doesn't return by the end of this year, I'll either have to marry Mr. Wharton or lose the plantation."

Andrew contemplated Raven's revelation for several minutes. He knew that arranged marriages were common, and the practice hadn't bothered him before. But he was horrified to learn that Raven Maury was being forced into an unwanted and, what seemed to be, unsuitable marriage. "And you don't favor the man?"

"Did you notice the three gentlemen who spoke to us just now? The one with the cane is Mr. Wharton, whom Uncle Peter has chosen for me. Of course, he doesn't think I'll accept the offer and he will get Pleasant Hill. I don't know what to do."

Andrew stared at her in consternation. "I'm so sorry! What can you do?" And even as he posed the question, he knew she had no legal right to change the situation.

"My only hope rests on Uncle William's

return. If he's alive, then Uncle Peter's appointment wouldn't be valid."

"Would William let you choose whom you want to marry?" Andrew asked, surprised at how much her answer meant to him.

"He wouldn't *make* me marry a man I didn't favor, but on the other hand, he wouldn't agree to a match he believed wasn't good for me. But Uncle Peter isn't interested in me. This is a ruse to get control of Pleasant Hill, which isn't an issue with Uncle William, who has his own property."

This answer disconcerted Andrew. He couldn't help but wonder if William Maury would consider him an unsuitable match for his niece. His thoughts continued to amaze him, for he had seldom contemplated marriage before.

"Please excuse me for bothering you with my affairs."

"I feel honored that you confided in me, and I want to offer a bit of encouragement. The return of your uncle isn't your only hope. God can intervene in any situation. I can't believe He wants you to marry a man who's objectionable to you. Don't give up yet."

"No, I won't." Looking toward the center of the square, Raven said, "The cockfighting has ended. Shall we go? The puppet show will start soon." A cloud had obliterated the sun, and Raven drew her cloak more tightly around her shoulders.

"It's getting colder," Andrew said, pulling his cocked hat lower on his forehead. "But I'm used to a cold, damp climate in London, so I think I can adapt to the change in weather here."

He stopped to buy sweet buns for them to eat during the show. They sat side by side before the makeshift stage, while the puppeteer amused the crowd with marionettes — wooden figures of a tortoise, a frog, and a rabbit. When he saw the figures, Andrew whispered, "I saw this in Paris last year. It's based on *The Race,* one of Aesop's fables."

The assistant stood to one side and read the story as the puppeteer manipulated the figures. "Three friends — a tortoise, a frog, and a hare — lived together in a big meadow. One day the hare said he was going to the forest and the frog said he would go with him. When the tortoise mentioned his intention of also going, the other two laughed at him, saying he was too slow and would never complete the journey.

"The tortoise said, 'We'll see about that. I'll run a race with you.'

"The frog and the hare thought it was a big joke, but when a crow came along, they told him to give the signal. He cawed loudly. The race started. The hare took off first, and he was soon out of sight, but knowing he was the fastest of the three, he lay down and took a nap. The frog jumped as fast as he could, although he knew he couldn't beat the hare. Still, he could move faster than the tortoise. When he saw the hare taking a nap, he decided to rest, too."

The puppeteer was skillful, and the puppets characterized the animals so expertly that the audience laughed constantly, but not loud enough to drown the voice of the assistant.

"The tortoise kept crawling along. He was tired, but he passed the sleeping hare and frog and finally got to the forest first. The hare and frog couldn't believe they had been beaten by the tortoise. The crow, who had been following the race, told them, 'I can tell you how he did it — by keeping at it and doing his best and never stopping to take a rest.' "

Raven laughed merrily at the antics of the puppets, and Andrew was happy they could share this light moment. They joined the rest of the audience in applauding the puppeteer and his assistant.

Raven turned to Andrew. "I didn't learn the truth of this fable until I came to live with my grandmother. I lived a life of leisure most of my childhood, accepting as my given right for slaves to wait on me."

"With your family having slaves, that seems a normal attitude to me."

"But Grandmother didn't grow up that way. She was only a baby when her parents came to Virginia, and by the time they paid the passage for their family, they were penniless. Her father was granted land, and the whole family had to work hard in the house and in the fields to make a home."

"She seems well positioned now."

Raven agreed by nodding. "My grandfather's family was more prosperous than hers, and when he died, he left her with a comfortable living. The cook and Ezekiel belong to her, but she's not comfortable about it — I'm sure that she has provided for their emancipation in her will. She enjoys the lifestyle she became accustomed to after her marriage, but she's never forgotten her beginnings. One day each month, she gives her slaves a day off and fends for herself. I had already been taught the things expected of young ladies — embroidery, some music, education, deportment — but in the past two years, I've learned to cook, clean house, and mend my own clothes." Laughing, she added, "Although I think it quite unlikely, Grandmother says if I should have inherited the desire to wander that crops up in the Maurys every generation or so, I might marry a man who would take me to live on the frontier."

"If that should happen, would you be prepared?"

"More prepared than I was before Grandmother taught me a few things. And it wasn't easy. I thought I would never learn to bake a cake, but like the tortoise, I kept trying, and I can turn out a pretty good cake now."

When she started to stand, Andrew put his hand on her elbow to assist her.

"I must go home now. Grandmother isn't feeling well, and although she doesn't want me to wait on her, fearing I'll catch what she has, I do want to be there if she needs me. Horse racing is next, so you may want to watch that."

"I don't know when I've spent a more pleasurable day, Miss Raven."

"It's been a good day for me, too. Thank you."

When Mattie approached, Andrew stepped aside and watched them as they disappeared quickly into the dispersing crowd. He inhaled a deep breath, wondering if this day marked a turning point in his life.

CHAPTER 5

Contemplating one of the happiest days she'd ever experienced, Raven walked home in a state of euphoria, thinking about Andrew. She was flattered by his interest in her, and she was surprised at her reaction to him.

Walking a few steps behind her, Mattie chattered about the fair, but Raven was too intent on her time spent with Andrew to pay much attention. She found her mind straying to a conversation with her uncle a few weeks before his departure.

Perhaps sensing that he might not return from his military expedition to the western frontier, Uncle William had asked her if there was some young man she fancied, so he could arrange a betrothal before he left. She honestly replied that she didn't know of anyone she wanted to marry. Because most girls her age were married and looking forward to setting up their nurseries, this

263

had puzzled Raven, especially since her best friend and cousin, Carolyn Gilmer, was betrothed.

"You have plenty of time," William had said. "I want to keep you with me as long as possible, but I feel a responsibility to arrange a good marriage for you. Let me know if you take an interest in anyone."

Now, she certainly had an interest in Andrew, and she fervently prayed that her uncle would return soon.

Her hopes suffered a setback when she and Mattie turned the corner on Francis Street and saw Uncle Peter's carriage parked in front of her grandmother's house. "God," she prayed silently, "give me some direction on how to handle this situation. I have to make a decision today."

When they walked up the steps, Mattie opened the door and, taking the liberty of a longtime companion, whispered, "Remember, they can't force you into marryin'."

Raven nodded that she understood and, confident that God would help her, she walked into the hallway, removed her coat, handed it to Mattie, took a deep breath, and moved into the living room. Expecting to see her uncle only, her confidence wavered when she saw that Mr. Wharton was also in the room. Thomasine was seated in her favorite chair, holding a handkerchief to her nose.

"Grandmother! You shouldn't be out of bed."

"Your uncle was quite insistent that he speak to us today, so I left my sickbed to receive him. I only hope none of you become ill."

In spite of the seriousness of the situation, Raven smothered a smile. By the tone of her voice, Raven suspected that Thomasine wouldn't really mind if her guests did get sick.

"Since his business is with me, I'll hear what he has to say so he can be on his way and you can go back to bed."

Peter Maury didn't resemble his two elder brothers in size or temperament. Although Raven had only a vague remembrance of her father, she knew he had been much like Uncle William, who was of medium height and brawny. He was good-natured and a smile always seemed to be lurking in his gray eyes. Pleasant Hill's slaves were devoted to him.

Peter, on the other hand, was tall and lanky in size and cantankerous in disposition. It was his opinion that William pampered the workers, and the time he had been in residence at Pleasant Hill had been an unpleasant experience for the slaves, a situation that annoyed Raven, but she was powerless to intervene.

"As I told you, the banns need to be read in church this Sunday if you and Mr. Wharton are to be wed before the first of the year. If you do not marry him, you know as well as I do that you are disinherited."

Raven cringed at the thought of losing her home. Again she offered up a prayer of desperation, and suddenly a possible way out of this situation flashed through her mind. Why hadn't she thought of it before?

Turning to the older man, she said, "Mr. Wharton, I respect you and I don't want to seem unkind, but I won't marry you. I can't imagine how our marriage could bring happiness to either of us. Why would you want to marry me when there are so many suitable unmarried women of your own age in Williamsburg?"

He cleared his throat and slanted a glance toward Peter. "You're a very comely young woman, Raven. Your presence in my home would brighten my declining years."

"But what kind of life would it be for Raven to spend her youth looking after an old man?" Thomasine said indignantly.

Raven had often wondered the same thing, and for the first time she wondered if

Peter was paying the man to offer for her. She had always considered Mr. Wharton to be well off financially, for he dressed well and had a modest home in Williamsburg. But she had heard that he spent a lot of time in the gambling rooms of the local taverns. Possibly, Peter had promised him a sum of money from the coffers of Pleasant Hill if he would offer for her, thinking he would have plenty of money when Raven refused to marry him.

For an instant, she contemplated marrying the man to spite her uncle, but she discarded that idea as an unchristian thought. Besides, marrying Mr. Wharton would punish her more than Uncle Peter.

But since she now believed she had another way out of the predicament, at least on a temporary basis, she said, "Regardless, sir, I won't marry you." She spoke to Mr. Wharton but kept her eye on her uncle.

A smile of victory lighted his eyes momentarily, but he spoke gravely, "Then you leave me no choice except to take other measures."

"I don't think so. I'll have grandmother's attorney look into it, but as I remember, Papa's will stated that I was to be disinherited *if* I married someone against my guardian's wishes. It didn't stipulate that I *had* to marry anyone my guardian chose for me. As long as I don't marry at all, you can't have me disinherited."

Thomasine burst into laughter, which provoked a bout of coughing, and she again covered her mouth with a handkerchief. From the quick look of surprise and anger that spread over Peter's face, Raven assumed he hadn't even thought of that possibility.

"We'll see about that," he said furiously, jumped to his feet, and started toward the door. "You'll come to regret this! When you find somebody you *do* want to marry, I'll not give my permission."

Thomasine lifted her handkerchief long enough to retort, "She can make her own choice when she comes of age."

Without answering, Peter left the house and slammed the door behind him. Mr. Wharton delayed long enough to say goodbye politely, but even he looked disappointed as he left the parlor. Mattie waited at the door. She winked at Raven, opened the door, and bowed him out of the house.

When Raven rejoined her grandmother, Thomasine's eyes sparkled above her handkerchief. "We could have saved ourselves a lot of worry if we'd thought of that before.

The only thing that bothers me — what's going to happen if you meet someone you want to marry?"

Andrew's compelling face flashed through Raven's mind. "I've put my future in God's hands. If that happens, I'll trust Him to bring Uncle William home. That is the only hope I have."

"At least we can enter into the joy of Christmas without knowing you're going to either lose Pleasant Hill or marry a man you don't favor." Thomasine struggled out of her chair. "Now, I'm going to bed. I gave the slaves the day off to enjoy the fair. You can prepare your own supper."

"I'll do that and bring you a tray, too. You don't seem infectious."

"I don't have any appetite, but I suppose I should eat something."

Feeling as if a burden had been lifted from her shoulders, Raven hurried upstairs, took off the clothing she'd worn to the fair, and put on a calico dress, an apron, and a mob-cap — garments she referred to as her "scullery maid garments."

When Thomasine had first mentioned that she was expected to learn basic housewifery skills, Raven was excited, thinking it would be a new source of entertainment. But after the first day, she'd learned a new meaning

269

of work. For months, she dreaded the workday, but eventually she had learned the wisdom of her grandmother's practice. For one thing, she appreciated the slaves much more than she ever had. In common with her acquaintances, she had always taken their service for granted. At the end of those workdays, she went to bed with a sense of accomplishment that compensated for the hard labor.

Throwing a shawl over her shoulders, she hurried to the kitchen. It was a spacious room with a huge stone-and-brick fireplace covering one wall. She stirred the coals on the hearth and added a few chunks of wood. She pulled the crane toward her and peered into the iron kettle hanging on a pothook. The water was warm, but not hot enough for tea, so she swung it over the fire. A skillet full of hash — a mixture of pork, potatoes, onions, and herbs — was on a three-legged trivet near the back of the fireplace. She pulled the trivet over the hottest part of the coals.

Raven could prepare a complete meal by herself, but she was pleased it wouldn't be necessary today. A loaf of fresh-baked bread and a raisin-and-apple pie were on the table. Raven smiled at this evidence of the cook's displeasure of someone else working in *her* kitchen! She also thought that Thomasine and Raven, being ladies, shouldn't be cooking.

When the kettle started steaming, she poured hot water over tea leaves, sliced some bread, and dipped up a portion of the stew on a pewter plate. She lit two myrtleberry candles and enjoyed their balsamic perfumed scent as she sat at the table. On workdays, she and grandmother ate in the dining room as usual, but today the cozy warmth of the kitchen was preferable to taking a cold walk to the usual formal room.

While she ate, Raven daydreamed of the hours she had spent with Andrew. After finishing her own meal, she washed the few utensils she'd used and prepared Grandmother's tray — a slice of buttered bread, a medium-sized piece of pie, and a pot of tea. Carefully banking the fire, she covered the tray with a warm cloth and hurried toward the house. She set the tray on a table outside her grandmother's door and opened the door quietly.

"I'm not sleeping," Thomasine said. "Leave the food on the hall table and I'll get it later."

Picking up the tray, Raven said, "You need your tea while it's hot. I'll bring it in and sit with you while you eat."

Thomasine didn't protest any further. She threw back the covers, put a shawl around her shoulders, and sat on the side of the bed. Raven put a small table in front of her to hold the tray. With a smile, her grandmother said, "I'll admit I have been lonely today. You can stay and tell me about your day, but keep your distance."

Raven sat in a high-backed chair not far from the bed. "It was more entertaining than the one last year."

"Last year, Braddock's defeat was too fresh in our minds for merrymaking."

"The puppet show was good, as was the militia band. And I was squired around by a very handsome man."

Thomasine lifted her eyebrows.

"Mr. Faulkner approached me early in the morning, and we spent the day together, but Mattie kept her eye on us so we were well chaperoned."

"And?"

"I enjoyed his company very much."

"We don't know much about him, my dear."

"I know. But he is related to the Byrd family and visited at Westover plantation before he arrived in Williamsburg. Besides, you heard the rector say his brother sent a letter of commendation."

"Just keep in mind that he is a stranger. I had a message from George. Your cousin, Carolyn, is coming tomorrow and she intends to stay until after Christmas. That should make you happy."

Raven clapped her hands. Because Uncle George owned a plantation a few miles from Pleasant Hill, Raven saw Carolyn often. They were as close as sisters. "Oh, it does! Carolyn and I have such good times when we're together. She can help me make decorations to use when the rest of her family come for Christmas. I'd intended to make them myself, but it will be more enjoyable to have Carolyn helping."

"I knew you would be pleased. And it will be a treat for me to have both of my granddaughters here at the same time."

"I'll have to put away the garments I have in the wardrobe in the spare bedchamber, for, as you know, Carolyn always travels with several portmanteaux full of clothing."

"Perhaps we should have the dressmaker make some new robes for you, too. You should have a special one for the Twelfth Night ball at the Apollo Room, as well as one for Christmas Eve."

"That would be nice," Raven agreed, wondering what kind of dress would please Andrew. She knew she had to stop thinking about him, and she blushed when she saw Thomasine watching her, a speculative gleam in her eyes. It was difficult to hide her thoughts! She knew that her grandmother's advice about caution was important to remember, but how could she tell that to her heart?

CHAPTER 6

Carolyn descended on them the next afternoon like a whirlwind. Thomasine and Raven lived a rather quiet life, but with Carolyn's boundless energy and cheery nature, there would be plenty of activity over the next few weeks. And that suited Raven. Now that she didn't have to worry about Uncle Peter's ownership of Pleasant Hill, she looked forward to some gaiety in the house.

Grandmother felt well enough to sit in the dining room for the evening meal, but she went to bed early. The two young girls turned in early, too, but they didn't plan to sleep. Raven knew that Carolyn would want to talk most of the night.

Mattie and Carolyn's maid helped the girls into night shifts and warm robes and then left the room. Raven said, "You go ahead to your own bed. I'll keep the fire burning and bank it before we settle down to sleep."

Fluffing the pillows behind her, Carolyn pulled a heavy blanket around her shoulders. "I had a letter from Oliver, and he'll be leaving England the last of March."

"So the date for your wedding will still be the first week in June?"

"Yes. It hasn't been easy for us to be separated for so many months, but he wanted to visit his ancestral home and relatives in England before he settled down. His mother intends for him to take over management of the plantation as soon as we're married. She's planning to move into their townhouse so I can become mistress of the plantation."

"That's very thoughtful of her."

"I thought so. I wish your marriage prospects were as good as mine."

"I'm more optimistic about my future than I was." She related her conference with her uncle, and Carolyn received the news with a frown.

"But that means you can't get married for five years or you'll lose Pleasant Hill to him."

Settling comfortably under the coverlet, Raven said, "I'd rather lose the plantation than marry someone objectionable to me, but I don't have to face that decision now."

The girls continued talking for some time about Carolyn's upcoming wedding. After Carolyn fell asleep, Raven lay awake into the night, wondering if she would ever be able to marry a man she truly loved.

The next morning, Raven and Carolyn, with Mattie following, set out to look for materials to make decorations. All three of them carried baskets, and they walked up and down the streets of Williamsburg gathering nuts, acorns, walnuts, and pinecones. They also visited a farmer on the edge of town to gather ears of corn from the large field behind his house. Promising to share some of their decorations with his wife, they filled Mattie's basket with three dozen ears of corn with the shucks still attached.

Returning home, they spread their supplies on a table in the large parlor. Using lots of glue, they formed the nuts into figures of children and birds, and Carolyn used a brush to dab paint on the ornaments to represent eyes and other features. At the end of the afternoon, they had about three dozen figures, which they would attach to garlands of pine and place around the house a few days before Christmas.

Thomasine checked on them by midafternoon. "Don't you think you've had enough work for today? Dinner will be ready soon."

"Do we have time for a short walk?" Raven asked. "I've been bending over the table and my whole body feels stiff."

"Yes, but don't take long."

They took coats from the hall tree, wrapped heavy shawls around their heads, and slipped their hands into muffs. As they left the house, Raven suggested, "Let's turn on Blair Street, walk along Duke of Gloucester Street, and pass by Market Square. That won't take long."

The sun did little to counteract the sharp wind so they walked briskly. They stopped once to peer in the milliner's window, for Carolyn had mentioned that she wanted to buy a new bonnet. As they resumed their walk, they came face-to-face with Andrew Faulkner.

"Oh!" Raven said, somewhat confused.

His eyes brightened with obvious pleasure when he greeted them. Raven stifled her confusion and smiled at him. "Mr. Faulkner, this is my cousin, Carolyn Gilmer. She'll be staying with us until after Christmas."

"It's a pleasure to meet both of you. Is your grandmother able for me to make a visit tomorrow afternoon?"

"She's feeling much better and none of us

have plans. We'll look forward to seeing you."

"I hope you enjoy your visit in Williamsburg, Miss Gilmer. Until tomorrow," he added and walked on down the street.

"And who is he?" Carolyn asked, her eyes wide open with curiosity.

"A newcomer to town from England." Briefly, Raven sketched the arrival of Andrew and mentioned that they'd entertained him for Sunday dinner. She said nothing about the day they'd spent together at the fair. Her feelings for Andrew were still too new, and his nearness was overwhelming. It would take time to realize what these strange emotions meant, and she wasn't yet ready to talk about them, even to her cousin.

The next morning was taken up by the seamstress, who measured both Raven and Carolyn for new gowns. Looking through the woman's sketches, Raven chose a blue silk, open-front sack gown with matching underskirt trimmed with pleated satin. Lace-edged gauze ruffles would be added at the neck and sleeves. She planned to have Mattie weave a string of pearls into her hair, which would be dressed in an elaborate style on top of her head. The seamstress would finish this dress before she started on the gown for the Twelfth Night ball.

Carolyn already had several new gowns made by the dressmaker on their plantation, but she couldn't resist ordering an oyster-colored satin gown, looped up in polonaise style with a small matching hat. The garment was fitted with gauze sleeves trimmed with satin ribbons and a pink pleated petticoat. Carolyn said she would wear the dress with a set of pearls, a gift from Oliver before he left for England. Thomasine insisted on a modest neckline for both of the girls, and Raven chose a mixed-flower posy for the front of her bodice.

When the seamstress packed up her fabrics and patterns and left, Raven and Carolyn flopped down on Raven's bed, their hands behind their heads.

"Ordering new gowns is not my favorite thing to do," Carolyn said.

"Nor mine," Raven agreed. "I'm tired, but we can't rest long. Andrew will be coming soon."

"And, of course, we can't keep the admirable Andrew waiting," Carolyn teased.

Raven closed her eyes and pretended to ignore her cousin. She would have to talk to Carolyn about her feelings for Andrew soon, for she wouldn't stop pestering until she had the whole story.

Not long after he arrived, Andrew was escorted into the parlor. After greetings were exchanged, Mattie brought in a silver tray holding a steaming pot of tea and a tray holding scones, china cups, and saucers.

"Shall I pour, ma'am?" she asked.

"No, thank you," Thomasine answered, "Raven will do that. You can pick up the tray later."

Andrew observed Raven under lowered eyelids. She poured the tea to each one's satisfaction and then moved the pot to a trivet on the hearth to keep the water hot. To counteract his awareness of Raven, Andrew turned to his hostess. After he complimented her on the quality of the scones, he said, "I've found that I may have to delay my plans to give music lessons."

Andrew perceived that Raven had cast a startled glance in his direction, and he quickly added, "Yesterday, the president of William and Mary College called on me and offered me a teaching position in the school."

"Why, that's wonderful! And you're interested?" Thomasine said, obviously pleased.

"Yes, to the extent that I'm going to try it.

I'm Cambridge-educated and I have the qualifications to teach, although I have no experience in the classroom because I continued to further my education through travel."

"What would you be teaching?" Raven asked, excited to think that Andrew was extending his stay in Virginia.

"The works of Shakespeare. And I have also been asked to organize a college choir. It seems that their last choirmaster has passed away. I will be hired on a temporary basis for a few months to see if I like the work and until the board members determine if they are pleased with my performance."

"This sounds like an excellent opportunity," Thomasine said. "It will give you a reason to stay in Virginia."

Andrew agreed by nodding, knowing that he already had one reason for taking up residence in Williamsburg.

"More tea?" Raven asked.

Thomasine asked for a refill, and Raven brought the kettle from the hearth. "There are more scones in the pantry," she said. "If you'll excuse me, I'll bring them."

Carolyn jumped up from the stool she had occupied near her grandmother's chair. "You've been serving, so I'll bring the scones."

Andrew wanted to reassure Raven about the music lessons so he said, "After I see how much time I'll be spending at the college, I'll arrange my presentations at the theater and schedule private lessons for those who are interested."

"We're too busy preparing for the festivities that lead up to Twelfth Night to concentrate on music lessons now anyway," Raven said.

"Which reminds me," Thomasine said, "unless you have already laid plans for Christmas, I'd like to invite you to dine with our family on Christmas Eve."

"My cousin extended an invitation to spend the holidays at Westover, but I haven't accepted his invitation. I'll be happy to observe the occasion with you."

"We don't do much merrymaking on Christmas Day, for it's a time of worship, but we are festive on Christmas Eve."

"That's when we light the Yule log," Raven said. "Would you like to go with us when we cut the log?"

"Yes. That would be a new experience for me."

"We'll let you know," she said.

"I'll be taking my leave now. Thank you again, Mrs. Gilmer, for another pleasant visit. I look forward to Christmas Eve. Farewell." Andrew had hoped for a private word with Raven, so he was pleased when she went to the door with him.

"May I ask what decision you've made concerning your uncle's demands?" He would have welcomed the answer to this question before he agreed to teach at William and Mary College, for while he wasn't sure of his feelings for Raven, he knew he wouldn't want to live in Virginia if she was married to another man.

Raven handed his coat to him and pulled a shawl from the hall tree. "Let's step outside for a few minutes."

Facing him on the steps, she said, "I told my uncle I wouldn't marry Mr. Wharton."

A hopeful glint flashed in his eyes, and he stepped closer to Raven.

She quickly lowered her thick, dark lashes. "It suddenly came to mind that as long as I don't marry *anyone,* my uncle can't steal my inheritance."

Andrew felt a wretchedness of mind he'd never experienced before. Feeling an acute sense of loss, he said quietly, "Does your property mean so much to you that you'd remain a spinster all of your life?"

"The restriction is only valid until I'm twenty-five."

Feeling somewhat better, Andrew asked, "And how old are you now?"

"Twenty!"

Andrew groaned audibly. His throat aching with anguish, he turned toward the steps. *Five years!* He had waited this long to lose his heart and he must wait five years more!

"Andrew," Raven said quietly. He stopped before he reached the sidewalk and looked up to where she stood, her long, tapering fingers gripping the iron handrail. "Have you forgotten already what you said — that Uncle William's return wasn't my only hope and that you didn't believe God would want me to marry a man objectionable to me? Your words encouraged me then, and I'm still holding on to the hope that He's in control of my life."

Andrew lifted Raven's right hand and daringly kissed her fingers. "Thank you," he said. "You've given me hope also. I'll call in a few days and let you know about my employment."

"I'll be waiting."

Andrew couldn't believe that he'd been plunged to the depth of despair and raised to new emotional heights in such a short period of time. When it seemed as if there was no hope for a future with Raven, he had been tempted to forget William and Mary College and Williamsburg and go back to England. From her words and the expression in her eyes, Andrew believed that Raven was also interested in him. He'd been given new hope for the future.

CHAPTER 7

The next Saturday, Thomasine hired a wagon and horses so that Ezekiel could go into the forest and haul in the Yule log. Raven sent a note to Andrew's lodgings, telling him they planned to start around nine o'clock. Dressed in their oldest gowns and wearing heavy coats and scarves, Raven and Carolyn were already seated in the wagon when he arrived. Bundled in a heavy coat, Thomasine was standing on the porch.

"Am I late?" Andrew asked.

"No," Carolyn said, "we're just overly eager to go."

Putting his foot on the small step, Andrew vaulted into the wagon. There was a layer of straw on the bottom of the wagon bed, and he sat down facing Carolyn and Raven. Ezekiel cracked a whip, the team leaned into their harnesses, and the wagon lurched away from the sidewalk.

Waving, Thomasine called, "Bring a good log."

"We will," Carolyn promised.

"I know the Yule log has been a part of English culture for several centuries," Andrew said, "but this is the first time I've ever participated in the ceremony. My father and I lived in cities and followed rather quiet lives. Tell me what the custom is in Williamsburg, and while you're at it, you might refresh my memory about the origin of the Yule log."

"The custom evolved from the Roman Saturnalia festival marking the beginning of the winter solstice," Raven explained. "And since the observance of Twelfth Night was a pagan practice, it was banned for years by the church. After a few hundred years when Christians decided it might be a way to convert pagans and hold them to the new faith, they started to observe a festival of feasting, family gatherings, and public gaiety during the time of the winter solstice."

"Here in Virginia, we don't do much feasting on Christmas Day now," Carolyn added. "It's more a time of worship."

"Our celebrations are reserved for Twelfth Night."

"It's that way in England, too. Yuletide covers the twelve days between Christmas

288

Day and Epiphany, January 6, the traditional observance of the wise men's visit to Jesus."

"We exchange gifts on Twelfth Night and attend a big party at the Apollo Room," Raven said. "We start burning the Yule log on Christmas Eve and keep it burning until the twelve days are over."

After they left town, Ezekiel followed a rutted road into the forest. Looking back over his shoulder, he said, "Miss Raven, your grandma said for me to cut a big oak log, but she didn't say how long it ought to be."

Laughing, Raven said, "About five feet long. Actually, if we take a log that comes to my shoulders, it will be the right size to fit into the fireplace."

"I know a good tree — one that toppled over in the high winds last month. We can cut a Yule log from it, and I'll come back later to chop the rest of it into firewood."

The fallen tree was lying on the bank of the James River, and a few dry leaves hung on its spreading branches. The cold wind that had chilled them as they were riding in the wagon didn't reach them in this secluded spot.

The sun was shining and the weather pleasant as Andrew helped Raven and Carolyn to the ground. Raven took two baskets from the wagon bed.

"We'll walk around and pick up pinecones and maybe find some red berries for decorations," Carolyn said.

"Don't go out of sight," Ezekiel cautioned them. "Miz Gilmer told me to take care of you," he added as he picked up an axe and started chopping branches off of the trunk.

"Can I be of any help?" Andrew asked.

Ezekiel's dark, sparkling eyes quickly appraised Andrew's garments. "Ever used an axe, Mr. Faulkner?"

Andrew laughed at the skeptical look on his face. "No — I haven't even held one in my hand."

"Then you'd better leave the choppin' to me."

"Surely I can do something," Andrew insisted.

"I'll be trimming off these branches until I can have a log the size the mistress wants. It would be helpful if you'd pull the branches out of my way when I cut them off and stack them to one side."

"I'll do my best."

While Andrew tugged and pulled at the heavy branches and piled them in the area the driver had indicated, he used muscles he didn't even know he had. Although he wore heavy gloves, within an hour, he sensed that blisters were forming on his hands. It was a relief when Ezekiel called, "That's all, Mr. Faulkner."

Andrew turned as Ezekiel gave the final blow and the desired log was severed from the rest of the trunk. Raven and Carolyn had just returned with their baskets full of pinecones and evergreen branches, and they cheered as the log fell away from the rest of the trunk.

"Grandmother will be very pleased with this log," Raven said. She turned to Andrew. "We'll light it when you're with us on Christmas Eve."

When Ezekiel bent over to pick up the log, Andrew said, "I'll help you." His body felt as if it had been stretched to the limit, but he wouldn't stand aside and let the slave lift the heavy log by himself. Summoning all the energy he had left, he picked up one end of the log and helped heave it into the wagon bed. It was even heavier than he'd expected, but it was gratifying to know he had been of some help. Ezekiel stabilized the log so it wouldn't shift from side to side as they traveled.

"We'll sit on the log," Raven said.

Andrew assisted Raven and Carolyn into the wagon; then he climbed in, too. He couldn't suppress a groan when the muscles of his legs tightened.

In concern, Raven turned to him. "Did you hurt yourself?"

With a wry smile, he said, "I hurt everywhere. Studying at Cambridge and becoming a musician didn't exactly fit me for outdoor work. I don't think I could have survived in the early days of this colony."

"I doubt that any of us would have. Most of the first settlers were gentlemen, who had no aptitude for hard labor, and the colony almost died out. But now that we're established, there's a place for people with a variety of skills. I feel sure that what you can teach is just as important as manual labor."

"Thank you for encouraging me. But while I was wrestling those tree trunks, I would have traded my college training for a strong back."

When they arrived at the house on Francis Street, Andrew helped Ezekiel carry the log into a shed behind the house. Refusing an invitation from Thomasine to eat with them, he returned to his room. His hands weren't blistered, but they were red and sore to the touch, and he hoped he wouldn't be called on to play a harpsichord soon.

He struggled out of his clothes, hung them in the wardrobe, and crawled into bed. He had never welcomed a soft bed more, but his last thought before sleep overtook him was the joy of spending another day in Raven's company. Despite the hardship of the day, he wasn't sorry he had come to Virginia.

Carolyn's parents didn't plan to come to Williamsburg on Christmas Day but intended to arrive for the Twelfth Night festivities, so Raven laid four settings as she prepared the table for dinner on Christmas Eve.

She handled the English-made china carefully for it had been a gift from her grandfather to Thomasine shortly before his death. Because it was the last present she'd had from him, Thomasine used it sparingly, wanting it to be intact to pass on to her oldest granddaughter, Carolyn. But Grandmother had compensated by promising Raven many other treasured items, such as the two crystal candelabras and the china tea service on the sideboard.

Raven was placing the napkins when Carolyn entered with a centerpiece of greenery, pinecones, and berries. Raven helped her carefully place it on the table to avoid breaking any of the china. They stood back to admire their handiwork.

"I doubt we did as well as Grandmother would have," Raven said, "but the table does look nice and festive."

"You're being too modest. I think the table setting is beautiful!"

Laughing at her cousin's self-praise, Raven answered, "We'll let Grandmother be the judge."

They walked into the big parlor where the Yule log had been placed in the fireplace. "Ezekiel will move Grandmother's chair in here," Raven said, as they pulled the settee and chairs into a semicircle before the fireplace. "We'll be spending a lot of time in this room for the next twelve days, so we want it as comfortable as possible."

"Let's get dressed," Carolyn suggested.

The room was getting dark and Raven said, "You go ahead. I'll light a few candles. I'll be there soon." She looked through the window into the gathering dusk, thinking about the sadness they had felt last year when they had to observe Christmas without William. Although she still didn't know that he was safe, Raven was content, believing that God was in control of her life. She still prayed that her uncle would return safely, but if not, she would accept it and whatever the future held for her.

■ ■ ■ ■

When Andrew entered the dining room with Thomasine on his arm, it was as if he had entered a new world. The faint scent of wood smoke teased his nostrils. Candlelight flooded the table in a faint glow. Silver candelabras gleamed on the mantelpiece.

After he seated his hostess at the head of the table, he bowed over Carolyn's uplifted hand and touched it to his lips. He moved on to where Raven stood by her chair, and a faint scent of perfume emanated from her as he took her hand. His lips lingered on her fingers, and he hoped that the candlelight didn't reveal the flush that he was sure had risen to his face. In this gracious atmosphere, Andrew understood how austere his life had been in a bachelor household with his father.

"Andrew," Thomasine said, "we're pleased to have you as our guest tonight, and since my son won't be coming for a few days, I'd appreciate it if you would act as our host." She motioned to the chair opposite hers.

Almost overcome by this gesture of welcome, Andrew stammered his thanks. "My father and I lived very simply so I don't have any experience at being a host. You'll have to tell me what to do."

"First, please pray a blessing on our food," Thomasine said.

When the prayer concluded, she said, "Let's have a drink of wassail while we wait for the food to be brought in from the kitchen."

Andrew picked up the glass to his right and sipped on the spicy liquid.

"This is Grandmother's own recipe, and she won't tell anyone the ingredients," Raven said, with an affectionate smile toward her grandmother.

"There's no secret," Thomasine said, smiling mysteriously. "It's made from sweet cider, sugar, roasted apples, and spices. I just won't tell anyone what spices I use."

The cook entered the room and placed a large platter holding a roasted goose in front of Andrew. He looked at it helplessly.

Raven touched his hand. "You don't have to carve it. Cook will do that, but she wants us to see how perfectly browned it is."

"If it tastes as good as it looks," Carolyn said, "it will be delicious."

They applauded the masterpiece she'd produced and, beaming, the cook removed the goose and carried it to the pantry to carve. Mattie entered and placed bowls of oyster soup before them.

When they finished the soup, the cook returned with a platter of sliced meat, surrounded by an herbed bread dressing with dried peaches in it. Andrew had no difficulty filling plates for his companions and passing them around the table. Thomasine and Raven guided Andrew through the four courses, and by the end of the meal, he knew he had managed quite well in the role Thomasine had asked him to fill.

After the sumptuous meal, they went into the parlor. Mattie followed with a tray of tea. The chairs formed a semicircle around the fireplace, where the Yule log waited. Raven noticed that Andrew stood until Thomasine sat in a chair to the right. He then assisted her and Carolyn to the settee directly in front of the fire before taking the chair on the left.

The three slaves stood behind them until Thomasine turned to Ezekiel. "Now, if you please."

Ezekiel stepped forward, knelt on the hearth, opened a pottery bowl, and poured ashes on the kindling that surrounded the Yule log.

"Those are ashes from last year's log," Raven whispered to Andrew.

Ezekiel lifted a thin sliver of dried pinewood, lighted it with a long taper, and touched it to several places. The kindling slowly burned until the log caught fire, and a collective sigh escaped the lips of the room's occupants. The Yule log would burn until Twelfth Night.

"Thank you, Ezekiel," Thomasine said. "Enjoy your meal and fellowship."

"I'll slip in later, ma'am, and watch through the night to see that the log is burning all right." She nodded her thanks.

"Merry Christmas, all of you," Raven said, and the slaves left to enjoy their private feast.

Thomasine took a Bible from a nearby table. "It's customary in our home to read the Christmas story from Matthew and Luke, and I will do that now."

As her grandmother read the familiar story, Raven experienced again the blessedness of how much God had loved His creation — to send His Son as a tiny baby destined to become the Savior of the world. When her grandmother came to the angel's song, " 'Glory to God in the highest, and on earth peace, good will toward men,' " all of a sudden Raven was conscious of an inner peace that she had seldom experienced. As swiftly as if on angels' wings, the grace of God washed over her soul, and her fears were replaced with an unquestionable faith in the future. She believed that Uncle William would return, but if not, God would direct her future in a way that would bring her contentment.

She jolted back to the present when Thomasine closed the Bible and said, "It's our custom to sing after the scripture reading, and if you will, Andrew, please play the harpsichord for us."

Standing, Andrew said, "I would be honored. What songs would you like?"

"You choose," Thomasine said. "If we know the songs we will sing with you. If not, we will listen."

Andrew played, not only hymns of the church but classical selections, as well, and sometimes he sang to his own accompaniment. If she knew the song, Raven hummed along with him. But mostly she listened, knowing instinctively that he had a great talent. If the trustees of the college had heard him play as well as sing, it didn't surprise her that they wanted him on the staff.

"I'll conclude by playing and singing a few lines of a song that may not be familiar to you. The melody is over one hundred years old, but the lyrics are fairly new."

The song was new to Raven, but she also

found confirmation for her newfound hope when Andrew sang:

"Hark the glad sound! The Savior comes,
The Savior promised long!
Let every heart prepare a throne,
And every voice a song.
He comes the broken heart to bind,
The bleeding soul to cure."

Andrew sat with bowed head after he finished, and the silence in the room was broken only by the crackling of the fire.

"Thank you, Andrew," Thomasine murmured. "Your words have brought peace to my heart."

"And your reading of the Christmas story to mine," he said as he acknowledged their thanks. "I must leave now, but thank you for making me feel so much a part of your home tonight."

"Don't leave just yet," Thomasine said. "I need Carolyn to help me with some preparations for tomorrow, but I'll have her bring you a cup of tea. Raven can keep you company while you enjoy it."

Raven was flustered at her grandmother's obvious attempt to give her time alone with Andrew, but he didn't seem to mind. When Thomasine and Carolyn left the room, timidly she pulled her skirts aside to indicate that he should sit beside her.

For a short time they sat in silence staring into the flames, but the peace of the moment was broken when Carolyn brought in a tray with two cups, tea leaves, and a small kettle of water. Andrew stood and helped Carolyn arrange the items on a table and placed it in front of Raven.

"Good night, Andrew," Carolyn said, favoring Raven with a conspiratorial look. Raven frowned at her.

After Raven prepared the tea to their tastes, she said, "I was impressed by your music tonight. God has given you a great talent."

"My father believed that, too, and from my childhood, he provided the best teachers available. It seems that I've spent most of my time learning to play instruments or taking voice lessons."

"But you haven't regretted it?"

"When I was a boy, there were times that I would have rather played with my friends than practice, but I'm not sorry now that my father insisted on a disciplined life."

"Have you composed any music?"

"A few sonatas, and they've been well received, but I'll never be a Bach or a Beethoven."

"God only wants you to be Andrew Faulkner."

"I know, and that's what I'm trying to be. But tonight as I enjoyed the graciousness of your home, I realized I've missed a lot."

Raven felt compelled to share with him the sense of peace and goodwill she had experienced during the evening. She concluded, "For two years I've fretted about the return of Uncle William, but I've had a good life with my grandmother. I'm convinced now that God holds the future in His hands, and I'm content with that."

"And will I have a part in that future?" Andrew whispered.

She looked up at him, and her eyes were full of half promises. "I hope so," she answered softly. "I pray that you will."

His fingers touched her face gently. He brushed her brow with a soft kiss and moved to her lips, which he pressed with a soul-reaching message. "I want to share your future," he said with his lips still close to hers, "for you see, Raven, I love you very much."

"God willing," she whispered, "we will spend many more Christmases together."

He stood and lifted her beside him. He embraced her briefly before he released her. "And now I must go."

Raven saw him to the door. After he left, promises filled her heart as she rested in the love of her heavenly Father and in His gift to her — the love of Andrew Faulkner.

CHAPTER 8

The days between Christmas Eve and Twelfth Day passed rapidly for Raven. They were either entertaining or being entertained each afternoon and night, and they saw Andrew every day.

After some hesitation, Thomasine had finally agreed for Raven to perform the minuet with Andrew as a feature of the Twelfth Night ball. They practiced for hours in the parlor, with the organist from Bruton Parish Church playing accompaniment for them.

Andrew encouraged Raven, insisting that she was mastering the steps, but the muscles in her feet and legs ached after each practice, and a few times she almost gave up. Eventually she was able to move through the series of required figures, one of which formed the letter *z*. During the performance, Raven and Andrew alternately joined hands, separated, passed, and circled each other. To remember all of the steps and to maintain a smooth up-and-down motion while at the same time keeping her upper body erect required all of Raven's determination and strength.

While Raven and Andrew practiced, the dressmaker spent hours in the upstairs bedroom completing the dress Raven would wear to the ball. It was the most elaborate gown Raven had ever worn — an open robe in champagne-colored taffeta with matching flounced petticoat, ribbons, and trimming. A series of ribbon bows decreased in size from décolletage to waist in a ladder-like formation down the center of the stomacher. Elbow-length sleeves were finished with three layers of lace ruffles. The seamstress wove pearls into the neck ruffle. Raven planned to wear her hair swept upward into a series of curls interwoven with pearls and lightly powdered.

When Twelfth Night finally came and Andrew led Raven out on the polished floor, she knew she had made a wise choice in her garments when he whispered, "You are beautiful! Don't be nervous about the steps — just follow my lead."

Raven felt as if she were walking on air as Andrew skillfully guided her around the floor. And their long hours of practice were rewarded by a thunderous applause which greeted them as they took bow after bow when the dance ended.

As Andrew lifted her from the last curtsy, the circle of merrymakers parted as if on cue, and Raven lifted startled eyes toward the doorway. Two men stood in the opening. One was an Indian, whose long breeches of animal's fur and bearskin robe around his shoulders proclaimed that he was not a Virginia native. The other man was dressed in fringed buckskin, his graying brown hair shoulder length.

When her eyes met his, Raven's hand flew to her mouth. "Uncle William!" she cried. She hurried across the floor to her uncle, holding out her hands. "It is really you?" Raven whispered. "Have you finally returned?"

Taking her hands, her long-lost uncle said, "I'm home at last, although I've often wondered if I would ever see this day." He held her away from him. "My little niece has grown into a beautiful woman while I've been away."

"Where have you been? What took you so long to return?"

"I'll tell you some things tonight, but I have to get some rest before I can relate all that has happened to me. My companion,

306

Silvertip, and I have had a long journey." He turned toward the door, but the Indian was gone.

"Where did he go?" William asked.

A man standing near the door said, "He slipped out the door when you went to meet Miss Raven."

Shaking his head, William said, "And I hoped to reward him for bringing me home. Without him I wouldn't have made it, and now I may never see him again."

As her uncle shook his head, Raven sensed that he had become fond of his guide.

Thomasine hurried toward him. "Welcome home, William. We've waited a long time for this day."

He kissed her cheek. "So have I, Thomasine. So have I."

"We can give you some food here or go to my home."

"I would prefer to go to your house." More quietly, he said, "After living in the wilderness for months, it will take awhile to get accustomed to large crowds."

A look of resignation flooded William's features when his friends crowded around him. "But where have you been?" one of them asked.

"Most of the time I've been in New France with the Ottawa Indians, but in their company I've traveled many miles of this continent."

"You must have had many marvelous experiences," a member of the House of Burgesses commented.

"It will take a lifetime to tell you all of the things I've seen. But will you arrange for me to speak to the House of Burgesses within a few days? I have information they should know."

The man readily agreed.

In spite of his obvious exhaustion, William circulated among the crowd, greeting former friends and neighbors, promising to tell them all about his experiences within a few days.

Taking charge of the situation, Thomasine said, "Gentlemen, please excuse us. William is exhausted and I've sent word for Ezekiel to bring the coach."

Andrew brought Raven's cloak, whispering, "I won't see you home, but I will speak with your uncle in a few days."

Her eyes filled with tears as she clasped his hand. "God has blessed me more than I deserve. He brought you to Virginia, and now my uncle has returned. I want you and Uncle William to meet as soon as possible. Promise to stop by tomorrow."

"I will. Classes start two days from now,

and I won't have much free time then."

Raven quickly followed William, Thomasine, and Carolyn out of the Apollo Room to the carriage where Ezekiel waited.

"Good to have you home, Mr. William," he said. "Almost like having one come back from the dead."

"That's the way I feel about it, Ezekiel. God has been with me all the way, or I wouldn't be here now."

"Raven," Thomasine said, "you and Carolyn take the seat on the left, and William may sit beside me."

After the women were seated, William stepped inside the carriage, sat down, and sighed. "This is the first time I've been in a carriage since I left Williamsburg. I've traveled thousands of miles by canoe and walked more miles than that, but I've never ridden in a wheeled vehicle."

"We're all curious about your adventures," Raven said, "but we won't pester you with questions until you've had a night's rest."

"It will be a pleasure to sleep in a bed again but not until I've had a good scrubbing and know I don't have any vermin on me. Just give me a blanket or two and I'll be comfortable anywhere."

Ezekiel stopped the horses and, yawning, William peered out. "That was a short trip."

William was behind Raven when they started up the steps and into the house. "I forgot to ask how things have gone at Pleasant Hill."

Laughing lightly, she said, "We'd better wait until tomorrow to talk about it."

Grimly, he answered, "I don't like the sound of that, but an absentee landlord leaves the way open to a lot of problems. It will take weeks for us to catch up on what's happened since I left."

She stood on tiptoes and kissed his whiskered cheek. "I've looked for you so long that I can't believe you are finally here. I've missed you so much."

"And I've missed you, too." He backed away when she would have kissed him again. "No more kisses until I've cleaned myself up, but I'll have to wear these buckskins until I go to Pleasant Hill after my clothes."

Raven wondered if he even had any clothes left at the plantation, but he mustn't know that tonight.

Thomasine came down the hall with a pillow and several blankets. "My son is about your size, and he keeps a few garments here so he won't have to bring anything when he comes to town. He intended to stay through Twelfth Night, but several of the slaves were sick so he left yesterday morning. I'll lay out a set of his clothes for you to wear tomorrow." She handed the bedcovers to him. "If you're determined to sleep on the floor, the parlor is the best place for that."

"I'll spread the blankets and be asleep in no time." He looked around the room, wonderingly. "I still find it hard to believe I'm back in civilization."

CHAPTER 9

Raven and Carolyn tiptoed around the house the next morning to avoid waking William. Thomasine had closed the door into the parlor, and the house was quiet. He slept until midmorning.

When he did get up, he apologized, "I didn't expect to sleep the clock around. Am I too late for breakfast?"

Raven thought he looked more like himself now that he'd rested.

"I told the cook to keep food warm for you. We'll send for it," Thomasine said.

"No, I'll go to the kitchen, eat my fill, and then have a bath."

"They're heating water for you, and Ezekiel will assist you. He'll bring the fresh garments."

The Yule log was no longer burning, and the parlor was getting cool. When William finished his bath and came into the house, Thomasine said, "Let's go to the sitting room so you can tell us about your experiences."

A knock sounded at the door, and Mattie hurried down the hallway.

"That may be Andrew. I invited him to come today," Raven said. "I knew he would want to hear your story. I hope that was all right," she added, looking at Thomasine.

"Certainly," she said and rose to welcome Andrew when she heard his voice.

"And who is Andrew?" William inquired, looking at Raven.

Her face warmed, and she failed to meet her uncle's eyes. "A friend. I hope you like him."

"But do *you* like him?" he asked with a significant lift of his shaggy gray brows.

Before she could answer, Andrew entered the room and Thomasine introduced him to William, adding, "Sit down, Andrew. William is ready to tell us about his adventures."

"I hardly know where to begin. I'm sure you've heard enough about Braddock's defeat and the events leading up to it, so I can skip that part. During the battle when Braddock was killed, I was taken prisoner by the Indians. Frankly, at that time I wished I had been killed in battle for I was convinced that I'd die a brutal death. However, when they started back to

Canada, they took me with them."

Raven listened breathlessly as her uncle talked for hours about his experiences — how he had been treated as a slave until one of the Indian children had fallen in a river and he'd jumped in and rescued her. "After that I thought they might release me, but the little girl became attached to me and she didn't want me to leave. The Indians have a tendency to pamper their children."

"But where did they take you?" Raven asked.

"Eventually to their village northeast of the big lakes, but first we crossed the river near where Braddock had fought, which the Indians call O–hi–o. We traveled westward for weeks and came to another large river, the Messipi. When we got to that river, they said it was still many moons' travel to another ocean. I picked up enough of the Indians' language to learn how large this continent really is."

"I've heard in England that you can cross this continent and reach the Orient," Andrew commented.

"That may be," William said. "I'll admit I was curious enough to keep going west and find out, but I was anxious about Raven. Also I gleaned a lot of information that the English need to know about French activities. That's why I want to talk to the Burgesses. The conflict between the French and British is heating up, and the outcome is going to determine whether the French or English control this continent."

He stood and stretched. "I'm about talked out. I haven't spoken English for so long, it's hard for me to remember my own native tongue."

Raven had noticed that he had stammered and faltered in his speech several times.

"I must go," Andrew said. "It was a pleasure to meet you, sir."

Raven walked to the door with him. "I'll come back in a few days and talk with him," he said quietly.

"I haven't told him about Uncle Peter yet, so wait a few days until I can pave the way." Raven glanced around the hallway, and seeing no one, she lifted her face to him. Andrew didn't disappoint her. He dropped a kiss on her upturned lips.

After Andrew left, Raven returned to the parlor.

"I want to take a walk around town and see what's happened since I've been gone," William said. "We were still several miles from Williamsburg when darkness fell last night, but without even knowing that it was Twelfth Night, I just had to come on in. I

315

paused long enough to change into better clothes than I'd been wearing on our long journey. I've never known why the Ottawas decided to release me, but the Frenchmen who came to the village seemed to resent me. I believe most of the Ottawas liked me, and they knew I wasn't safe. One morning before dawn, Silvertip tapped me on the shoulder and told me to prepare to travel. I wasn't even allowed to say good-bye."

"May I walk with you?" Raven said.

"Yes, we still have much to say to each other."

"I'll bring my cloak from upstairs."

Few people were on the streets, and at first, William seemed content to comment on the changes that had taken place in Williamsburg. Finally, he said, "I might as well hear it — what's wrong at Pleasant Hill?"

"I can sum it up in two words — Uncle Peter. A few weeks after the remnants of Braddock's army returned and you didn't show up, he had himself appointed as my guardian. He moved to the plantation and discharged your overseer. I've only been to the plantation once in the past year because I was afraid he might keep me there against my will if I went again."

A grim look passed over William's features, which boded no good for his younger brother. "I should have anticipated that, I suppose, and appointed Thomasine as your guardian in case I didn't survive the expedition."

"Mattie goes to see her family on some of her days off, and she reports that the slaves are mistreated. Even though I'm twenty now, I didn't know what I could do."

"There was nothing you could do. Peter always had a mean streak."

"And —"

"You don't mean there's more!"

"Yes. You remember, of course, that provision in Papa's will that I couldn't marry without my guardian's permission. About a year ago, Uncle Peter accepted a marriage offer for me from Mr. Wharton."

"Wharton! You don't mean Daniel Wharton!"

"That's the one."

"Why, the man's a wastrel. He gambled away the fortune he inherited from his wife."

"I think Uncle Peter was gambling, too — believing that I wouldn't accept the offer so he'd get the plantation."

She continued to explain how Thomasine had gotten a year's extension of Peter's authority. "Then I suddenly realized that as long as I didn't marry *anyone* until I was twenty-five, I wouldn't be disinherited."

"Was Peter at the ball last night?"

"I didn't see him."

"I'm going to Pleasant Hill today and evict him."

"Will you let me go with you?"

He shook his head. "There might be some fighting. I don't want you there." They were nearing Francis Street, and William stopped. "I sense that there's something between you and Andrew Faulkner. Is that true?"

"Yes." Although she knew she was blushing, she looked him in the eyes, explaining about Andrew's arrival in Williamsburg, his profession, and his employment at William and Mary College. "He's indicated that he wants to speak to you."

"Let me take care of Peter first, and then I'll talk with Andrew." He shook his head. "During the past two years, I've wondered if I shouldn't have left the fighting to others and stayed home and looked after you and your property until you were wed. I've betrayed the trust your father placed in me. But hindsight is better than foresight. And I *have* learned a lot of important information that will help the English in the war with France that's going on in Europe now and will soon spread to the colonies."

"Not in Virginia!"

"That's possible. I've seen enough of this

continent to know what a prize it is, and England and France both want it. I'm not saying that there will be fighting in the streets of Williamsburg, because I think the conflict will be mostly on the frontier and in the northern colonies. Both the English and the French are courting the Indians, trying to get certain tribes to fight with them. That's what I need to report to the House of Burgesses, so they can act on what I've learned."

"Look!" Raven pointed. The Indian who'd accompanied William last night was standing in front of Thomasine's house.

William hurried forward and raised his right arm. The Indian then grasped his outstretched hand.

"Silvertip! I thought you'd gone away."

The Indian shook his head, and to Raven's surprise, answered in English, "Stayed in woods."

"I'm glad you did stay. You can go with me today, but you must eat first." He turned to Raven. "This is Silvertip. He's a good man to have at one's side in a fight. I doubt Peter will put up much of a struggle about leaving if Silvertip is with me. Will Thomasine mind if I take him to the kitchen to eat?"

"Of course not! I'll tell her."

"After he's eaten, I'll stop by a friend's house and get the bag of gold I asked him to keep for me until I returned. He whispered to me last night that the gold is still in his safe, so I'll have funds to rent a couple of horses. We'll leave for Pleasant Hill right away. Don't be worried if I don't come back for a few days."

Raven didn't worry over the next few days, for she had sized up Silvertip and believed that he would be a good ally in a fight — but she was on tenterhooks, curious about what was happening in her home. She was also lonely because once the Christmas season was over, Carolyn had returned home. Andrew was busy preparing his schedule for the new school term, and she hadn't had any time alone with him.

It was late afternoon of the third day when William returned from Pleasant Hill. Raven met him at the front door. "How did everything go?"

William's expression clouded in anger. "Peter is gone, and I don't think he'll show his face in Virginia again. The house and furnishings are intact, but the place is filthy. The fields have been neglected. He hadn't found a large amount of your money that I'd stashed away before I left, so you're not penniless. We swung by my holdings, and the overseer had everything in good condition, as your place would have been if Peter hadn't made the man leave. It will be a few weeks before we can move back to the plantation, but you'll soon be going home."

Raven was excited at the prospect of returning to Pleasant Hill, but she knew in her heart that any true *home* for her now had to include Andrew.

Andrew came calling that night after Raven let him know that William had returned. William asked to see him privately, and Andrew knew he was in for a grilling. But when they went into the living room, William was silent.

Andrew was uncomfortable, so he finally said, "Sir, I have become quite fond of your niece during our short acquaintance. In fact, I love her, and I would like your permission to approach her about marriage."

"And what would you have done if I hadn't returned?"

"I would have gotten permission from her grandmother to keep company, and we would have waited until she was twenty-five, when she could have married without permission."

"I have learned from Raven that she shares your feelings, and thus far I can see no reason to discourage you." Andrew smiled widely, and William held up his hand. "But at this point, I don't know enough about you to give my permission for you to wed. You've only been in Virginia a few weeks, and for all I know you may have a hidden past. When I joined Braddock's expedition, I failed the trust my brother placed in me when he made me Raven's guardian. I'm determined I won't do that again."

Gravely, Andrew said, "Although I want to marry Raven right away, I commend you for your caution. There must be some channel between Virginia and the colonies so that you can check up on my character and that of my father. We weren't wealthy, although we had a comfortable existence, and I'm far from penniless. I'm convinced that you won't find any personal reasons to reject my suit. Perhaps you will want to start with Mr. Byrd, a kinsman of mine."

"I propose an understanding between you and Raven for six months, during which you may spend time together under limited supervision. Meanwhile, I will investigate your background and observe your actions before I make my decision as to the wisdom of this marriage. Does that suit?"

"Yes sir. I consider that fair — exactly what I would do if I were in your position."

William went to the door and called across the hall, "Raven, will you join us?"

Her heart hammering, Raven walked slowly into the room. Her eyes connected with Andrew's immediately, trying to learn if William's decision had pleased him. William's back was to them, and Andrew nodded slightly. She flashed him a smile.

When they were all seated, William explained in detail the conversation he'd had with Andrew. "Do these arrangements meet with your approval?" he asked. He then added with a smile, "You're not dealing with Peter now, and although I'm your guardian, I won't force a situation on you that you find unpleasant. Do you think my decision is fair enough?"

"Yes, I do. The six months will go rapidly, and we'll have a wedding planned before then. I'm convinced that you won't find anything in Andrew's background to make you change your mind."

"I pray that is so." He stood and walked toward the hallway. "You have fifteen minutes," he said and closed the door.

Knowing there was little time to waste,

Raven was pleased when Andrew gathered her into a close embrace and looked into her face.

"I love you, Raven, and I want you to become my wife. Will you marry me?"

Without a moment's hesitation, she answered, "Yes. I believe our marriage is one that was meant to be. Just as God made Eve for Adam, so he made us for each other."

"Because we know it will be six months before we can actually become man and wife, would it be wrong if we made our vows before God now?"

"No, I don't believe so."

"Then, I take thee, Raven, to be my wedded wife, to have and to hold from this day forward, for better for worse, for richer for poorer, in sickness and in health, to love and to cherish, 'til death us do part, according to God's holy ordinance; and thereto I plight thee my troth."

As Raven repeated the same words she had heard from Andrew, she knew that God had already placed His blessing on their life together and that the ceremony at Pleasant Hill in a few months would bind them lawfully before God and others and serve as a celebration of their becoming man and wife.

Raven's lips seemed to find their way instinctively to Andrew's as he lowered his head. She lost track of time then, and it seemed only a moment before William's knock sounded on the door. Andrew kissed Raven once again, then put his arm around her. Her heart soared with love and gratitude to God as she and Andrew walked into the future . . . together.

■ ■ ■ ■

BROKEN HEARTS
BY LAURALEE BLISS

■ ■ ■ ■

To Robin Bayne,
who travels often to Williamsburg.
Thanks for being such a
great writing friend.

He healeth the broken in heart,
and bindeth up their wounds.

PSALM 147:3

CHAPTER 1

Williamsburg, Virginia Colony, 1775

Mary Farthington wandered about her plantation home on a cold and dreary winter's night. Kate had already gone to bed and, without the chatter of the young girl to occupy her mind, Mary was left alone with a multitude of memories. She gazed out the window where the frost had carved intricate patterns like leaves onto the glass. Everything appeared dark as it did many months ago when it all happened. How she hated the night. It seemed to perpetuate the dream of that terrible day.

She could still see the driver standing in the doorway of the home, his hands clutching his cocked hat, his face contorted in pain. "Mrs. Farthington . . . ," he began, "I don't know how to tell you this. This is the hardest thing I have ever done. May the Almighty give me the courage."

Mary didn't even wait to hear his words.

Instead she looked beyond the man, expecting to find David's broad form alighting from the carriage, his arms ready to enfold her in a loving embrace. Yet all she saw before her startled gaze was the driver and an empty carriage.

"We didn't even see them until it was too late," the man said. "They came up quickly on their horses. They called for the master, asking why he was aiding traitors of the crown. They said his support of such men meant that he, too, was a traitor."

Mary remembered clutching her throat as fear washed over her. She knew of David's passion for the cause of liberty. He spoke of it often, of men who shared in the dream of a country free from the demands of England that sought to choke the very life from them. David was well aware that his vocal leaning for a rebellion would be met with anger by those who still held loyalties to England. "Did they arrest my husband?" she asked softly.

"If only that were so, madam," the man said. "It would be much easier. They . . . they said the master deserved a traitor's death. The master tried to talk to them. They had no ear to listen and no heart either. They took him and . . ."

"David?" She could still hear her voice in

her mind, calling his name. She ran out into the darkness, searching for him.

When she returned, sensing the emptiness like a cold, dark grave, the man continued in a hollow voice. "They thought he was one of those involved with the gunpowder incident in Williamsburg. They thought he had helped summon the militia to fight the governor. I'm so sorry."

The man then produced something Mary had forgotten about, even as tears began to fill her eyes in remembrance. He handed her the bisque head of a doll — the doll David was bringing back as a present for Kate, one they were to hide away until Christmas. Mary didn't even possess the whole doll either but only this fragment, still intact. It was all that remained of David's important errand that night, an errand that sent him to heaven's throne rather than back into her arms.

Mary withdrew from the window. David knew the dangers of his patriotism. He swore to uphold the cause, no matter what. Now it had cost him his life. *Dear God, may he not have died in vain. May the colonies see the dawn of freedom as he so wanted. It's all I can hope for.*

She went then and brought out the doll's head, looking at the charming face painted on the silken surface. She must do something with the doll that Kate dearly desired. The Christmas season would soon be upon them. There was no time to order another doll and have it sent here from England. Not that she would want anything else from a land that bred hateful men who took the life of her husband. Perhaps she could find someone in Williamsburg willing to help her. Someone who could fashion a doll's body for the head so Kate might have the one present David wanted to give her. Maybe a man who was also a fierce patriot, like David. Maybe that would bring peace to their family and laughter within their home.

Kate ceased to laugh or sing since hearing of her father's entrance into heaven. She could not understand why he didn't return. How does one explain to an eight-year-old girl that evil men had killed her father, but God had His purposes and that he was in a better place? Mary tried to explain it all, but the words were difficult. The young girl could sense Mary's struggle in trying to understand what no one else could.

"Mother?" a young voice suddenly called out. Mary looked up from her contemplation to find that Kate had arisen from bed, wiping the sleep from her eyes. "Is it morning?"

Mary quickly hid the doll's head inside her embroidery basket. "Oh no, my darling. You have only just gone to sleep."

"I want it to be morning," the young girl protested. "Please let it be morning, Mother."

Mary came and gathered her daughter in her arms. "It will be soon, I promise."

"Is it morning where Father is?" Kate wondered.

"Oh, yes. In heaven, morning comes every day, all day long. There is no night, only day forever. And he's with the angels right now, singing a beautiful hymn to the Lord, just like I read to you from the Bible, remember?"

Kate leaned her weary head on Mary's shoulder. "I wish God didn't need Father in heaven, Mother. We need him here, too."

"I know," Mary told her, "but we must be strong. And I believe with all my heart our morning is coming, if we're patient. And it will be a beautiful morning with sunshine and the birds singing, just the way we both want it to be."

She gently took up Kate's hand and led her back to bed. Ever since David's passing, Kate insisted on sleeping in Mary's room in a trundle bed. Mary made no comment about it; rather, she liked having her daughter near her. It helped pass an otherwise lonely night without David by her side. And she sensed a greater bond with her daughter during these long days and now long nights. "Go to sleep," she said softly, stroking her daughter's fine brown hair. "And when morning comes, I will wake you."

Kate snuggled under the covers. Mary looked down at her, resolved she would soon have the sweet doll beside her — a friend, a companion, the doll David wanted her to have above all other possessions. She would go to Williamsburg at first light and seek out a craftsman willing to help her.

"I hope we can continue to speak civilly to one another, even if you appear deaf to everything I have to say."

He stood still, the hammer poised in his hand, before he let it fall upon the chisel. "I never declared I would no longer speak to you, Jonas, though I can disagree with you."

"Disagree you may, but if you don't join us in our stand, there will be more difficulty to come. Already a den of thieves is stirring as it did this past spring. And you have done nothing, have you, John? When we saw this town nearly laid to waste by those marauding militia, you stayed silent, even as you do now."

"My beliefs are between my Lord and me. To Him alone do I swear my allegiance and not to any man. Or any cause for that matter. That is the way I wish to leave it." John Maxwell glanced out the corner of his eye at his older brother, Jonas, who stared at him, even as Jonas held a pewter mug of some potent brew.

Jonas thrust the liquid down his throat, wiping the sleeve of his blouse across his face. "You can't hide under the banner of your religion forever. You will have to choose. And you will choose on the side of your king and your country, I'm certain."

John didn't look up again until he heard the patter of footsteps, the door to the shop close, and then blessed silence. He wiped away the droplets of sweat that collected on his brow, thankful his brother had left.

The moment Jonas had stepped inside, darkness had invaded the shop. John sensed the turmoil that still remained. It was hard to forget the conflict of last spring, with the royal governor, Dunmore, stealing the town's gunpowder and then the militia coming in force to take it back. John thought surely the rebellion had arrived at the doorstep of Williamsburg and all would dissolve into chaos. But when the militia proved victorious, those who followed the governor, including Jonas and his friends, became irate and rebellious. Bands of Tories roamed the streets. Fear was written on the faces of the town's inhabitants. There had been little semblance of peace since.

For now, John only wanted to forget the incident with Jonas and concentrate on his task of finishing the desk for a wealthy family who had ordered it. Instead he found Jonas's words reverberating in his mind.

How do I tell Jonas the Almighty alone begs us to choose in the matter of life? He asks us to choose either life or death. And what have you chosen, my brother? Have you chosen some army of your own making and not God's holy army? If so, what will become of it in the end? Again he wiped away the sweat, hoping as well to remove the sting of the meeting. How he prayed Jonas would not seek him out to debate matters of state with him. And yet his brother seemed to come at the most inopportune time, like today when there was much work to be done.

John looked down at the desk, wondering how he would ever finish the project with these delays. He sighed once more, taking his chisel to a panel to chip away the wood, when he heard a rustle and the sound of footsteps enter his shop. *Please, let it not be Jonas returning with his friends. I can't bear it.* "I'm quite busy," he declared without looking up. "You may take your conversation elsewhere. I have no time for it."

"I'm sorry to have disturbed you."

His head jerked upward at the soft voice, only to find a woman whirling about, her skirts flaring, ready to leave his shop. Begging forgiveness from God for his poor manner, he immediately called to her. "Forgive me, please, madam. Do you need help?"

She paused and turned, clutching a small handbag close to her. "I'm sorry to have disturbed you," she said again.

"You are not disturbing me. I only thought it might be —" He nearly shared about the ill manner of his brother with a perfect stranger before catching himself and swallowing down the words. "I have much on my mind."

"Yes, I can see you are very busy. I had hoped to seek out your skill, but perhaps there is another craftsman in Williamsburg who can help me."

"Please, Mrs. . . ."

"Mrs. Farthington of Highland Grove plantation."

"Yes, I know of it. A grand place by the

James River."

"Grand, I suppose. Too large for me to manage anymore without my husband. I will likely have to sell next spring."

John wondered about the statement and where her husband could be but decided not to pursue such personal questions. "What can I do for you?" He saw her open the handbag hanging over her arm and withdraw a delicate bisque head.

"I'm looking for someone to make a doll for my daughter using this piece I have. It's for the coming holiday."

John carefully took the doll's head, gazing at the cheerful face painted on the smooth surface. "Why not order a new doll, madam?"

She shook her head. Were those tears gathering in the corners of her hazel-colored eyes? "No, I can't. The doll must have this head alone."

Her insistence intrigued him. "As you wish. I'm not certain I can help you, madam, but I can try."

"I understand." She took the doll's head from his outstretched hand and placed it back in the bag. "I see you are quite busy. I shall inquire elsewhere." She fastened the cloak beneath her chin. "Good day."

"Please wait. I would very much like to

try and help, madam, if you would allow me."

Mrs. Farthington hesitated. "This is too important to be taken so frivolously. The doll is for my daughter, and it will mean everything to her."

"If you would allow me to keep the doll's head in my possession, I will do my utmost to help."

With what seemed like great reluctance, Mrs. Farthington once more handed him the doll's head, this time in the small handbag. "When might I expect it to be completed?"

"That I can't say, madam. But I will do what I can to see that your daughter has it for the festivities, God be willing."

She nodded, appearing satisfied by this statement. He saw her gather herself together as if every movement took great effort and concentration. If only he could see beyond her outward appearance to what lay in her heart. Not that he had many answers to life's difficulties, but he did serve an Almighty God in whom he placed his many burdens. Surely she had burdens as well, especially after her comment about selling her grand home.

"Are you a Christian, madam?" he suddenly asked. His face warmed as she stared at him. "I only say this as I have entrusted unto Him my greatest burdens in life. And it seems you also carry a few?"

"Sir, I have trusted more than you could possibly know, with life and with death. And I've had to carry them, too . . . alone. Good day." She nodded and left in a flourish, her skirts swirling about her, her feet scuffing up straw and wood chips scattered on the wood floor.

John felt sad for having spoken so openly. He looked inside the bag to see the painted eyes staring up at him. The head of a doll brought by a fine lady with a broken heart. How were they intertwined? And what could he do to help mend the pieces? At least he would do what he could to construct the doll. Maybe that would open a door to other secrets buried within.

CHAPTER 2

John found sleep difficult that night. All he could think about was Mrs. Farthington bringing the doll's head to him that day at the shop, along with a heart of sorrow to match. He lit a candle and stood to his feet. The floorboards were cold. Wind passed easily through the cracks in the walls. Winter had been teasing them with cold temperatures and brisk winds that blew from the north. Not many weeks from now the holidays would be upon them — Christmas and the festivities that followed. Fruited wreaths and pine garland gaily decorating the doors. The Yule log burning in the fireplace. The singings and the playing of instruments. And all the food and drink one could hold. It seemed difficult to believe that the time had come. Where had the year gone?

Only a few months before, he had taken over much of the cabinetmaking business from his mentor, Aaron Longworth, who taught him everything he knew during his years as an apprentice. Now that John had become a journeyman and nearing the revered title of master of his work, he found himself busy with requests, mostly from wealthy families within Williamsburg. Tables, dressers, desks, a dining room set — but he never had a request to make a doll before. Nor did he know in the slightest how he would create such a thing and fit it with the bisque head given to him. Furniture was his specialty. But it appeared God desired him to seek out other areas of skill, even if they were untested, to help someone in need.

John took out the small doll's head, looking at the brightly painted blue eyes and tiny red lips. He then took out a sheet of parchment and a quill to begin sketching ideas. He would need to find a good piece of wood that could easily be carved and yet was strong enough to hold the doll's head in position. He would make the arms and legs with tiny moveable joints.

As he began drawing the design, he became more and more excited, not only over the idea of making the doll but seeing the joy on the face of Mrs. Farthington's daughter when she received the finished prize.

How he would love to see that day.

John shook his head. How did he expect to witness such a thing? To presume he would be invited to partake in the holiday festivities with Mrs. Farthington and her daughter? A ludicrous notion, to be sure. But he would not even mind being a small mouse in the corner of a great room to see the joy on the young girl's face at that moment. Such a sight would bring much satisfaction.

Suddenly John heard a knock on the door of his humble dwelling. He rented two rooms from the Longworths, situated below the main level of the house. He hoped he had not awakened them with his midnight musings. He owed the family much, not only to Mr. Longworth for his tutelage in the workings of furniture making but also for providing him a place to live.

He opened the door to see Mr. Longworth clad in his nightshirt, holding a lantern. "You're up late, John."

"I couldn't sleep, sir." He stepped aside, allowing the man in. At once he went to the fireplace where a few embers glowed like jewels and stoked a fire. He put a kettle on a hook. "I hope I didn't disturb you. Can I make you a cup of tea?"

"No, indeed. I must return soon or Mrs.

Longworth will wonder what has become of me." He strode over, holding the lantern higher to study the parchment on the small desk. "And what is this?"

"A woman came to see me in the shop today — a Mrs. Farthington. She asked if I might make a wooden doll to fit the bisque head she has. It's to be a present for her daughter."

"Did you say a Mrs. Farthington? Hmm . . . of all the people."

"Sir?"

"Surely you heard what happened to her husband."

"I don't believe I have, sir."

"About the Farthingtons last spring? The tragedy with her husband? He was found dead on the road to Williamsburg. It was not an accident, either."

John stared in disbelief. "You mean Mrs. Farthington's husband was murdered?"

"His life was taken by Tory sympathizers, from what I've heard. Some believed he was involved with the colonial militia who had recovered the powder that was stolen from the town's magazine. He was quite a staunch, vocal patriot for the cause of liberty. And as you know, there are bands of Tories roaming about who desire to silence such voices, especially after what happened with Lord Dunmore."

John knew all too well what others thought but kept such knowledge buried inside him.

Mr. Longworth glanced down once more at the drawing. "This is a good thing you are doing, young John Maxwell. We need to help those who grieve."

"I had no idea she had been through such suffering, sir. I pray God will guide my hands and my head with this task. I hope to do a careful job, for the sake of the little girl." *And especially a little girl who no longer has a father's lap to sit on.* The mere idea sent a wave of distress washing over him.

"And so you shall. But you must also have your rest so the mind works quicker."

He nodded. "Yes, I will seek rest."

The man smiled before heading for the door. "If you need any help with your task, I will gladly give assistance. Mr. Farthington left not only a grieving wife but a sad daughter, as well. I think a finely crafted doll would bring her much joy."

"I'm certain it will, sir. Thank you for your offer of help." John waited until the man had closed the door behind him before returning to the design. Now more thoughts plagued him besides the simple doll constructed out of wood. The tragedy concerning Mrs. Farthington's husband. The Tories responsible for the deed, perhaps still roaming about Williamsburg at this very moment. He gnawed on his bottom lip. It made little sense to dwell on it. Many people were restless these days, with those who felt led to separate themselves from England against those who wished to stay. Now the tide of war was sweeping across the land. He wondered where he stood in all this, just as his brother Jonas inquired. Where was his heart? What did he believe? Where did he stand in light of this conflict?

I stand in hope, he decided, looking over his simple design for the doll, *and I trust in God's guidance.* Now God had given him an even greater task — not only to make the doll, but the importance of making it to the best of his ability for a little girl who had lost her father. *Almighty God, make me worthy of this task,* he prayed softly. *And help me know what to do concerning the sorrow of Mrs. Farthington.*

The next morning, John had all but forgotten about the desk he was to have ready and instead searched around his shop for the perfect piece of wood to begin carving the doll. Only when William Geddy came by to inquire about the desk for his mother did John remember his other duties. He put aside the small piece of wood he had been whittling to show the gentleman what he had done.

"I see little progress of late, Mr. Maxwell," William said. "It's almost as if you are distracted. Could it be a young lady of Williamsburg, perhaps?"

John felt the heat in his face. "No, sir." He brought forth the piece of wood and the diagram he had drawn. "Rather, I'm making a doll for Mrs. Farthington's daughter."

William paused. "A noble thing indeed, young man, to care for a widow's needs. But do not forget others as well to whom you owe your talent. And I promised to pay you handsomely for the desk."

"Yes, sir. I will have it ready soon."

William nodded and strode out of the shop. Only then did John survey the untidiness of the shop and realized he may have taken on too much. With the holidays approaching, everyone wanted their furniture pieces completed speedily. He would ask Mr. Longworth for assistance, but John felt it a measure of defeat that might keep him from the status of master if he asked for help. He wanted to own this shop one day. If Mr. Longworth knew he had fallen behind in the work, he might never attain the revered title of master. Instead John continued in what he was given, trusting God with the time and praying his tools would accomplish miracles.

A few days later, John had just put the finishing touches on the desk when he heard the shuffle of steps inside the shop. He looked up to see Mrs. Farthington standing in the doorway, her face partially hidden by a straw bonnet. She led by the hand a young girl who gazed about the shop in interest.

"This is my daughter, Kate," Mrs. Farthington introduced.

"What is this place, Mother?" Kate inquired. "There are tables and chairs here. And look!" She pointed in glee at the desk John had just finished. "It looks like the one at home."

Mrs. Farthington smiled. "Yes, darling. Mr. Maxwell makes furniture."

"Are we having something made?"

"In a way. It's a surprise. You will see it at Christmas."

The young girl tugged even harder on her mother's hand, jumping about in excitement. The sight made John smile, especially in wake of the family's trying circumstances. How good it was to see a bit of joy this day.

"And how is our surprise faring, Mr. Maxwell?" she hedged.

"It's coming along quite well, madam. You'll be pleased, I'm sure."

"Are we having a new desk made, Mother?" Kate asked.

"No, but don't ask me any more questions or it will ruin the surprise. We must stop by the millinery shop now to see about your new dress. I'm certain Mr. Maxwell has much to do."

"Actually, I've just finished the desk. Would you like to see the secret drawers I made?" he asked Kate.

She nodded, her eyes widening in anticipation. He stretched out his arms, slowly lifting her up and over a workbench and placing her on the ground before the desk. He opened the front doors to the piece. She clapped her hands at the array of tiny drawers inside, along with another door. She opened it as he instructed, only to find still smaller drawers within.

"Oh, Mother, what fun! I want a desk just like this."

Mrs. Farthington laughed. "We have too much furniture as it is, dear one."

"I will be delivering it to the Geddy family," John said.

"We know them well!" Mrs. Farthington exclaimed. "They made our silverware and candlesticks. The sons are wonderful silversmiths, just like their father who has since departed, may God bless him."

"Would you like to accompany me when I deliver the piece? Then you can show them the secret drawers, little Kate."

"Please, Mother?"

Mrs. Farthington paused, seemingly considering this request. "I hope we will not be an intrusion, sir," she said, as John called for a servant of Mr. Longworth to help him carry the desk to an awaiting wagon.

"No indeed, madam. And while your daughter is occupied with the piece, I might have a chance to share with you the progress of our secret."

She nodded knowingly. Once the desk was secured within the wagon, John helped each of them up to the seat, with Kate in between. He looked down upon the girl, thinking of her bright eyes and sweet smile come Christmas when she would receive the doll. What great sadness her mother and she must have suffered these many months. And how grateful he was to be called upon to bring some happiness into their lives.

They did not have far to travel, just down the street and around the corner to the Geddy home. Williamsburg was alive with townspeople in wagons, carriages, and on foot, tending to their duties of the day. From afar John could hear the drum and fife of some military parade. He glanced over at Mrs. Farthington to see a look of distress on her face. Her lips began to move in silent prayer, as if the sounds brought forth a painful memory.

Soon they had ridden away from it all and to the Geddy house, where they were hailed by several servants and the family's other son, David Geddy. "So you've finished the desk for my mother at last," he observed. "A fine job indeed, Mr. Maxwell. She will be most pleased."

"Now I will show you the secret drawers!" Kate announced to David Geddy, who whirled at the sound of her young voice. "May I, Mr. Maxwell?"

"I'm sure Mr. Geddy is interested."

David Geddy laughed. "I would be pleased to see them indeed, thank you."

While Kate engaged the man, showing him the drawers and proclaiming her excitement, John turned to Mrs. Farthington. "The doll is coming along well," he said in a low voice. "The plans are drawn. I will construct the body of fine wood and make moveable joints. And I believe the master's wife will gladly sew the clothing."

"How lovely, Mr. Maxwell. I knew you would do well with the task." He saw a smile break forth on her lips. He didn't realize until then how attractive she was. He would have gazed at her more, but he heard Kate and David Geddy returning.

"I like the drawers very much," David said. "Excellent places for Mother to keep her secrets, no doubt. Either my brother or I will be by the shop with your payment, Mr. Maxwell. Thank you, and good day."

John once more took up the girl in his arms and brought her to the wagon. "Now shall we see if the bakery has made any fine ginger cakes this day?"

Kate clapped her hands in delight. John ushered the team of horses back down Nicholson Street and toward the delicious aroma wafting from the town bakery.

"You are very kind, Mr. Maxwell," Mrs. Farthington began.

"It's a small thing really, especially after all you have been through —" He paused.

She turned then, her eyes narrowing slightly. "You know about my husband?"

"I was told by my master, Mr. Longworth. I'm deeply sorry."

She sighed. "Thank you. He believed in freedom, but that freedom cost him and all of us dearly. I only pray the dream of freedom does come true. Then I will know he did not die in vain."

"Are you talking about Father?" Kate asked.

Mrs. Farthington hugged her daughter close. "Yes, darling. Your dear, brave father, who is now with God and His angels."

"I pray Father will come back to us, Mr. Maxwell," Kate said matter-of-factly. "I pray for it every night. Mother says that God hears prayers. She said to me that God's own Son came back to life. He even brought people back to life, like a little girl once. He can bring Father back, too. I know it."

John glanced at Mrs. Farthington to see her mouth twitch in discomfort. "But your father's soul is alive, dear one," John said gently. "He is more alive than any of us, in the Lord's great and glorious home. A mansion, if you will, just as our Savior Christ has been preparing for all of us."

"But Father is not here. I want him here with us, in our home, instead." Her cheerful countenance quickly deteriorated into a look of unhappiness.

"No, he's not here. But I'm certain he's mindful of you and what you do. And he wants you to take care of your mother. To be a good girl and mind her. And be patient and kind."

"I will," Kate promised. At that moment the girl snuggled against John's arm while he held the reins. "I can smell the ginger cookies," she declared as the wagon stopped before the bakery.

When John returned with cookies for each, a smile again appeared on Kate's face. "These are so good. Mother, if Father can't come back from heaven, maybe you can marry Mr. Maxwell instead."

John stared in astonishment until he was suddenly beset with a choking cough.

Her mother's face turned as red as cranberries. "Katherine Marie . . . you don't know of what you speak!" she managed to say.

"I know that I like Mr. Maxwell very much. I think he would make a fine father."

John didn't know what to think or say. Instead he made haste with the wagon, back to his establishment. The ride was quiet until he drew the wagon to a stop and assisted the mother and daughter safely to solid ground.

"I hope you will forgive my daughter's zeal," Mrs. Farthington said softly.

Was that a tremor he saw in the corner of her mouth? "There is nothing to forgive, madam. She misses her father and rightly so."

"Yes, and you have been very kind to her. More than any man since his death. I fear it brought hope in her heart."

"A delay of hope makes one's heart ill. I'm glad I was able to bring hope instead."

Mrs. Farthington appeared startled by the comment. She flushed red. "Well, thank you again." She took up Kate's hand, even as the young girl waved good-bye with the other hand.

John watched the mother and daughter hurry down the street toward the millinery shop. He shook his head. To have the girl come out and speak of marriage like she did, he could not have been more stunned than if he had been dumped in a trough of cold water. Not that the Lord had never whispered thoughts of marriage when John beheld the fine young ladies at church or those he saw in his shop. He knew, too, that he was older than most men who had married. None had waited as long as he had for a wife.

Now John stumbled back into his shop, wondering what to make of the encounter and the girl who had spoken her mind so openly . . . as if the word of the Lord were on her lips.

CHAPTER 3

Mary could not believe what Kate had said. She did not know how she would ever speak to Mr. Maxwell after what happened. For many days afterward she stayed close to the plantation, unwilling to venture to Williamsburg and meet with the man face-to-face, even if she was curious about the doll's progress. How could Kate say such a thing? As if she needed to marry anyone right now, though many of Mary's friends asked her that very question from time to time. They claimed it was unwise for a young widow with a child to remain unmarried for long, especially with the rebellion in their land. Nor was it wise for her daughter to be without the care and devotion of a father.

For a time Mary listened and smiled when her friends encouraged her to seek another. But this was the first time Kate had spoken about such a possibility. She had thought David's death too recent to force a new father upon her daughter, but maybe she had been wrong. Maybe Kate was ready to accept another father into her heart. Now she must determine if she, likewise, was ready for a husband.

Mary thought often of John Maxwell since that day when they delivered the desk to the Geddy house. She felt humbled in his presence, especially a skilled craftsman like he who could make such marvelous pieces. Her late husband did little such work. Rather, David roamed the countryside, espousing his patriotic beliefs. He traveled to Charlottesville and other places in Virginia, attending meetings with like-minded men. When news came of battles in far-off places like Lexington and Concord in Massachusetts, David was eager to find out all he could. Then followed the gunpowder stolen by the British governor in Williamsburg. The incident sent David off in a wave of fury, determined to take back the gunpowder at all cost. Not long after, he paid the ultimate price for his fervor on a lonely country road.

Now it was John Maxwell who hoped to provide the dear object David wanted Kate to have for Christmas — a lovely doll with a fine bisque head. Mary sighed. She realized soon she would need to venture to Williamsburg and see about the doll. If only there weren't the incident of Kate's words clouding the meeting. Would John Maxwell think she was pursuing a husband if she came to his shop, despite her honorable intentions? *If only this hadn't happened,* Mary thought in frustration. But it had, and she would need to show herself again before the man and pray for the words to say, even though they felt choked up inside.

Mary sent word to her neighbor, a kind woman without any children of her own, to watch Kate while she went to Williamsburg.

"You seem to be going to town quite a bit, Mary," Abigail Williams noted when Mary stopped by to leave Kate with her. "Do you have something you wish to share?" She poured Mary a spot of tea that a servant brought out on a tray.

Oh, dear, Mary thought, trying to lift the teacup with a steady hand. Had Kate already told her about Mr. Maxwell? "I'm having something made for Kate. The cabinetmaker in Williamsburg is fashioning a doll using the head from the doll David was to give Kate when he returned from his trip."

"I remember the doll your husband was to bring. How nice that you found someone who could make another."

"It's a surprise, so I'm going to Williamsburg to check on the doll's progress."

Abigail sipped on her tea. "It seems Kate is already taken with a particular cabinetmaker in town. When she came into my home, she described how a man let you see the desk he had made and then bought you both ginger cakes."

"Yes, Mr. Maxwell has been kind. But so are many men of business."

Abigail smiled. "He is also very good at what he does, Mary. He would provide well for you and Kate. Furniture making brings in a good deal of money. From what others have said, Mr. Maxwell's work is extraordinary."

Mary began feeling as warm as the teacup in her hands. She set the cup down carefully on a small table. "I'm sorry, Abigail, but I have no interest in seeking a husband. It's too soon."

"Surely you must think of Kate . . . and yourself. It would be a good match. The cabinetmaker is older, too, but he remains unmarried."

"Thank you, Abigail, but I prefer to wait on the Lord as I have done with everything in my life. When the time is right, I will know."

Abigail looked away, appearing vexed that

Mary did not accept her wise and true counsel. Yet Mary could not simply bow to what everyone thought she should do with her life. She had her own feelings to consider. Her heart, after all, had been broken in the aftermath of David's demise. God must restore her heart so she could love another. Now was not that time. "Thank you for the tea and for looking after Kate."

Abigail nodded and said no more, even as Mary put on her cloak. She went out to the carriage where the servant stood waiting to take her to Williamsburg. She tried not to think about the conversation but instead looked at the bare trees framing the river and the few farms that dotted the brown land. She wished spring were here, both in the landscape and in her heart.

When the servant stopped the carriage before the cabinetmaker's shop, Mary could not bring herself to venture inside. Instead she peered in the window, framed by a few evergreens that gave the shop a festive appearance. She could see Mr. Maxwell's solid frame and his large hands hard at work creating another masterpiece. No doubt the man had little time to spare, making a trivial thing like a doll. There were much more important tasks to accomplish than devoting himself to a mere toy. Perhaps she should take his advice and try to buy a doll. Then she would not have to come here and stir up everyone's expectations about her future.

"Good day, Mrs. Farthington," a friendly voice greeted her. She turned to see Mrs. Carter with several of her children, their hands full of brown packages from a day of shopping. "Are you seeking Mr. Maxwell? I do believe he is in his shop today."

"Yes, I . . . uh . . ." Mary managed a smile. "Yes, I need to ask about an item he is making for me. A pleasure to see you." She hurried inside the shop to avoid further conversation with the woman who also knew Abigail well. For all she knew they would soon talk to each other about her and the cabinetmaker. The mere thought made her blush. Oh, why did life have to suddenly become so complicated?

John Maxwell looked up upon her entry and gave her a warm smile. "Good day, Mrs. Farthington."

"Good day. I . . ." She hesitated. "I — I have decided to do something else with the doll. May I have the doll's head returned to me, please?"

In an instant his smile faded into a picture of confusion. "I don't understand. The plans for the doll are coming along very well. Let me show you what I've done so far. I think you will be pleased with it."

Mary tried to contain herself as Mr. Maxwell hurried to bring forth what he had made — a carved body with one leg attached.

"See how well the joint moves?" he said to her, demonstrating it. "Much better, I daresay, than any doll you can buy in England."

"Yes, it's excellent work. I only fear —" She paused. *What is it you fear, Mary? Happiness? Love?* "I know you are a very busy man, with many orders for the upcoming holiday. I don't want you to fall behind because of this doll. I would just as soon take it elsewhere."

"You're mistaken, madam. I find my work with the doll a pleasant diversion. It brings me much happiness, especially after meeting your daughter. She is a wonderful child and deserving of whatever skill I can give."

Oh, dear, Mary thought. How could she possibly not have him finish the work on the doll simply because of her own uncertainty in matters of life? After all, he had only been courteous and kind. Her friends were, as well — looking after her well-being, trying their utmost to restore her happiness. "I think the doll looks wonderful, Mr.

Maxwell. Of course you may continue, if you have the time."

He sighed. "Thank you. I feared I had done something to displease you. I do want to complete this project. It is unlike anything I have ever done." He acknowledged the chair he was building. "While I do like making furniture, working with the doll has brought my creativity to a place of detail, and one I have enjoyed. Even Master Longworth found the doll interesting, as he has never made one himself. Perhaps it might even establish me enough so that the shop finally becomes mine."

Mary could see the joy in his face and how much the doll meant to him. "I'm very glad." She hesitated. "And thank you, too, for the time we had together the other day. Kate talks about it constantly."

"I'm glad, madam. I enjoyed it as well. In fact, I would be most pleased to do it again. Are you in town often? Or shall I drive out to your home to pick you up?"

Oh, dear, Mary thought. Was she ready for this? Certainly Abigail would laud such an occurrence. "I'm not certain, Mr. Maxwell."

"Of course. I only wish to help."

Mary averted her gaze when he stared at her. She thought of Abigail's words, how he would provide for them, that they were the perfect match. *But I'm not ready, am I Lord?* "I — I have business at the store, sir. If you will excuse me?"

"Allow me to walk you there." He removed his carpenter's apron before she could say anything else.

She nodded and allowed him to open the door of the shop for her. "The windows look quite festive," Mary commented.

"Mrs. Longworth insisted on the greenery. Though many shops display green boughs and fruited wreaths, I fear I lack the skill in such decoration. It indeed takes a woman's touch to bring forth beauty." He walked alongside her, his hands at his sides, keeping a respectful distance from her even as he asked questions about her life.

Mary talked of growing up in Pennsylvania and her family that still lived there, meeting David when she came here to Williamsburg, and the whirl of their courtship when he announced their marriage in a week's time. She hoped she had not been too personal, revealing such details, but John Maxwell seemed interested in every word. "And what of you? Have you lived here in Williamsburg long?"

"All my life, madam. My father worked as a carpenter here. He helped build many of the homes on the outskirts of Williamsburg.

I suppose watching him work with wood aided my interest — though I had no interest in building homes. I enjoy carving wood instead. In fact, I should one day like to show you a Noah's Ark that I made. When you return, perhaps?" His voice turned eager. "When might that be?"

"Soon," she said, pushing open the door to the store.

"How soon?"

She hesitated. "Tomorrow. I shall come tomorrow." Disappearing inside the store, Mary could not believe her boldness. How could she come again and so soon? But Mr. Maxwell intrigued her. She enjoyed their conversation. She wanted to come, as often as possible, to discover more about him, to talk over things with a man. There was nothing about him that raised concern; rather his interest in her and his devotion to Kate seemed unmistakable. In all these signs, she found the makings of an endearing heart.

Mary returned as promised the next day, and the day after, as well. On that particular day, Mr. Maxwell took her hand in his in a move that startled her. "Mr. Maxwell!" she began. "What are you doing, sir?"

"I have something to show you."

Mary glanced around to make certain no one was watching. She followed him hesitantly as he led her to one of the finer brick homes and then to an entrance in the rear of the home. Her face began to warm. "I don't think this is proper, sir."

"Wait here. I shall be just a moment."

Mary could not believe she was standing before the man's humble dwelling. At least she stood behind the main house and away from curiosity seekers meandering along the main road. She could just imagine the gossip that would stir in the streets — a widow waiting before the door of an unmarried man's home.

Just as she was about to leave, Mr. Maxwell came out, carrying a small wooden box. "Come see," he told her with a smile as he began unloading the contents.

Mary became entranced by the small ark and the animals carved out of wood. The whimsical faces displayed their anticipation in joining their master within the safety of the ark. "How wonderful, Mr. Maxwell. You made all these?" She picked up a lion to examine it.

"Yes, about two years ago, along with some wooden horses and other animals on wheels that children can roll along."

"You should make more toys. You would

sell them certainly, especially this time of year."

"Perhaps," he said, watching her.

She turned a horse over in her hand, looking at the face painted on the carved head before placing it with the others. "This is a delight."

"Then take the set, madam. It's yours."

Mary whirled, clutching the hood of her cloak about her face. "What did you say?"

"Take it . . . for Kate. She would like it, I'm sure. Wouldn't she?"

"I–I'm certain she would. But I can't accept this, Mr. Maxwell. At least let me pay you for it."

"There's no need. She's a sweet child, and I'm truly sorry for all you have been through. If this brings a bit of joy to your home, then that is payment enough."

Mary didn't know what to say. Even as Mr. Maxwell began packing the set back into the box, she fought for the words. "I — I'm speechless, sir," she finally whispered.

"It's but a small token, really. I've often wondered who might enjoy the Noah's Ark. I kept it until the time was right. I knew when I saw Kate and you the other day that the Noah's Ark had finally found a home."

"But I still would like her to have the doll," Mary continued as they made their way back up the steps to the road.

"Of course. I will make it, and she will love it, as well. I wish for nothing more."

Mary did not doubt his sincerity as he carefully placed the wooden box into the carriage. She had never met a man like him. "Thank you again for such a wonderful gift."

"You're most welcome."

He offered her his hand. Only then did Mary realize he was offering to help her into the carriage. She accepted it with thanks.

When the carriage pulled away, she could not help but watch his figure slowly fade from view as he remained transfixed before his shop. At her feet rested the beloved Noah's Ark. Kate would be so excited. And when she learned who had made it, it would no doubt renew her fervor for a father. *Could John Maxwell be that man for us?* Mary wondered. *Oh, how can I even consider such a thing?* But he had been the perfect gentleman, kind and considerate, thinking of ways to bless them. She should at least consider where this was leading and in which direction the Lord was sending her.

When Mary arrived home, she showed Kate the gift from John Maxwell. The girl clapped her hands in delight before taking out each animal to examine it. "This is wonderful, Mother! Thank you!"

"You needn't thank me, darling. It's Mr. Maxwell we must thank."

Kate looked up then, her eyes widening. "Mr. Maxwell! He made this? I thought he makes desks with secret drawers."

Mary laughed. "He thought you would enjoy having this. We will think of it as an early gift to celebrate the coming holiday."

"Oh, Mother, I told you he was the nicest man," she said with a sigh. "Please, can we invite him here for a visit?"

Mary stepped back, startled once more by her daughter's boldness. "I don't know, Kate."

"But look at all the nice things he has done. Please, Mother?"

Mary could never say no to such pleading, not when it came to Kate's happiness and when she had lost so much at a young age. "I will send a messenger to invite Mr. Maxwell to dinner, if that's what you want."

Kate sighed in contentment as she placed all the wooden figures on the floor, arranging them in a parade. "And now you can read me the story of Noah," she decided.

Mary couldn't help but smile as she retrieved the family Bible. She had nothing to fear. God was doing something wonderful in their lives. She would embrace it all, including the kindness of John Maxwell, if she could muster the strength to look beyond the past to the future.

CHAPTER 4

John was taken aback by the dinner invitation to Highland Grove plantation and the home of Mrs. Farthington. He had not considered that giving the Noah's Ark would bring about such an invitation, though secretly he was glad for it. He wanted to spend more time with the woman and her daughter. They seemed so in want. He could not ignore it, nor could he ignore the feelings in his heart after everything that had happened. Kate's words, for example. The way Mrs. Farthington appeared when he gave her the Noah's Ark — her eyes sparkling like the stars of heaven, her lips upturned in a smile of joy. The times they spent in conversation, walking the streets of Williamsburg. And wondering if the doll would be the final event in bringing them closer than ever before.

He glanced at a small looking glass to check his appearance. The blouse and lace cravat looked pleasant enough. He possessed a gentleman's coat, as well, given to him by his mentor, Mr. Longworth. With the money from the desk, he had purchased new boots. He liked his appearance and hoped Mrs. Farthington would, as well.

He hesitated. Why would he be concerned if she found him presentable? He still knew so little about her, only that her heart had been broken last spring. Not that he had any inkling that he could be the repairer of such a breach. But he felt the Lord drawing upon his heart to help. And if he could be of any assistance to the family, especially with the holidays drawing near, he would avail himself.

Perhaps he could ask Mrs. Longworth if he might invite Mrs. Farthington and her daughter to their gathering at Christmas. He would very much like to escort them to church for the service and sit opposite Mrs. Farthington during the family dinner. And it would please him to hear Kate's exclamation when she received the doll.

John toyed with the cravat once more, then ventured out into the chilly afternoon. His horse was waiting for him, one he borrowed from the master for this ride. He looked forward to the day when he owned his home and a team of horses. Soon it would come, if all went as planned and the shop became his.

He sighed, gazing at the blue skies above. A fine day for a ride. He didn't often find himself on the main road heading out of Williamsburg. It proved a pleasant diversion from the shop where he labored in making furniture, with wood chips flying in the air. Instead he took the time to enjoy the scents of winter — the cold air mixed with the fragrance of pine trees that grew in abundance.

During the ride, John thought back over his life. While God had blessed him greatly in his work, he did miss having a family of his own. The Longworths had been his family since he became an apprentice, but now he sensed a need to look elsewhere. He wondered if this road could be leading him to a new family and a new purpose in life.

When he arrived at the plantation, little Kate burst out of the house, flying down the stairs, startling the horse he rode. He managed to calm the animal before dismounting. "What a fine greeting," he told her as her little arms came about his coat. "To what do I owe this pleasure?"

"You know . . . for being so kind to Mother and me. Look, Mother! Here is Mr. Maxwell."

John stared at the fine and delicate form standing in the doorway of the large home, set off by pillars arrayed along the front portico. She wore a light blue satin polonaise gown, her hair swept off her shoulders into a bun, a lace pinner cap atop her head.

"Welcome to Highland Grove, Mr. Maxwell."

"A beautiful place, madam." He lifted his cocked hat and performed a regal bow. Kate giggled before taking up his hand and leading him inside. He wanted to remark to Mrs. Farthington that she looked beautiful as well but held the comment in his heart for the time being. Maybe one day there would be an opportunity for him to make such comments and she would receive them with a smile.

"I must show you where the Noah's Ark is," Kate said. John didn't even have time to see the interior of the home, including the fine furniture from England which he would have liked to inspect for its craftsmanship. Kate had all but taken him from such things to her own little world. She led him to a table in the main sitting room where she had displayed the Noah's Ark for all to see. "Noah is ready to have the animals come inside the ark to protect them from the rain," she explained. "Mother told me the story."

"A fine story it is, as are many in the Bible. I like the story of David doing away with the giant. It does us well to know that God helps us win over our enemies, no matter how big they are."

"I know that story. But how can a boy kill a giant?" Kate shook her head, her curly locks swaying as she did. "It's too terrible, Mr. Maxwell."

"But necessary. God has His plans. And sometimes those plans mean destroying the enemy."

"Like the enemy that took away Father?" She paused. "I would like them to be punished for what they did."

For a moment John didn't know what to say. "We must put it in God's hands, dear one," he told her. "Just as our lives are at this moment."

A servant appeared in the room, motioning to Kate to help her serve the refreshments. John suddenly found himself alone with Mrs. Farthington, who had ventured inside, calmly watching his interaction with her daughter from afar. He hesitated, wondering how much she had witnessed and if she had overheard the comments about her husband.

"She likes the Noah's Ark very much,"

Mrs. Farthington noted. "All she talks about is you, Mr. Maxwell. I daresay she has no other friend."

"Oh, come, she must have many friends," John said, finding his way to a chair.

"We speak to very few people. There are our family friends, of course. But no men, certainly."

John stirred at this. No men . . . and no man for this fine lady either. "It must be difficult after the passing of your husband," he started.

"My husband would want us to go on — to live and have hope for ourselves and our country. He would be sad indeed if he thought his passing kept us from enjoying God's blessings. I know Kate is certainly ready for such things." John saw her gaze settle on him. "Perhaps that's why she found in you a kindred soul, Mr. Maxwell. She has seen that another man does care for her and wishes to make her happy, just like her father."

"I don't suppose you could call me John."

She straightened, her eyes widening. "I . . . ," she began, "I — suppose I could . . . John. And you may call me Mary."

He smiled, and to his delight, she returned the smile. When Kate entered the sitting room, balancing a tray of crumpets, followed by the servant carrying tea, he continued to sense Mary's gaze on him. He had only been here but a short time and already they were taken with each other in ways he had not anticipated. He thought Mary might still be consumed by her husband. Or the family still wrought with pain. But there was none of that. Only an eagerness to live.

Kate filled the atmosphere with her sweet chatter as she talked about finding a nest of rabbits behind the house, her pony, and again about the Noah's Ark that had become her pride and joy. "When can I come help you in your shop, Mr. Maxwell?"

Her question caught him off guard. "I don't understand."

"I helped you the other day with the desk. Don't you need a helper?"

John chuckled. "Some days I do," he confessed.

"My darling, Mr. Maxwell doesn't allow young girls to help him in his shop," Mary admonished.

"But why not? I would like to make things. He could teach me."

"There is plenty to learn here — such as sewing or making candles or even making a wreath for the front door. I can show you how with boughs of boxwood and holly."

Kate wriggled up her face and crossed her arms.

"I see there is much more to your daughter's opinions than meets the eye," John observed with a chuckle.

"She has the spirit of her father in her — to do new things, no matter how unseemly they might be." Mary went on to explain to the young girl the work a fine lady would pursue. Kate only shook her head, insisting she would like to make things like the Noah's Ark and the desk with the secret drawers.

"Perhaps you can come one day and watch me work," John finally told her. "I will even show you how to make one of Noah's animals. Would you like that?"

"Oh, yes," she said with a sigh. "Tomorrow."

John couldn't help but laugh at the child's eagerness. When he looked over at Mary, her face glowed. She appeared relaxed and confident as she stood to her feet to give him a tour of the plantation. Kate ran off to check the den of baby rabbits in the field while John and Mary toured the house and the large barns.

"Your husband kept this place immaculate," John perceived.

"Yes, he did. But I fear it's slowly dying as

time goes by. Several of the buildings are in need of repair. If there is another harsh winter, I'm not certain what will happen. I've looked over the books and fear we may need to sell come spring. This is far too large a place for me to manage all by myself."

"Times and seasons do change. I will help, though, in any way I can."

"You already have, John. More than you know. But I know, too, that I must be ready for change. To give up the life I led here and embrace the future. Only . . ." She paused. "I don't know what that future holds. I fear at times for our country. I know there is a war going on now. What will become of us, John? Will we find our freedom as a country? It was the dearest wish of my husband, but I don't know."

"None of us really know. Only God knows."

"And what about you, John? Are you for the cause of liberty?"

The question caught him off guard. "Am I for the cause of liberty?" he repeated. He sensed at once the conflict that arose from another such question — after the challenge put forth by his brother, Jonas, when Jonas inquired about his stand on similar issues. "Of course I desire freedom for all who are held captive."

"And do you believe England holds us captive?"

He hesitated. "I will admit I'm not privy to all the goings on of this conflict as your husband once was. Perhaps because I've found myself helping people with their furniture or even making a doll. I find such things more useful to the common man rather than trying to decide what the future of the colonies should be."

Immediately after he said these words, a distance formed between them. No doubt Mary held firmly to the cause of liberty. After all, her husband gave his life for it. But John was not that kind of man. He had no patriotic fervor. He was but a humble cabinetmaker, looking to be a master of his work.

She turned from him to gaze at the fields beyond the barn and the browning grasses that swayed in the wind. "I shouldn't think you would hold to everything my husband believed in," she said at last. "I suppose I think all men should be as patriotic as he, and that's wrong."

"Madam, if you mean do I love this land, I do indeed. Do I care to have us separate from England? If it be God's will that we become a nation unto Him, then I support it wholeheartedly. But my heart is not in the conflict itself. I will instead leave that to others more gifted than I in such matters."

"Then I will leave such matters to God as well, sir."

When she turned back, he could not help but stare at her eyes that appeared softer and her cheeks tinted by the wind. When he stepped forward, she didn't move. Nor did she stir when his arms slowly came around her and his lips found hers. When they parted, she drew in a breath. Her cheeks reddened even further, like berries on the holly bushes.

"Please spend Christmas with me," he asked softly. "I would like nothing better than to have you and Kate with me at the services and then at the holiday feast with the Longworths."

"But the family you stay with —"

"They are a good and godly family who would be very happy to have you. Say you will spend it with us, and it will be your gift to me. And I will treasure it."

He saw the hazel color of her eyes turn cloudy, veiled by her tears. "Thank you, John, for thinking of us. I know Kate will be happy."

"And you can give her the doll."

"The doll . . ." Her voice seemed to fade

away. "The doll that was supposed to be a reminder of her father, John."

"Of course it is. Just as Kate is a reminder of your husband. Her fine spirit pays tribute to his memory. There is no abandoning it. You will carry it forever. But there are new memories that can also come forth, just as Kate was wise to see. We must continue on with life, even as you said earlier this day."

"I suppose you're right."

"Then we will allow God to guide us. He has brought us together, and His love will keep us."

Suddenly the bell sounded from the kitchen. "Dinner is ready," Mary whispered.

John gave her another kiss. "I've waited a long time to dine in the presence of a lovely lady," he told her with a smile.

When they took their seats, John could not tear his gaze from Mary, who sat opposite him at the dinner table. Only when he felt a tap on his knee did he look beneath the table to discover that Kate had slipped out of her chair.

"Kate, whatever are you doing under there?" Mary said in alarm. "Go back to your chair at once."

"I only wanted to know if Mr. Maxwell could see me," she said. "He only seems to see you, Mother."

"If you must know, you have a beautiful mother," John added with a laugh. "And you may be pleased to know that you'll be seeing more of me, Kate. I have invited you both to spend Christmas with me in Williamsburg."

Kate crawled out from under the table and clapped her hands. "Oh, Mother! Did you know?"

"Yes, darling. I thought it would be nice to spend it with the family where John . . . that is, Mr. Maxwell is staying. Their name is Longworth. We will go to church with him, too."

"Oh, it will be grand. Mr. Maxwell, everything is so wonderful since you came here. Please don't ever leave."

"That will depend on your mother."

Kate looked over at Mary, who was trying to spoon up some peanut soup. "Mother? You will not send him away, will you?"

"Darling, I would be foolish to do such a thing."

John could not have been happier. The dinner went beyond all his expectations. Now his help of a needy family had given way to feelings he did not even think would come to light. Later, when John said good-bye, he noticed the sparkle in Mary's eyes and the warmth rising in his own heart. God was performing a great work indeed. He only hoped and prayed he was the man Mary and Kate needed in their lives.

John had plenty of time to mull over the day on the long ride back to Williamsburg. The sun had already set, with only the glow of a crescent moon to illuminate the road. When he finally arrived back in town, he headed directly for the Longworth house to find it aglow with lanterns. Several horses were tethered to posts nearby. To his startled surprise, several men appeared to be accosting the master on the doorstep. He stared at the scene in disbelief before dismounting in a hurry, running to Mr. Longworth's aid. "What is the meaning of this?"

"This man participated in a meeting with the militia a fortnight ago," a man said.

"And if I did, is giving support to our town militia now a crime?" Mr. Longworth asked.

"It is if these meetings are to usurp the authority of the crown," said the man. "And if such meetings seek to undermine the governor's authority, which these men have done in the past, then it is also a treasonous act."

"I recognize you," John said. "You stand with Jonas. Where is he?"

"Who are you?"

"His brother, John. I will speak to him and ask why you are confronting this man in such a fashion."

Just then a familiar voice bit the air. "John, need we say anything else to you?"

John whirled to find Jonas appear out of the darkness, his rigid face barely illuminated by the lantern he held.

"Yet look at what you have become," Jonas continued in an icy voice. "You play the role of a cabinetmaker by day but then keep company with a traitor's widow. We have seen you with her, walking these very streets, a spectacle to behold before all the eyes of Williamsburg. It's plain to see now where your true loyalties lie, even if you refuse to confess it."

"And I see where yours lie, as well. I do not fight for a cause but for the needy and the oppressed. And whom do you fight for, Jonas? Whose side are you on?"

"My lord, King George, to whom we owe our allegiance."

"There is only one King of heaven and of earth. And you must make Him King of your heart and soul lest you be condemned forever."

Jonas stepped forward then, his eyes narrowing. "You don't understand, do you? A traitor's death awaits all whose loyalties are in doubt. We will do what we must to remove this scourge from the colonies, even as we did with that widow's husband."

John stared in disbelief. The horror of those words sliced him like the blade of a sword. "No! It was you, wasn't it? You — you and your men killed David Farthington!"

"He was a traitor. He deserved a traitor's death."

"How could you do such a thing? Leave a widow and a small girl to fend for themselves in this land? And you call your actions noble? Why, you're murderers!"

Jonas clenched his hand. The lantern swayed. "And you seek to murder your own loyalty, John. You would kill and destroy everything you are just as quickly, even as you toy with treason this moment by keeping company with that traitor's widow." He held up his hand. "This is my warning to you both. You walk a dangerous path. Do not associate any longer with such people, either of you, or you will face the wrath of Lord Dunmore and the King of England. I have said it." He whirled, the lantern light fading quickly in the distance.

John stared after the men, too overcome to know what to do or think. When he looked back to address his mentor, Mr.

Longworth had quickly disappeared into his home, bolting the door behind him. John closed his eyes, fighting to contain the wave of distress over this meeting. *Oh God, what shall I do now?*

CHAPTER 5

Mary never thought she could know love so quickly, but it had happened. Love, like a breath from heaven, bringing with it the scent of flowers, of trees, of a warm spring after the cold of winter faded away. John was the perfect man to fall in love with. Everything about him moved her — his tenderness, his kind demeanor around her daughter, his merciful heart. She felt young and carefree around him — younger, perhaps, than Kate, who laughed and sang these days as if she, too, had been reborn.

Even her friend, Abigail, remarked at how happy Mary seemed to be. As they visited, she asked if a man could possibly be the reason why.

"Oh, I must tell you of him," Mary said, watching a smile break out on her friend's face. "Yes, it's John Maxwell, the gifted cabinetmaker of Williamsburg."

"I knew he was a blessing of God!" Abigail said in glee, giving Mary a swift embrace. "When I first heard how he cared for you both, I knew God's will was at work. How wonderful indeed."

"He also invited us to spend Christmas with him and the Longworths. Kate is so excited." Mary glanced down at her hands that trembled slightly in her lap. "I must say, I'm eager, as well. To go to church with a man, to sit by him while we sing hymns of praise to God and read from the holy scriptures — it's a dream come true, Abigail."

"I'm so happy for you, Mary, I cannot say."

Mary could say little either with her heart overflowing, keeping her too overwhelmed even to speak. How she wished it were already Christmas. But she would see John again before that time, she was certain. She could not stay far from him, not after everything that had happened. Oh, how she prayed they would meet again soon. Perhaps she might feign another errand to town, this time an errand of love.

A few days later, Mary noticed a wagon coming fast and furious on the road to her home. A black man sat in the seat, and beside him, a strange woman in a dark cloak. The woman appeared in distress.

"I must speak to you," she said in a shaky voice when she arrived.

Mary led the way to the sitting room. When Mary offered tea, the woman shook her head.

"There is so little time. I only pray to God no one has seen me. I — I don't know what to do." She twisted her hands, looking about fearfully. "I — I am Mrs. Longworth."

Mary straightened. "Why, yes! Your husband mentors Mr. Maxwell, does he not?"

She nodded and dabbed her eyes with a handkerchief. "I'm so fearful. I don't know what to do. I thought perhaps your husband once had communication with the militia. Maybe the militia can stop them — if you knew where to send word? Or tell me where the captain might be, and I will do the errand myself."

"I don't understand, Mrs. Longworth."

"Those men, the Tories. They threatened to hurt my poor husband. He didn't do anything wrong. He only went to the meeting because a friend asked him. He didn't know it was a political meeting. They found out and now they say he is a traitor. They will do what they did to your husband! Oh, what will I do?"

Mary stared. "I don't know what to say, Mrs. Longworth."

"I would have gone to Mr. Maxwell about it, but I can't. For all I know, he could be one of them."

"What? Of course not. John is no Tory."

"How do you know? His brother is. It was his brother who killed your husband, you know."

Mary sat back in her chair, even as a feeling of numbness swept over her. "That's not true. It can't be true. You must be mistaken."

"If only I were. Mr. Maxwell even said it. My husband heard it all. Mr. Maxwell's brother killed your husband. And they even mentioned Mr. Maxwell spending time with you — the widow of a traitor."

No! Oh dearest God, help me! Mary felt weak. She shook her head. "You must have heard in error. John is only kind and helpful."

"Perhaps, but his blood runs with that of the Tories. Even now I'm convincing my husband to dismiss Mr. Maxwell. He will bring those men down upon our house if he stays." She lowered her head. "My husband does think highly of Mr. Maxwell. Like a son, really. But I can't allow us to be harmed."

Mary shook her head, unable to believe what she was hearing. How could this be . . . and when God was in the midst of restoration through the bonds of love? She wanted to shout aloud to the Maker of heaven and earth with the shattering plea of *Why?* How like Job when his pleas reached heaven. Why had this come upon her?

"I don't know what to say or think," Mary mourned. "Nor do I know anything about the militia, you see. I don't seem to know anything anymore. Not even about the man I'm supposed to love. What can I do?"

Mrs. Longworth sensed the despair and hastily gathered her wraps. "Forgive me, I must go. I'm truly sorry for all this, but I believed you should know, Mrs. Farthington. I don't know but the Tories might even come here, especially knowing that you and Mr. Maxwell have been seeing each other. My husband even heard their warnings. Do what you must to protect yourself. And I will do what I can to find the captain of the militia."

Mary followed Mrs. Longworth to the wagon, then stared after it as it rattled away, returning in haste to Williamsburg. She stumbled along the path back to the house. How could this have come upon her? The man making the doll for dear Kate and the man she kissed, now the very man whose brother took the life of her husband? If John knew such a terrible thing, why did he keep it from her? She pondered this fact. Perhaps there was a certain truth to Mrs. Longworth's words. Perhaps John was an informant for his brother, sent to find out about the patriots that David knew. Anger rose up within her, along with a determination to meet this new challenge placed before her, even though her heart had once more been shattered into a thousand shards.

"Mary!" Abigail called out as she hurried down the road from her home, staring after the racing wagon. "What's wrong? Is there bad news?"

Mary fell into Abigail's arms, crying. Abigail escorted her gently into the house and to the sitting room. "What happened?"

Between her sobs, Mary revealed everything.

Abigail shook her head. "I don't believe it. Mr. Maxwell is only a good Christian man. There is no such deceit about him. And he is most certainly not a Tory."

"But his brother took the life of my husband! And he kept it from me! For all I know he was sent to seek things from me — to spy on me. He could not even espouse the cause of liberty, you know. He said as much to me when I asked him during his visit here. Now I know why — because his family are evil Tories seeking our destruction."

"Have you any proof at all to these claims that he is involved? Or are you only distressed that you fell in love with a man who has this unfortunate link to your husband's death?"

Mary looked away. At that moment she envisioned the way John looked at her while inviting her to spend Christmas with him. His face revealed such tenderness and devotion that it nearly took her breath away. But she dare not make him a part of any new memories. He was linked to the memories of old — to dreadful, terrible memories bathed in blood. There was no future to grasp. "I do not love him," she declared.

"How can you say that? You know it isn't true. I've seen it in your eyes and heard it in your voice. Go seek the truth for yourself. Speak to him."

Mary whirled. "How can I do that? Bare my soul once more before a man whose only desire is to use me?"

"I believe you will discover that John is, like you, burdened by a terrible sin in his family. And likely he is as distressed as you are over such news. Comfort each other and don't tear each other apart."

She shook her head. "I can't. Nor will I

put Kate in danger. I have no choice but to leave this place at once. I have family in Pennsylvania. I will go there immediately." She stood to her feet and called for the servants.

"Mary, please. Consider what you are doing. . . ."

Abigail's voice faded as the pain of betrayal filled the void. Mary would hear and see no more. Everything was blanketed by a cloud of grief without end. She would seek the sunlight elsewhere.

John spent the night and all the next day prostrate before God, asking, pleading, inquiring. He could not bring himself to work even though orders awaited his attention. When a knock came on his door, he ignored it. He could do nothing but pray . . . for the Longworths . . . for his wayward brother . . . for Mary. Never did he find himself in such turmoil. And what of Mary? What if she were to find out that his own flesh and blood had killed her husband?

She cannot know, he decided. There were many times in scripture that God didn't want knowledge to come forth, realizing its consequences. So it was with this. Such knowledge would prove too painful. It would destroy all that had begun to sprout in their hearts, along with withering the hope and joy growing inside a young girl.

Again came the incessant knocking on his door. He wanted to ignore it but, instead, came weightily to his feet. He peered out the window. A woman stood there, holding the hood of her cloak tight about her head to protect her from the wind. Immediately he opened the door.

"Mr. Maxwell? John Maxwell?"

"Yes, I'm John Maxwell."

"I'm Mrs. Turner, a friend of Mary Farthington."

"Yes, good day. I would invite you in out of the cold, but —"

"I do understand. Gather your cloak, sir. I must speak to you, please. It's most urgent."

John grabbed for his cloak, throwing it about him and joining her outside in the blustery day. They walked the paths surrounding the Longworth home. "You must go at once to see Mary, sir. She is determined to leave."

"She is leaving? But why? Where?"

"She knows about your brother. And she fears you also are a Tory, seeking to use her for knowledge."

John rubbed a hand across his face. His worst fear had come true. "How did she find out about my brother?"

"A Mrs. Longworth came to see her. She was most distressed."

John understood well the turmoil in the family since the news came forth. He had seen the Longworths conversing, and he knew it was about him. When Mr. Longworth suggested he not go to the shop today, John abided by his wisdom. He had no desire to work anyway and decided it would do him better to spend a Sabbath rest before God, seeking His will. But now he wondered where the seeking had led on the heels of this disturbing news.

"As God is my witness, Mrs. Turner, I am not a Tory. I have never agreed with my brother on his political views. My views are only of my God. And when I heard what Jonas had done . . ." His voice began to choke as his throat closed over. "I — I have been on my knees all night in prayer and repentance for it. I don't know what else I can do."

"There is something you can do. Go see Mary at once, sir. Talk to her."

"And tell her what? That my brother murdered her husband? That I sought myself as a substitute perhaps for her dead husband, only to see it now lay to waste? She already believes I'm to blame when I'm innocent." He began to pace. "All I have ever tried to do is bring her and her daughter a bit of happiness. And now look what's happened." In these words he sensed his own despair rising up.

"But you are a godly man, sir. You have spent the night before God's throne, seeking His wisdom, as you have said. Is He not able then to affect this when you cannot? Or can you say your faith has waned, as well?"

The cold of the day bit hard as his flesh likewise grappled with what lay before him. He shivered. Oh, if he didn't have the sting of Jonas's sin on him. If he had not already fallen in love with Mary and was close to finishing the doll for Kate. If all these things had not come about.

But life was a struggle, a battle even as battle lines were being drawn in this country to determine freedom or tyranny. And now he faced a battle for the heart and soul. Would it likewise bring forth freedom for them all? Or would Jonas succeed in destroying more lives?

When Mrs. Turner left, John returned to his dwelling to ponder her words. How could he bring himself to see Mary after all that had become known?

He ventured over to a wooden crate and looked at the doll. The arms and legs had each been carefully carved, attached by their wooden joints to the body. He picked up the doll then, moving each of the joints, seeing in his dreams Kate's smile when she beheld the doll on Christmas morn. He picked up the bisque head next, the only thing left after an awful encounter on a dark road that ended a life.

He sat down to look at the doll's head and the body. Taking out a small box of tools he kept inside his home, he began working with the doll. The work made him feel better, as if God were reconstructing the limp body of those who had suffered so greatly. Could He mend the broken pieces back together? Could He complete a work of restoration?

When John had the head of the doll affixed in place, he could not have been more pleased with the results. It was a great achievement for him. Perhaps even a symbol of the work that God would do in their lives, despite the fractures caused by the past.

He stood to his feet then and fetched his cloak. He would visit Mrs. Mercer at the millinery shop and see if she could make a dress for the doll. He would not ask Mrs. Longworth, who had not spoken to him since her husband's confrontation with Jonas. The less he interacted with them at this time, the better.

When he arrived, Mrs. Mercer agreed to sew clothes for the doll. Yet he perceived a distance in their meeting as well as coolness in their conversation. Could it be that everyone knew about Jonas? That nothing was hidden? That it had been shouted from the housetops, and now his reputation had likewise been soiled?

A fury rose up within John. How he wanted to see Jonas right now, to tell him how angry he was. But his own brother had threatened him. *I, too, am a victim and have seen my life cast before my eyes. It is true that enemies can be members of one's household.* He walked the deserted streets of Williamsburg, deep in thought. Even the greenery decorating the windows of the homes for the upcoming festivities failed to cheer him.

He paused when he came to the town magazine, the storehouse for the gunpowder — the place that had begun the circle of violence which now seemed unending. He watched then as several men came out of the magazine, speaking to one another. They were not dressed as British regulars but in commoners' clothing with their cocked hats, carrying rifles. Militia, he was certain. John glanced about the street for any observers but saw no one. Murmuring a prayer on his lips, he approached the men.

An hour later John was on a horse in the company of the men, riding out of Williamsburg. As he hurried to do what he knew he must, John prayed Mary would not leave, and all this would instead lead them back into each other's arms.

CHAPTER 6

"I don't want to leave!" Kate wailed. "Please, Mother!"

"It's for the best," Mary only said, watching the servants scurry about, folding clothing and stowing away valuables into crates. "I have a sister in Pennsylvania who has never seen you. It will do us well to leave and begin elsewhere. Perhaps this is our time."

"But I want to be here for Christmas! Mr. Maxwell invited us. I want to go to church with him."

Mary sighed. How she wanted to tell Kate what had happened, but she knew she could never do such a thing. To tell Kate that John might very well be involved with her own father's death would prove too much. Even Mary found herself overwhelmed by it all. "I don't think we will ever see him again," she said quietly.

"But why? I don't understand. Why won't

we see him? He was just here for a visit. We all talked and laughed."

Mary closed her eyes, trying hard not to think about that time, especially in the barn when he had taken her in his arms and kissed her. Why had she allowed herself to fall in love so easily? She had taken his embrace willingly, perhaps even as a lamb to the slaughter. And now what did she have left? Only the nightmare that his flesh and blood killed David. The mere notion made the anger burn hot inside her, and her hands work even quicker to assemble their belongings. "I will talk no more of it," she said to Kate. "Go pack your things."

Mary worked steadily awhile longer before looking about to find Kate still standing there, the girl's arms folded in defiance. "I won't go. I won't have someone else taken from me. I won't."

"Kate, you must believe me when I say that Mr. Maxwell is not the man you think he is." She sighed. "He — he knows things about your father that he won't tell me. I had to hear of it from a stranger." She nearly gasped at the thought.

Kate stared at her. "What things? Who sent Father away to heaven?"

Mary nodded. "I cannot say, but I was upset to learn it. That's why we must leave.

It could be dangerous for us to stay here. You must believe me that this is for the best. We will have a wonderful Christmas with your aunt in Pennsylvania. She even has a daughter about your age. Please gather your things so we can leave as soon as possible."

Kate turned, her feet shuffling along the floor, her head drooping in despair. If only there were some way to lift her spirits.

Mary froze at that moment. The doll — the precious doll still in John Maxwell's possession. She pressed her lips tightly together and hurried to find her cloak. She must get the doll back before they left. It was the only item of value she desired. Not her jewels, her dresses, nor even the furniture. None of it mattered. But she would have the doll.

Before she left for Williamsburg, Mary looked through David's collection of weapons and selected the smallest of them, a pistol. She shuddered. David would never forgive her for taking it. She didn't know how she would forgive herself. But there were other things more important now. She would do what she must to get the doll back.

Mary hurried to Williamsburg, paying little heed to the people who looked on her as a frenzied woman on horseback, galloping along the main street of town. She came at once to the Longworth home. Before she headed for John's door behind the dwelling, she took out the pistol and hid it in a long pocket tied around her skirt. Her hand shook as she touched the weapon. She didn't know if she even had the courage to use it, but she would do what she must to protect herself and Kate.

She hurried to John's door, murmuring a prayer under her breath. After ceaseless knocking, she determined he was not at home. She realized then she would have to confront him at his place of business and with a gun hidden away in her pocket. How could she do this? But at that moment, all she could think about was the bisque doll head. She had no choice. She strode to her horse, unwound the reins from the post, and prepared to mount when she heard a gentleman address her.

"Mrs. Farthington?" Mary turned to see Mr. Longworth approaching her. "Are you looking for John Maxwell?"

"I . . ." She hesitated. "Yes. I need to speak to him."

"He is at the courthouse right now, but I'm certain he will be returning soon."

"Why is he at the courthouse? Is he in trouble?"

Mr. Longworth shook his head "Oh, no. I

believe he should explain it all to you himself. But I can say it is most urgent business."

Mary didn't know what to make of this. She felt once more for the pistol at her side. Slowly she took it out and hid it in a saddlebag. For some reason she didn't feel the need to carry it. Whatever John was up to, she was uncertain, but a meeting at the courthouse might signify something important. She would go immediately and find out what was happening.

When she had mounted the horse and took up the reins, preparing to venture out, she caught sight of a man hurrying down the road. When their gazes met, the man froze in his stance.

"Mary."

Mary could not tear her eyes from him. John Maxwell. He stared wide-eyed, his lips parted, his face ashen. Slowly he approached. "I — I heard you were leaving. Your friend, Mrs. Turner, told me."

"Abigail came here?"

"She — she said I should speak to you. I was about to come out to your home as soon as I arrived back."

"You are not welcome at my home, Mr. Maxwell," she said evenly. She looked away, to the houses across the street and the trickle of smoke curling out of the chimneys. "In fact, you are not welcome at all in my family. I only came for the doll that belongs to me. And I will have it, sir. Do not deny me this."

"Of course. It's finished. I will go get it." He hurried past her and moments later returned, carrying a long wooden box. "I'm certain Kate will be happy with it. And you needn't pay me. It is a gift."

Mary hesitated for only a moment and then took it from him, placing the box on her lap. When she gripped the reins to wheel the horse about, he took hold of the bridle. "What are you doing?" She tried to push his hand away.

"Before you leave, I must tell you something."

"Thank you for the doll, but there is nothing left to be said. Please let go of my horse."

"There is much to say, if you will listen for a moment. I wanted to tell you that you no longer need live in fear. The enemy has been brought to justice."

Mary looked down at him to see his dark eyes staring up at her. For a moment the sight of his handsome features of dark hair and eyes and his rugged complexion caught her breath. She relaxed in the saddle. "I don't understand."

John released his hold on the bridle. "I found several soldiers on duty by the magazine. From them, I was able to see the captain of the militia in this region. I told him what happened. They arrested those responsible for your husband's murder." He looked away. "And yes, I'm sad to confess, my brother was among them."

Mary opened her mouth but no words would come out.

"I was at the courthouse this morning for their trial. My brother all but cursed my name. I told him I would pray for him. He threatened me with my life, but there's nothing more he can do to either of us. He is now in the gaol and will likely face death." John's gaze once more found her face. "Mary, I'm so sorry for all of this. I do understand why you can't remain here. Fond as I am of you both, I'm most willing for you to depart and find a place of peace. It's all I have ever hoped or wanted."

Again Mary tried to speak, but heaviness gripped her throat. Instead she took up the reins, and with a snap, directed the horse down the road and away from John Maxwell. Even then she could picture him standing on the street, his face sad, his hands limp at his sides. But she didn't know what else to do. There was nothing else to do but leave and find love and peace elsewhere. Where, she didn't know.

Don't leave! Please come back! Oh, how he wanted her to stay. His words had been untrue when he claimed he understood Mary's need to leave. Love had come quickly for them both. Love when they walked the streets of Williamsburg or shared in the Noah's Ark with Kate between them. And then the tender touch of their kiss.

Now love had departed just as quickly as it came. There was no return for Mary Farthington or her sweet daughter. He had done all he could.

John tried to move toward the shop where he might bury himself in his work, but his feet were slow to respond. Not only that, but several townspeople stopped him, asking about the arrest of the Tories. He gave them little information, directing them instead to seek out the magistrate. He didn't wish to become a public spectacle but hurried to his shop to hide from the inquiries. He would lose himself in the task of furniture making. It was his only escape from the pain and confusion of a time unlike any other in his life.

He fumbled to light a lantern. Just then he heard a rustle. Every part of his being tensed. He thought back to Jonas's warning. *You will be punished for this, John,* the man had snarled. *I have friends. And it won't be me hanging from a tree either.* John trembled. This might very well be his time. He had no defense but God alone.

The lantern swayed in his trembling hand as he held it up. "Who's there?" he asked, trying to steady his voice. He expected to find the muzzle of a weapon pointing at him.

Out of the shadows came a figure. He drew back until his eyes adjusted to the dim light. He saw a figure dressed in a hooded cloak. Slowly the figure drew back the hood.

"Mary!" he gasped.

"John!" She hurried toward him. He put down the lantern and gathered her in his arms, holding her close. Her tears dampened his blouse.

"There's no need to cry," he assured her. "I'm so glad you came back."

"I've needed to cry for a long time. Even when David died, the tears were difficult to shed. So much has been kept inside me. But you've been so gentle and kind to both Kate and me. How could I ever think you were . . ." She hesitated.

"All is forgiven."

She stepped back, wiping the tears from her face. "If only I can forgive myself. I thought you were a Tory, that you had come to spy on us, even to cause us harm."

John sighed. "Oh, Mary, if you could only know the truth about me."

"I do know, John. Even though my own hurt blinded me to it, others believed in you. My friend, Abigail. Kate, who would not let you go." She paused. "Oh, my poor Kate. I — I told her you had something to do with her father's death. What will I say to her now? How can I change my foolish words?"

"I believe Kate will receive whatever we tell her. She is a very intelligent child. A blessing." He took Mary again in his arms. "I will kiss you and court you and then marry you, Mary Farthington, if it be God's will. Though I know we have only been together a short time."

"It doesn't matter. God has bestowed a blessing, and you, John Maxwell, are a blessing. When Kate receives her doll on Christmas, she will be blessed, as well. Though . . ." Mary paused. "I won't tell her about the doll's head. I wish it to be from your heart alone."

"But Mary . . . your husband wanted her to have it. The doll is really from his heart."

"My husband is with the Lord, John. I want her to know the doll is from the man who will be her father, just as she wisely spoke that day in the wagon."

"Mary, Mary, you are my delight," he murmured. He could not help but kiss her to confirm his words. "Now I must open up the shop for business. It is unseemly for us to be here together alone, as you know."

"I will return home at once and tell Kate the news — that we will be having Christmas with you after all." Mary gave him a lasting smile before leaving the shop.

John could only shake his head, marveling as he leaned against a post to watch the woman he loved mount her horse and trot up the road in a hurry. He prayed, too, for Kate, that all would be well, that she would accept them, and that they would indeed have a most wondrous Christmas.

Suddenly, Mary turned the horse about and came back to his door. "Sir, I must ask. Do you dare close the shop?"

John straightened in curiosity. "Close the shop?"

"I do so want Kate to see us both together. I think it would do her well if she does. And we can set everything in order."

John agreed, wasting no time retrieving his own cloak and locking the shop door. He saddled a horse. "We will go immediately," he told her, "and we will pray that everything goes well."

"Amen," she breathed. "God, I pray for Your hand to be upon us and that You will guide us to a peaceful end."

CHAPTER 7

John enjoyed Mary's company as they rode toward Highland Grove. On his lap rested the wooden box that contained the precious doll. John was pleased with the results and knew Kate would be happy. The seamstress at the millinery shop gave the doll a tiny polonaise gown of robin's egg blue to match the doll's eyes. A tiny pinner cap rested on the doll's blond curls. Wee black satin slippers donned the wooden feet he had carved. What a delight for any dear girl, but especially for Kate in whom he owed the love that had sprouted between Mary and he. And to think that God could use the innocence and friendliness of the young girl to bring two people together. It was the essence of the Christmas spirit — that a child might lead them, as a little Child did long ago, sent to this earth to turn people's hearts toward God.

They arrived to the road leading to Highland Grove only to find the carriage of Abigail Turner before the main house. Mary gave John a look of distress before hurrying into the home.

"Abigail!" she called when she saw her friend appear.

"Oh, Mary. We don't know where Kate is. She has disappeared!"

John followed Mary to the front portico to hear Abigail's words. He didn't even wait to hear more but immediately began searching the outer buildings for her. *Oh God, please. Not another lost soul, and the young girl at that. Keep her safe, I pray. Restore her to us.*

He called her name, but only the whinny of the horses and the play of the wind in the eaves of the barn met his ears. He heard footsteps then and whirled to find Mary behind him.

"John, what shall I do?" she cried, the tears spilling down her cheeks. "The servants have searched the house but found no sign of her. I know she was upset that we were going to Pennsylvania. She begged me not to leave. And then I told her about you. This is all my fault!"

"We will find her, Mary. We must. I will travel the road and look there."

"If anything happens to her, I will cease

to live," Mary fretted.

John took her hand, squeezing it gently, then hurried to his horse. Like her, he, too, was grieved in spirit and prayed for God's intervention.

He rode swiftly, scouring the countryside for the tiny figure. The winter chill bit through his cloak. He could not bear to think of Kate lost if night were to approach. Cold and alone, she could very well freeze to death. He forced away the fear and set his sights high in determination to find her.

John decided to retrace the journey back toward Williamsburg. The town lay eight miles distant, but perhaps she had headed in that direction. They had passed a few wagons heading for town when they rode by on their way to Highland Grove. If he could catch up with one of the wagons, perhaps the driver might recall if he had seen a young girl on the road.

He urged the horse forward, galloping with great speed, and soon caught up with one of the rickety wagons heading toward town. "Sir, if you please!" John shouted above the sound of the creaking wagon wheels.

The driver immediately halted the wagon.

"Sir, I'm looking for a young girl about eight years of age. Her name is Katherine

Farthington." Just then he caught sight of a face peering out from among the many parcels in the back of the wagon. A set of tiny blue eyes gazed at him. "Kate?"

"I picked her up all right," the man said. "She told me she had family in Williamsburg."

"Where are you going, Kate? Your mother is very worried."

"Please don't send me to Pennsylvania, Mr. Maxwell," she begged. "I — I will live with you. You said I could come watch you work."

John dismounted from his horse and helped Kate out of the cart, thanking the driver.

"I know what Mother told me — that you knew about Father and who took him away. But I have no one else. I don't want to leave here. I know you're a kind man, even if Mother doesn't think so."

John gave her a swift embrace before leading her by the hand over to his horse. "Your mother is worried nearly to the point of being ill, young one. We must return immediately."

"I won't go to Pennsylvania," she declared again.

John looked at her and suddenly chuckled. "Can this be the spirit of your father rising up within you?"

She stared at him, wide-eyed. "What? I don't understand."

"I know that your father was also outspoken about what he wished to do in life. But come, you need not fear. Your mother is not going to Pennsylvania."

Kate clapped her hands. "What did you say to her, Mr. Maxwell?"

"I told her the truth, dear one. And I made certain the men who took your father away were punished, just as you once asked. They are in the gaol in Williamsburg, even as we speak."

All at once he felt the warmth of a small embrace as Kate threw her arms around him. "I knew you were a good man. I think, too, that God heard my prayer about bringing back Father. He just brought him back in another way."

John patted her head before helping her astride the horse and heading back for her home. Never had he heard such words of confirmation and from one so young. It was indeed the truth of scripture come to life — that the kingdom of God can be found in young ones who speak far greater wisdom than any adult.

When they arrived back, Mary swooped her child up in her arms, kissing her, telling her how dreadfully sorry she was for the words she had spoken. When Kate told her mother how she had planned to live with John in Williamsburg, Mary could only look at John in wonder and surprise.

"I had no idea she would do something like run away," Mary murmured after telling Kate to go ask the servant for a cookie. "She does love you so."

"Kate has led in the matters of the heart more than any child I have ever met." John took Mary's hand in his. "And so what shall we do about that heart, Mary? We can't disappoint her."

"I will do whatever the Lord wills," came her gentle reply.

"Since there is no other family but your daughter, and she has given her consent most openly," he said, chuckling softly, "I do humbly ask if I might court you. How I want to take this time to learn all the wonderful things there are to know about you, although my heart has told me much already."

"Yes," Mary agreed with a smile. "John, you don't know how my heart wanted to believe in you, though my mind would not. Even when Mrs. Longworth shared about your brother, I didn't want to believe you were to blame. Nor did I want to leave this place either. Even though I did come back to Williamsburg for the doll, I suppose I also wanted to see if there was a light still burning between us."

"It burns fairly bright, my dear. And brighter still as we discover all there is to discover."

When news came to the Longworths of John's involvement in rallying the militia and finding the men responsible for the atrocities that had happened within Williamsburg, the couple once again invited John and his guests for Christmas. When he came to their home to inquire about the preparations for the holiday, Mrs. Longworth bestowed an uncustomary embrace before fetching him a mug of hot punch. "I pray you will forgive me for my doubts, John," she said softly.

"There is nothing to forgive."

"But there is. I went to Mary Farthington and said things I should never have said." She glanced over at her husband, who nodded. "I know that my husband was very angry with me for what I did. It was wrong to have cast seeds of doubt, especially between the both of you."

"Mrs. Longworth, all is forgiven. I'm grateful you have opened your hearts and your home to the Farthingtons and to me. I can never repay your kindnesses to me over these many years. You both mean everything to me, and I can only offer you my thanks."

Aaron Longworth came forward then. "I'm glad to hear you say these things, John, for you mean so much to the both of us." He drew in a breath. "That's why I'm most happy to give you my place of business."

John stared. "Sir?"

He extended his hand. "Congratulations, new master of the cabinetmaking shop."

John could barely shake the hand offered him. "Sir, this is such a surprise!"

Aaron smiled. "But well deserving. And no one will do better than you for all of Williamsburg."

"Thank you, sir." He left that day in a cloud, not of sadness, but in awe and amazement over what God had done.

A few days later, John arrived at Highland Grove to fetch the Farthingtons for the noonday service at the church. He found them both in new dresses and carrying a basket full of packages.

A few flakes of snow began falling from the sky above. "How wonderful," Mary said with a sigh, taking her seat beside John. "How I love the snow, especially during this time of year."

"I love having you by my side," he told her, giving her a kiss on her cheek, to the giggles of Kate. "Ah, I think we have a spy among us."

"I see everything!" Kate said with a laugh, poking John in the arm.

The ride to Williamsburg was serenaded with the singing of favorite hymns until John pulled the carriage before the Longworth home. There they were met with warm embraces and smiles as they gathered to make their way to church for the service.

John sat beside Mary, listening intently to the sermon that spoke of God's love in the Babe born long ago and how they must seek His love in these difficult times. He thought then of Jonas. Even though Jonas refused to see him the other day when he came to visit the gaol, John begged the jailor to give Jonas a present. It was his Testament, given in the hope that God's word might break through to the man's heart. John lowered his face, lost in thought, until he heard Mary's gentle voice in his ear.

"Emmanuel. God is with us," she said. "Do not ever forget, John."

He squeezed her hand and then stood to sing the hymn with the rest of the congregation. When they departed the church, everyone was in good spirits, anticipating the sumptuous feast of roast goose and plum pudding. Inside the Longworth home, the Yule log burned cheerily where the families gathered to enjoy its warmth.

Just then John felt a light tap on his shoulder. It was Mary with a gift for him, wrapped in brown paper. He took the package with a smile and unwrapped it to find a new apron for him to wear in the shop. "Thank you so much, my dear."

Mary then took his package and unwrapped a beautiful shawl he had bought for her at the millinery shop. The threads glimmered in the candlelight of the room. "I will treasure this always," she said to him, draping the shawl, which set off her forest green gown, around her shoulders.

John then slipped out of the room and returned with the long wooden box. He found Kate staring at the burning Yule log, singing one of the hymns they had sung in church that day. "Kate, I have a special surprise for you." He laid the box carefully in her lap. "This is from your mother and me."

Kate looked up in surprise. "For me!" she exclaimed, nearly wrenching the cover from the box. There lay the doll in a bed of soft cloths, dressed in the light blue satin gown, with a necklace of tiny pearls about her throat. The doll's face beamed back at Kate, who carefully took the doll into her arms. "She is so beautiful, Mr. Maxwell. The most beautiful doll there is."

John looked to Mary, wondering if she would explain about the doll and how a part of it belonged to the one her father was bringing her for Christmas. Mary said nothing but only asked her daughter, "Do you like the doll, darling?"

"I love her. I'm going to name her Sarah."

"A fine name," John said with a smile.

Just then Kate came and put her arms around his waist. "Thank you," she said. "Even if Mother doesn't marry you, I will still think of you as my father."

"Well, you may not need to wait very long, young one. Your mother and I have come to an agreement of courtship. And if all goes well, I believe this spring you may have your wish."

Kate stepped back, staring at them. "Do you mean it?"

"How would you like a cabinetmaker for a father?" Mary wondered.

"Oh, I would love it just fine! And maybe he can make me my own bed, and I will have my own room. Not that I don't like being with you, Mother. But I think I would like to have my own room come spring."

Mary laughed, gathering the girl in her arms to bestow a kiss. She looked over at John with love in her eyes and a peace that surpassed all understanding.

Later, John and Mary found a place of refuge in a side room as the rest of the family gathered before the fire to watch a servant roast chestnuts. Mary thanked him for the doll and for everything else he had done for them.

"A small matter, Mary."

"No, a large matter, sir, in more ways than I could've ever thought. You see, when I first came seeking a man to make a doll for Kate, I decided I would like a patriot to make it. A memory, if you will, in honor of my husband. And I did receive my wish. You are a patriot, John, whether you wish to be or not."

"Perhaps," he said thoughtfully. "My only concern was that I follow the Lord's will for my life. And His will appeared to extend to the battle for this country when I saw the enemy engage in evil. But I will never be an orator or any such men as you have undoubtedly encountered."

"No, and you shouldn't be. There are other patriots, too — patriots of the heart.

And you are still the thoughtful cabinet-maker with people's happiness your greatest goal."

He took her hand. "The only goal I wish to pursue right now is the one standing in all her beauty before me. We will have our wedding come spring. And I will make you the finest furniture. Whatever your heart desires, I will craft for you out of the best wood."

Mary shook her head as her fingers lightly stroked his face. "Make not furniture, darling, but carve the finest heart of love." She gave him a kiss. "That will do me very well."

ABOUT THE AUTHORS

Lauralee Bliss resides with her family near Charlottesville, Virginia, in the foothills of the Blue Ridge Mountains — a place of inspiration for many of her contemporary and historical novels. Aside from writing, Lauralee enjoys hiking, gardening, roaming yard sales, and traveling. She invites you to visit her Web site at www.lauraleebliss.com.

Irene B. Brand taught public schools in West Virginia for twenty-three years before she retired in 1989 to devote full time to writing. She has a Master's Degree in History and taught the subject for several years. Her first two historical novels also featured life in Colonial America. Fifteen of her forty-three published books have had a historical theme, ranging from 300 AD, during the reign of Constantine, to the Klondike gold rush of 1896.

Irene has been a Christian and active

member of her local Baptist church since she was eleven years old, and her commitments there continue to be her major priority. She lives in her native West Virginia with her husband, Rod.